A
Pacific Northwest
Publisher

Printed and bound in the United States.

Contact the author or the publisher for permissions.

ISBN-10: 0985902825
ISBN-13: 978-0-9859028-2-7

Published by:

Broken Publications
PO Box 685
Eatonville, WA 98328

www.BrokenPublications.com

Edited & formatted for print & eBook by:

Jennifer-Crystal Johnson
www.JenniferCrystalJohnson.com

Book Cover art by Wallace Piatt
www.WallaceisArt.com

The Monk
by James G. Piatt

The Monk

Table of Contents

Evil Realities

In the darkness of eddying pools, into
The depths of things
Unseen and unwanted,
Comes the truth of evil realities. They
Disturb the night dreams
Of innocent young,
Cause nightmares in the elderly:

In the dim ornate naves
With pious candles
Glimmering, and voices climbing
To the heavens,
Prayers of innocent children
With naïve minds, once
Unaware of sinister men, cry out.

Foul acts
Of the robed
Will haunt future
Dreams, as the
Children live their lives
Recalling scarlet-laced memories
Of sinful behaviors which will
Disturb their waking lives,

Forever, and forever, and forever....

Introduction

It is well-known in high-level scientific and military circles that mind control has been in use since the 1950's. During the Vietnam War, for example, it was reported in some secret communiqués that a device called the Rambo Chip was injected into soldiers to increase the flow of adrenaline into the bloodstream to increase their fighting ability.

The technology, which linked a human brain directly to a computer vis-à-vis brain implants, was said to have taken place in the 70's in the state of Ohio. The implanting of electrodes into the brains of prisoners as well as nursing home patients also took place in Stockholm, Sweden in 1973. There has been secret testimony that mind control systems were used to modify human behavior under the auspices of the CIA and the military dating back as early as the 1960's. It has also been speculated that brain control methods were used on prisoners in a Utah prison as recently as the early 1980's.

Many in the scientific community believe that thought control signals can be transmitted successfully from hundreds of miles above the earth with sophisticated transmitting equipment that now exists. It is also believed that orbiting satellites could accomplish a human brain-satellite interfacing feat with ease.

This story concerns a group in the Pentagon who wished to use such a system in their war on terror, and the inner conflict of a Benedictine Monk who wants to use the brain control system to fulfill his psychotic need for vengeance.

Chapter One
The Experiments

A silhouette carrying the shield of death
Is riding with Satan on his left, and
A shape with a bloody scythe is riding
On his right, the World will never be the same.

It was during a typical storm in the springtime that four men, inside a secret hidden laboratory near La Mans, France, were observing an experiment. The results of the test could determine how most non-nation oriented battles might be conducted in the future.

Father Dumas wrinkled his wide brow as he looked at the stark white, pristine walls of the laboratory. He had the impression they were melting before his eyes. His thoughts were propelled chaotically into the past and the room seemed to spin. He felt faint and leaned against the cold walls to steady himself.

Dumas, in the past, had been a moral man, a kind man, a good Catholic. However, after the horrible events involving his beloved family, his mind had been submerged in a deep depression and malevolent thoughts constantly crossed the threshold of sanity in his brain. As a child, he was an introspective loner and had profound thoughts about God and goodness. He also had a deep tenderness toward his siblings. He was solidly built and had a penchant for revenge if any of his brothers or sisters were harmed. Many of the boys in school felt his wrath, and physical blows if they offended his sisters or brothers. He was also very intelligent and had a proclivity for the sciences, in which he excelled in Catholic schools and universities.

After graduating with a *Licencie' en Science* from the *Université de Paris*, he started his own bio-technical corporation. He had been a successful CEO of the firm for many years prior to the terrible incident involving his sister and his three nephews. The nefarious incident turned his life upside down and infused dark feelings of revenge into his mind.

He entered the *Abbaye de Solesmes* Monastery to escape the images of the horror that had occurred and to remove the evil thoughts that oscillated back and forth in his mind like a frantic pendulum. His thoughts continually vacillated between that which was horribly malevolent and that which was spiritual, and finally resulted in a psychotic breakdown.

Years after the ghastly events, and after attempting to assuage his feelings of hatred by continually praying in his cell at the Abbaye, a blood-lust darkness prevailed in his brain. It had overtaken any moral lightness and a nefarious plan for vengeance formed in his brain. Today, after the conclusion of two years of research, a malevolent darkness was present. He looked forward to the results, and especially to the beginning of his actions of reprisal against those who had perpetrated the terrible acts against his loved ones.

* * *

The rain was pelting the metal sides of the small, isolated laboratory like bits of cold hatred. The laboratory was not far from his old corporation where the plan had originated and come to fruition. The rain made a loud, eerie, almost unearthly metallic *ping*. The fierce animal growl of thunder in the hills was like the muted roar of an enraged lion.

Dumas and a man named Gary Hart were standing by the back wall in the small laboratory encased in stark, glossy-white enameled walls and decontaminated, slick light gray linoleum floors. Shiny stainless steel cages were located along the edges of the room. Two of the cages were covered with sinister black cloths while others were uncovered and empty. On a small stainless steel table rested an odd-looking laptop computer. Two scientists clad in long white laboratory coats were standing anxiously by the computer.

The short, corpulent Frenchman with dark hair and black, somnolent eyes wearing a strangely vague look was dressed in a long, white lab coat over a dark blue cashmere suit. He had removed his black Monk's robe, which was his primary wear prior to the tests. He was nervous and the logical part of his mind, for some reason, was at odds with the warring forces in his right brain. He shook his head to rid his mind of the conflict. A tall, aloof man with dark brown short hair named Gary Hart wore his white lab coat over a dull gray wool suit. He was sporting dark glasses and wore the bored yet lethal expression of an intelligence agent. The two watched silently and intently as the test procedures began to unfold. One of the cages was uncovered and a small gray and white cat was taken out.

The two French scientists, Drs. Pierre Fourner and Leon Billen, were adjusting a tiny electronic receiving module in the base of the small, docile cat's brain.

"Pierre, push the module a bit to the right."

"Yes, it does fit better that way. Do you have the frequency set?"

"I'll turn the dial a bit more. Ah, yes; that is perfect."

Dumas sighed. Pierre went to the laptop computer and typed in a series of cryptic instructions.

"Leon, you can uncover the cage now."

Leon walked over to the cage and uncovered it. It contained a huge, menacing-looking pit bull that had been starved for over two weeks.

"Pierre, please activate the transmitter in the computer."

Pierre readjusted the computer, setting a dial to a specific frequency. He then sent a message.

"I am sending instructions to be transmitted to the mid-brain of the other animal now."

What was going to happen was mind control at the peak of development and, if successful, could alter the direction of all military conflicts in the future. That was the plan of the military and intelligence community. However, Dumas' plan was very different; it had been from the beginning, unbeknown to the others.

Dumas nodded slightly and said to the man in the dark glasses, "As far back as 1948, over sixty years ago, Norbert Weiner published his book *Cybernetics*, in which he defined in basic terms the highly-developed procedure now being tested. This system is the most technically sophisticated neurological computer-animal interface message and command system in the world at this time. This latest brain-computer system will link the brain of the cat, through an implanted microchip, to that small laptop computer you see on the table. A transmitter is set at a specific frequency to elicit specific behaviors from coded messages from the computer.

"The process was initially called electromagnetic stimulation. It was hypothesized in the 50's that it would be able to change a person's brainwaves and affect cerebral-muscular activity at will. We will know for sure if these new tests are successful that their premise was totally accurate. Since the 1960's, influencing brain functions has become an important goal of military and intelligence agencies, but had never been perfected... that is, until now. The procedure now being tested advances the almost fifty-year-old theory to the ultimate degree, making it a fact.

"Dr. Carl Sanders, who first invented the interface biotic device that could be injected into the brain, was my inspiration for my highly sophisticated and much smaller device." He lowered his voice to a whisper. "A tiny device, radically smaller than those used on the cat, is the major part of the new secret human-computer project. Eventually, if the present animal tests are successful with the larger transplants - which I feel they will be - the miniature devices I designed in my corporation's laboratory, measuring only 50 micrometers, will be embedded in other brains for future testing. The brains to be used for the final testing are located in a cerebrally highly-developed test animal.... The final test will take place with humans."

The man in the dark glasses nodded slightly. The monk suddenly frowned as a moral jolt occurred in his brain and clashed with his dark intentions. He shook his head again, refocused, then sighed and watched the test.

When Pierre activated the transmitter located inside the computer, not only did the cat's brain receive instructions, but an increase in adrenalin activated a microscopic but extremely concentrated amount of Phencyclidine (PCP) that had also been planted in the brain module.

"Mr. Hart, inside the brain module is a highly concentrated and chemically reconfigured amount of PCP. When it is activated, it will stimulate the brain and allow the body to withstand extreme pain without debilitating it."

"It has been changed from the original PCP?" Hart asked.

"Yes. Not only does it remove pain, it also gives the body tremendous, almost superhuman, strength."

Leon smiled at Dumas, then at the taciturn, Hart, who stood quietly leaning against the white wall with no expression on his face.

Pierre looked up. "Are you ready, Leon?"

"Yes, type in the instructions," he ordered as he looked at the huge, starving pit bull that was growling and lunging at the sides of the large cage. It saw the cat and started frothing at the mouth. In a few microseconds, the message that had been typed into the laptop with a specific frequency targeted to the microchip was transmitted to the small cat's brain. She was then thrown into the cage. The pit bull growled with its huge mouth frothing and charged at the small cat.

The dog's vicious lunge coincided microseconds after the instructions from the computer were received in the brain of the cat. The cat snarled ferociously and leaped easily on top of the pit bull. The cat sunk its claws into the dog's back and its teeth sunk into the neck. The huge dog thrashed around, frantically trying to knock the cat of its back. The cat continued to tear at the dog's neck, burrowing into its brain stem. The dog continued thrashing, snarling, and growling, but the cat remained firmly on the dog's back. Near the end, the snarling diminished and only a small whimpering was heard. In another few seconds, the huge dog lay dead.

Another signal was sent to the cat's brain and the cat, looking at the dead dog benignly, ambled over to the far corner of the cage. The demure cat meowed softly and started preening and washing the blood off of her whiskers and face.

Dumas shook his head and patted the two scientists on the back. "You have done well, my friends. You have proved that the system works perfectly."

Pierre and Leon smiled with satisfaction. Pierre looked at the dead dog and shook his head.

"It is unbelievable, Monsieur Dumas, just think what we can do with animals in battle with these modules implanted in their brains. We will have a whole new battalion of fearless warriors. We can significantly diminish the number of our soldiers killed going to war, the loss of human lives will eventually be minimal," stated the naïve scientist, Leon.

Pierre nodded his head as he looked at Dumas. "Your idea for this project will pay great dividends, Monsieur Dumas. The world will be a better and safer place."

Dumas' face darkened, then he frowned and nodded his head. "It only took ten million dollars and two years of research by brilliant scientists like you, my friends. Time, money, and brilliant scientists have always been the answer to man's problems. Just look at the atomic bomb!"

After he said that, he frowned as if caught up in the irony and bowed to the two scientists. He shook their hands then took off his lab coat, picked up the laptop computer and the brain embedding devices, and placed them in a metal case. He looked at the man in the dark glasses that had not moved from his spot.

Hart nodded his head. "You can leave now, Dumas. I have something to discuss with the scientists." He then motioned for him to leave.

Dumas wrinkled his brow, but then shrugged and went out to his black Mercedes Benz. He sighed and drove slowly down the road. Uncontrollable, bitter tears starting flowing from his dark eyes as the clash between good and evil began to take place deep within his brain once again. He knew that his plan would succeed now, and all he had to do was take control of the computer when he had the opportunity and not allow the military and intelligence agencies get it. He also needed to keep the horrible event concerning his family firmly in place in his mind so he would not waver from his plan.

Hart looked at the two scientists with cold, indifferent eyes. He nodded calmly at them. "Gentlemen, you have done your nation and mine a great service. However, I am afraid we must make sure no one ever hears of these experiments. I am sorry about what I am about to do. Please do not take this personally."

He took out a Glock 29 with a silencer on the barrel.

"What... what are you doing?" Leon yelled.

Pierre lunged for the gun, but Hart shot him and then Leon at point blank range before they could respond further. Their bodies fell like bloody, splintered dolls to the white tiled floor, making the scene look like a grotesque Dali painting. Their vacant eyes stared back at agent Hart with incredulous, unvoiced questions.

Hart searched through all of the desks and cabinets and retrieved the rest of the lab notes and scientific data on the tests. He took the computer logs and the remaining notes the scientists had written on the experiments over the past two years, stuffed them in an attaché case, and placed them in his leased Citroën. Then, to make sure that no one would ever know what had happened in the laboratory, he went back with thirty pounds of plastic explosives strapped to timers. He placed the wads of explosives all around the inside and outside of the lab. He waited for about fifteen minutes, nodded casually to himself, and drove off.

After about thirty minutes, he looked back in the direction of the laboratory and saw a huge cloud of black smoke streaming above a copse of trees. The laboratory had exploded in a gigantic red ball of fire. The blast left nothing but a large, gaping hole with white and gray ashes covering seared earth. Only an ominous atmosphere of evil was left to permeate the blackened soil.

As he continued driving, he shook his head and said out loud, "The world will never be the same again!" He then accelerated and headed away from the conflagration.

He made a phone call. The person on the other end of the line was smiling as Hart finished the conversation. The final phase of the military plan was now underway. At least that was what Hart and the other man believed. They, and the others involved, had no idea what Dumas had planned for the brain-control system.

Chapter Two
The Abbaye Saint-Pierre de Solesmes

Because of the dark images emerging
In his mind, and the revulsion of undeserved
Deaths, his soul echoed the nightmares of
All people who were compelled to aid in
The death of the innocent, he wondered if
He would ever find comfort, in his driven
Struggle, to find revenge.

It was a week after the successful animal tests and the explosion in the laboratory near Le Mans that three figures, one wearing a brown friar's robe and the others in dark gray suits, were whispering in shadowy, muted tones with their heads huddled together. It was night and the moon-streaked sky was overcast with blotches of ghostly, dark clouds, remnants of the last spring rain. The moon was striving, with little luck, to escape the ebony pall which covered its illumination, and only its misty silhouette could be seen. The men were veiled in blurred, dim shadows of the northern transept of the Abbaye Saint-Pierre de Solesmes.

The famous Abbaye, which held the haunting, pious voices of Benedictine monks, had a profusion of beautifully and intricately carved scenes of the religious life. The area in which they were huddled together held sculptures of religious scenes involving Mary, the mother of Christ, amounting to over one hundred. The three dark shadows of men were clustered together next to the lower center portion near the beautifully carved entombment of Our Lady. Haunting and muffled voices singing beautiful Gregorian prayer chants were drifting rhythmically down the halls like precious jeweled poems.

The beautiful, haunting voices emanated from the nave of the Abbaye church, as they did every evening and often many times during the day. The nefarious dialogue was taking place in the presence of the lovely spiritual and stirring Gregorian chants, accompanied by Mary's sad and accusing marble eyes gazing out from the scene of the Ecstasy of Our Lady. Their conversation was defiant of all religious precepts. All those who are profoundly religious would consider it blasphemy and would acknowledge it openly as that, if they had witnessed it.

"*Qeul est le mode?*" The General asked in crude French with an American accent. His voice was gruff yet displayed enthusiasm.

"*Monsieur Bourne, s'il vous plait, parlez en Aglais, nous ne voulons pas etre avons surpris,*" the Benedictine Monk called Dumas instructed quietly.

"Sorry, Dumas. What is the status?" General Bourne asked gruffly, softer this time and in English.

"The laboratory tests had excellent results, Monsieur."

Hart remarked, "The PCP component added to the final element of the controlled behavior. The test cat's tremendous strength and immunity to pain was unbelievable."

"When will the new tests start?" the General asked.

"The next two tests using humans will be underway in a very short time. We will know for sure if my microminiaturized modules and the procedure function on a complex and more highly developed brain after these tests. What happens with mice and even with the more developed brain of a cat is not always an indicator that the system will work with a higher order animal, as you well know."

"The two scientists felt that if it worked with the cat, it would work well with higher order animals. Of course, they had no knowledge that those would be humans," Gary Hart stated without emotion.

"Yes, yes, I understand. I don't understand, though, why you had to assassinate the scientists. They were innocent and dedicated!" The square-bodied monk whispered angrily in English with his gravely French accented voice.

"It was unfortunate, Father Dumas, but necessary, especially since they knew that the system might work well on higher order animals. I am sure they would not stop at monkeys with their assumptions. It would eventually occur to them that humans would be a possible target as well," the General said as he shrugged his shoulders as if to remove any blame that might have fallen on him. "You must realize that we couldn't allow that to happen."

Hart looked at Dumas. "Yes, we cannot allow anyone to know what the project is about. The two scientists had intimate knowledge of the possible use of the system with high-level species, even though they only worked with lower order animals. They had to be eliminated."

"Our national security was at stake!" the General said soberly. "We could not allow top secret information on the brain-control project to eventually leak out. It was necessary that Hart eliminate them."

Dumas looked at the two men, shook his head, then sighed. "Yes, yes, I understand, but it is a very sad thing. But to get on with the other subject, we will learn soon if my microminiaturized devices and the PCP component will work on humans as favorably as the larger ones worked on the animals. The system will be deemed to be a success or a failure based on these final tests."

"Will the test subjects be the ones I suggested?" the General asked.

"Yes, General. Sister Murphy of St. Cecillian's Abbaye and Sister Mary Adair of *L'Abbaye Notre-Dame de Wisques*, the ones you met a few months ago and suggested for the trials. I hope that they will remain safe," Dumas stated as he looked warily over at Hart with his dark eyes.

"Ah yes, my two phlegmatic nuns. I am glad you finally came around to those two. It will be much easier to use them since you know them and can get close to them without any suspicions. At this point, using strangers could be very problematic and we don't need any new problems now. The decision will turn out to be a good one, Dumas, you will see. No one will suspect two shy nuns," General Bourne replied and looked at Hart. "We will not have to harm the ladies at all. There will be no need since they will be unable to remember anything about what they did!"

"Yes, that is true. I suppose they will be fine," Dumas said reluctantly as he shifted his weight, trying to reconcile the two antithetical thoughts of good and evil battling within the lobes of his brain.

"Isn't the *Abbaye Sainte-Cécile de Solesmes* a Benedictine Abbaye?"

"Yes, General, I am a Benedictine monk as well," Dumas stated, emerging from his dark and conflicting thoughts.

"You are the ones that use the Gregorian chant as your mode of prayer?"

"Yes, the Benedictines, both the men and the women, use the chant as a form of prayer. I am surprised a Protestant like you would know that much about Catholics."

"I have an interest in all religions, Father Dumas. My choice of the two sisters has to do with their placid demeanor, not that they are Catholics. Protestants are too full of opinions, too active, not like your quiet, obedient, and pious sisters."

"I see," the Monk stated with a hidden irritability as he nodded and looked over at Hart. He personally didn't believe that Protestants had any opinions of their own. In his mind, he felt they believed blindly in what their leaders said, even if facts proved otherwise.

Hart was placid and cold and had no reaction to what Dumas or the General had said. Dumas sighed and glanced into Mary's all-knowing cold marble eyes staring down at him again. He felt they were personally staring at him, accusing him, and he felt uncomfortable. A cold set of images crossed the threshold of his conscious brain and a frozen revulsion entered his being, causing him to be resolute in his personal task again. All recriminations of what he was going to do or what others would do disappeared into a dark, hollow pit within his mid-brain, the place where hot and angry emotions breed.

The three men continued talking without paying any attention to the enchanting pious music flowing into their ears or perceiving the holy beauty of Mary with their eyes. Father Dumas, however, could not keep the stare of the deeply embedded holy eyes or the melodic prayers from entering his being. He remembered the evangelical expression of charity written in the chapter on good zeal in Saint Benedict's Rule:

"Just as there is an evil zeal of bitterness which separates from God and leads to Hell, there is a good zeal which separates from evil and leads to God and life everlasting. Let monks, therefore, exercise this zeal with the most fervent love."

He looked up at the carved statue of Mary staring at him with accusing marble eyes again. Cold tears dropped from his eyes and down his square cheeks like tiny rivulets of sin. He crossed himself and sighed. There were too many times lately when he questioned what he had done and what he was going to do. However, when the dark internal images of the horrible past events entered his mind, his heart hardened and he justified his task as a holy one.

He had to avenge the innocent dead. It was the only way to soothe the intense iciness within his soul. Fortunately for him, the tears were unseen by the other two men because of the faintly lit area and dark shadows. The other two men with souls of ice had no use for any sentimentality. They viewed such things as weaknesses and abhorred such weaknesses in any man.

* * *

It was the following week when Sister Murphy was on her knees with a scrub brush and a pail of soapy water, washing the marble tiled floors in one area of the St. Cecillian's Abbaye's hallways. She was chanting a prayer and smiling. Sister Murphy was small and had a tiny bobbin of a nose, which sat quietly above a pair of rosebud lips.

She felt a slight prick, then a sharp pat on the back of her neck. She jumped up, startled, and grabbed her neck. She saw the square physique of Father Dumas looming behind her. He smiled and said in French, "I am so sorry, Sister, there was a mosquito on your neck. I swatted it away. I am so sorry if I startled you."

"Oh... oh no, thank you Father. The mosquitoes have been terrible this year and seem to be unaffected by the new screens we put on the bottom windows. I do not know why they are here so early; they usually don't start to arrive until the first of July. I am afraid we will have to use some type of pesticide in the summer months. Of course, Mother Bertrand is against using any harsh chemicals, especially to kill something. You know how she abhors the killing of anything, even insects." She spoke in Irish-accented French and shrugged her small shoulders timidly as she smiled.

Dumas flinched slightly. "Yes, well I would imagine something will have to be done," Father Dumas stated benignly in his gravely voice.

He then bowed to the sister and ambled slowly down the long marbled hall. He had in his closed hand a tiny, odd-looking metal syringe that had embedded a microminiaturized device between the base of Sister Murphy's skull and her first vertebrae. In a short time, there would be no trace of the insertion mark, just a tiny red dot that would be mistaken for a mosquito bite. When the module reached its destination, the sister would be under the control of computer instructions when nefarious hands typed on a computer. The instructions would be relayed to the sister's brain, making her a slave to the message.

* * *

Later on in the following week in *L'Abbaye Notre-Dame de Wisques,* Sister Mary Adair, a tall fair-haired nun with a somber demeanor and an active brain, was walking down the tiled hallway with pale cream-colored arches. The arches cast numinous shadows high above her covered head. She had just finished a meeting with the Metanexus group and was deep in serious contemplation over what had been said when someone approached her silently from behind. She did not hear the person, only felt a slight prick followed by a sharp slap on her neck. She jerked around immediately putting her hand on her neck. She saw a short square-bodied Monk from her group, Father Dumas. She rubbed her hand on her neck and looked curiously at the Father.

"Father Dumas, what are you doing?" she asked somewhat angrily in her Scottish-accented French.

"I'm so sorry to alarm you, Sister Adair! You had a huge mosquito on your neck and I swatted it away. I am so sorry if I startled you!" Father Dumas stated, innocently smiling at her.

"Oh... oh no, I'm fine. Thank you, Father, the mosquitoes have been very bothersome this month. I heard that they are even more terrible at St. Cecillian's Abbaye in Solesmes as well. I wonder if it is global warming?"

"Yes, I heard that the mosquitoes were also bad there, Sister. I suppose global warming has a lot to do with it. Did you enjoy the lecture by the Australian Bishop this morning?"

"It was very interesting, but I am not sure if our more fundamentalist Benedictines or possibly even the Pope will approve. Probably only the liberal Jesuits could accept all of his progressive theories."

"Yes, I suppose that is true. The good Bishop was a bit over the top for most Catholics. I guess, though, we must have progress, Sister Adair. Many in the faith believe that the Bible and science must be merged in totality. What that means, if I understand what the Bishop said, is that much of what has been professed theologically in the past must now be thoroughly researched. I suppose all of it must be methodically, and scientifically tested, and then modified according to the results of the scientific protocols. With all of the turmoil in the church today, perhaps some drastic measures should be taken to restore the faith and stop the bleeding of the numbers of our parishioners. The Church is down over two million in numbers as of 2008, and the number keeps swelling as the Americans keep finding more of those horrible pedophile Priests in their midst. The dropping of attendance has been happening in Europe for decades, but now even more. It is a shame since we have so very few weekly attendees to begin with!"

"Perhaps you are correct, Father. I can't understand how any Priest can be so evil! What type of person would join the Church and profess through sacred vows the very thing they desecrate?" She sighed and looked sorrowfully at the dark Monk. "But in regards to the Bishop's message, for a long time we Catholics have taken much of the Bible to be symbolic or allegorical anyway. It is not like we have, for a long time, truly believed that many of the allegories are factual like most of the Protestants, especially the Fundamentalists do."

"That is true, Sister. We have never viewed the totality of the Bible as factually true, only allegorically true! I find it difficult to understand the mentality of the Protestant Fundamentalists who interpret all things in the Bible as factually true." The sister nodded her head in agreement. Dumas continued. "Most in the Protestant churches, especially the Fundamentalists, don't even accept the most obvious contradictions in the Bible. Can you believe they still accept as true that Adam and Eve were real humans, and lived in a real garden, probably in Mesopotamia along the Tigris and Euphrates rivers? How naïve, religiously, can people be? It also amazes me how they can believe in the beginning that the only humans on earth were Adam and Eve, and eventually their children."

"Yes, I know, Father. Who did they think Cain married after he killed Able and was thrown out of the garden? Do they believe that he started his family with an ape? Many Protestants also actually believe that Noah built a wooden ark and saved all of the species in the world when a flood covered all of the earth. It is a scientific fact that only a portion of that specific area was flooded, and some low lying areas in other parts of the world." Sister Adair started shaking her head back and forth disbelievingly. "A ship the size of a modern luxury liner couldn't even *hold* all of the species!"

Father Dumas nodded again. "Many also believe that the earth is only 10,000 years old, even though carbon dating has been around for a long, long time which totally repudiates that theory. It appears that science is a totally misunderstood and unacceptable anomaly to them. Some of the Christians today feel that anything scientific is false. They won't even acknowledge that a child in the womb has gills and a tail at one time in the early stages, even though X-Rays have shown it to be a fact!"

Sister nodded. "The majority of elementary children, with just a few years of biological science education, know better than that. The allegation that the world is only 10,000 years old is truly absurd! I think it is fear, Father. Many of the Protestant religions are based on fear. You know, fire and brimstone where sinners will burn in agony forever. I had a grandfather who was a Pentecostal preacher. He preached all about burning in Hell's molten sulfur for one's sins! Can you imagine our God allowing such suffering to occur?"

"I am sure those types of Christians don't agree about the gills and tail, either. I am also sure few people in general, except scientists and doctors, know about those facts." Father Dumas laughed. "It seems it is easier for them to believe in a Hell that is a place of fire and brimstone. It does seem to contradict their theology, though, since they believe that everyone is forgiven without even any acts on their part."

"Yes, I suppose so, Father. The Biblical interpretations of many Protestant churches appear to be quite contradictory. I am sure it is based on fear, they are quite un-scientific, fearful, and naïve a lot of the time. It is like they wish to go back to the 1500's. One does wonder how they can accept that Cain, the hideous murderer of his brother Abel, was the foundation of their purist civilization! I just hope that the Catholic hierarchy does not attempt to stop this progressive movement in the church by hidden and nefarious means, like the Fundamentalist churches in America do when they disagree," Sister Adair stated tensely. "I can't believe they murder abortion doctors and profess they are pro-life! They also support wars and profess they are pro-life! And, they wholeheartedly support the murdering of criminals and profess they are pro-life! What a hypocritical religious belief system." She then crossed herself and sighed. "Anyway, I hope the powers at the Vatican don't stifle this merging of science and religion movement."

"Well, I guess only time will tell, Sister. If the Pope disagrees, that would not be advantageous to the science-theology merger. I am pleased that many of you Benedictine Sisters are in line with progressive thought, but I guess that is not unlike your beginnings. St. Benedict's rule was in many ways innovative in monastic life by replacing strictness with moderation. Well, Sister, I must be going now. I have a meeting in an hour and I must travel miles to get there."

"Goodbye, Father," she stated as she rubbed the back of her neck again and continued walking down the beautiful marbled hall with its carved marble statues. She was once again in serious thought as the knowing marble eyes of the carved figures gazed down at her. They seemed to be watching her sadly as she walked and knew what lay ahead for her.

Father Dumas nodded to himself as he walked out of the Abbaye. "If only she knew the truth, the poor, poor child would lay supine in front of the altar of Christ with tears of blood flowing from her sad eyes! God, forgive me!" His mind then strayed back to dark, malevolent images embedded in his brain and the eyes of the marble statues no longer entered into his soul. As he thought about the horrible incidents, he became resolute in his deadly goal once again.

* * *

A few days later, an American named Steven Bourne, Technical Manager of InfoSec at NSA who was staying at The Grand Hotel of Solesme near the Abbaye, made a phone call.

"Did you get the job accomplished, Father Dumas?"

"Yes, General Bourne. I am at looking at the latest computer readouts now. I was able to place the modules in each of the Sisters' brains without their knowledge, and the implants appear to be 100% successful." The Monk with the gravely voice answered more sadly than one would presume. His thoughts kept swinging back and forth from the darkness to the light, like an insane pendulum. His mood swings appeared to be getting worse and it was upsetting the equilibrium in his brain.

"Good, when will the tests commence?" Borne asked.

"In a few days. I will be satisfied then that the implants will have traveled to their designated spot in the mid-brain, near the hypothalamus. They should be fully ready to receive the messages from the computer at that time. The time I am giving the implants to migrate to the proper area in the brain is probably much longer than needed as it might only take a few hours, or even minutes, but I want to be totally sure."

"Yes, that is a good idea; this final test is crucial. We don't need to hurry things up and make some critical mistakes. Call me when the test starts."

"Yes, General, I will call immediately when the tests start. In regards to the targets, the two scientists, are you positive that such severe actions are required on such important innocents? Is it necessary to assassinate them?" Dumas asked almost in a whisper, the moral light side of his brain asking the question.

"I am very positive, Father, the security of three nations depends upon keeping the project totally secret. The two targets know all about the project, they have from the start. They could, even though innocently, or accidentally, aware others of the project through unrestricted speech. Remember, Dumas, they are not only scientists, but politicians as well. We all know what politicians will do to impress others. One must always protect the many at the expense of the few!"

Father Dumas sighed and then said to himself, *"Non omnia Possumus Omne."* He figured Virgil was correct.

General Bourne frowned slightly as he hung up the phone. "Ah, Dumas, you are sometimes too much the priestly monk! Let us hope you stay on the task and don't allow your moral conscience to sidetrack you!"

Father Dumas shivered and headed out to his car to drive back to the *Abbaye Saint-Pierre de Solesmes*. He figured the long drive would give his mind time to remove moral questions attempting to penetrate his soul and change his mind. He wondered as he drove, as he often did lately, if what he was doing was right. Then the black images of the terror perpetuated upon his family penetrated his brain in cold waves of hate from the deep recesses of his memory. His heart hardened and he became resolute in his task once again.

His mind seemed to sway more violently lately between sanity and insanity. It was as if he were two people, not one. He was becoming more and more weary from trying to control his oscillating brain, and his schizophrenia was increasing.

He watched as the sun started to disappear into the watery darkness of the orange horizon. His mind went over and over the horrible past incidents. He visualized the revulsion on their poor little faces and grimaced. He gritted his teeth and pushed down the accelerator so the speed of the automobile would drown out the sinister images, but to no avail. The images kept him resolute upon accomplishing the nefarious tasks ahead.

Chapter Three
The Old Spies

In love's sweet garden hopes do grow
Among the roses and pansies low,
In the soft, warm soil of our affection
Amid the dreams of soft perfection,
We will live and love under cerulean sky

Where wrens and hummingbirds softly fly,
Our thoughts and dreams build a nest awry,
Gaudy bird-like memoirs become confection,
                    In love's sweet garden,

A scarlet kiss and shared caress,
Lovingly shared without excess,
Our soft touch and words of love,
Is a beam of light to all above, and
A true reminder to those below,
                    In love's sweet garden—

At about the same time Dumas was driving back to the *Abbaye Saint-Pierre de Solesmes*, three elderly retired intelligence veterans were eating their bimonthly dinner at Edward Jones' manor house in London. They were all about seventy years old. They were discussing what Ephraim Yatom's half-French nephew on his sister's side, Claude Lambert, had told him a day ago.

Thomas 'Teddy' Dell, 72, retired from the CIA in 1986. Edward Jones, 70, retired from MI6 in 1988, and Ephraim Yatom 70, retired from Mossad in 1990. They had been close contacts throughout their careers as spies. They became even closer friends when they retired. This became especially true when all of their wives died several years ago in a single automobile accident coming home from a shopping spree in London. The original group was six, but three of the oldest ex-spies in their group died two years earlier; now only the three remained. Now that they were also without their wives, only their camaraderie kept them from despondency.

Teddy Dell was originally with the OSS. His job was collecting and analyzing data on foreign nations. He also collected data on some high-level civilians. Near the end of his career, he was assigned as a CIA desk liaison agent for ten years. He was stationed at the CIA headquarters at Langley in Virginia doing mostly analyst work. He thought it was quite boring.

Edward Jones was initially with MI5, then transferred to SIS and to MI6. He was involved in informational operations as well as field analysis.

Ephraim Yatom was an intelligence agent at the Institute for Intelligence and Special Tasks for Mossad, the Israeli secret service. He eventually transferred to the Research Department at MI5 in London after being assigned there temporarily by Mossad. He ultimately became a British citizen.

The three old spies had first met on special undercover assignments in Moscow before and during the Cold War. The three friends had been underground agents there for five years. All of the retired agents now lived in London and spent most of their time reminiscing, complaining about how boring things were, drinking wine, and wondering about women.

Ephraim spoke first, after finishing a juicy bite of filet mignon and sipping his Bordeaux. "Claude Lambert, my French nephew from the *Renseignements Généraux* (RG), is the one who contacted me the other day. He overheard a conversation on one of his bugged phones. It was a phone call between Marion Bartlet, the 2nd Assistant Director of MI6, and David Steinfeld, 3rd Assistant Director of Metsada. They were discussing some new secret computer project that was being conducted by the Pentagon. They may be involved in something that is simply called the Pentagon Project. However, the details of the project itself or the description of project was not discussed. They said something about someone at the Abbaye at Solesmes being involved as well. I don't know how that could be; the only people there are Benedictine monks! Maybe they are in cahoots with the Catholics to take over the world." They all laughed.

"My nephew also said that a group of civilians might be in cahoots with the Military and Intelligence community as well. I guess he is going to beef up his surveillance on both of the directors and anyone else they contact. It seems the higher ups in the RG want to learn more about what the project is all about and who is affected by it now." Laughing, he added, "You know how spies are, they can't even stay away from spying on each other when there are secrets flying around. I personally think we ought to get involved too! I am bored as hell sitting around all day, and one can only drink so much wine! Well, maybe that is not true, but I am definitely bored!"

"That is interesting Ephraim, but I can't believe something is going on at the Pentagon that we haven't heard about from some of our old intelligence sources!" Teddy exclaimed. "How did the RG figure the American Department of Defense kept it all so hush-hush?"

"He had no idea!" Ephraim answered, shrugging his shoulders. "Maybe it's just the stupid, innocent name. The Pentagon Project, Jeez that could be a new hot dog cooker for their high-tech cafeteria." They all chuckled again. They then toasted each other with their glasses of wine. It was the fourth toast of the evening. They did that quite frequently, especially when they got bored, which was quite often during the past several boring years.

"What was your nephew doing bugging the phones of directors of foreign intelligence agencies in the first place? That was a little arrogant, as well as somewhat diplomatically touchy, wasn't it?" Edward asked.

"Claude said there had been some odd things going on during the early part of the year. The French Intelligence felt it all to be somewhat strange. It involved contact between two high-level French scientific diplomats and the two foreign directors. For some reason, probably indolence, the RG brass never cancelled the bugged phones. That was even after their field agents satisfied them that everything seemed to be satisfactory, security-wise that is. He stated that there were some recent contacts between the two directors and America's NSA during the past two months. That event occurred just as they were going to finally cancel the bugging of the phones."

Ephraim took a sip of wine, smiled, and continued.

"He also mentioned that it appeared that there is a citizen group that is involved is the group that is very secretive and unknown to the general public. I don't know how that could be nowadays, though. You know with Wikileaks, tweetering, and all the chatter going on over the Internet! He said he had names of some agents in the intelligence community that might also be involved. One is George Jones, an MI6 agent, another is Meir Shavit of Metsada, and the other is Gary Hart of the CIA who is based with NSA at the Pentagon. It doesn't sound like a hot dog cooker project to me!"

Teddy Dell shook his head. "That is somewhat odd, isn't it? I can't imagine three intelligence agencies in three different nations being involved in a secret American project. Intelligence agencies, especially foreign ones, still don't cooperate that much with each other, even now. Hell, they don't even cooperate within their own agencies that much, contrary to what the public is told!" He laughed.

"Claude doesn't figure it is some silly Illuminati conspiracy plot, or a UFO plot taking place out in the desert, I hope!" Teddy chuckled.

"Oh, no. Claude considers the Illuminati organization to be a silly myth perpetrated by crazy authors that write conspiracy novels. However, he feels there is something going on among some very powerful people in three countries; some seem to be military while others are not. He considers that somewhat out of the ordinary. He feels that since they are directors and agents in the intelligence community, this issue is somewhat more questionable and very problematic." Ephraim looked at the others. "Yeah, you know, that does sound like a conspiracy, doesn't it! I think I need another glass of wine. Does anyone have a conspiracy toast?" He laughed.

"How about, here's to them, who when they get bored, drink!"

"Here, here!" the three old spies bellowed, somewhat tipsy.

"All of that information is interesting. However, we are too damn old to get involved in espionage work again! Our legs aren't what they used to be! Anyway, we don't know for sure if something nefarious is actually occurring. However, I am also too damn bored *not* to do something to get my blood flowing again! Especially since I am too old to chase women!"

"Well, what do you say? Should we get involved?" Teddy asked.

"With women?" They all laughed again.

"No, with the investigation!"

"Jeez, at our ages we need something to keep our man-child alive, especially since I think one of my other man things is dead!" Edward remarked.

The three old spies looked at Edward, roared, opened another bottle of wine, and gave another toast. This time they tearfully toasted to dead man-things.

"Okay Edward, don't get maudlin on us now," Ephraim stated.

"Say!" Edward began with a light in his eyes. "I have a young nephew who loves conspiracy theories, if we actually have one! He is one of those crazy novelists who write books about conspiracy theories, clandestine plots, nefarious CIA undertakings, and things like that. He would probably love to get involved in a case that can add to his repertoire of knowledge for his next book."

"That sounds good to me, Edward. We can try to snoop around for some data for him so we can stay in the game, too!" Ephraim added with a grin as he stroked his bald head. "Is that your nephew James Jones, the lawyer in Bristol?"

"No, this is my nephew David Alistair Heywood, my younger sister's son," Edward informed. "He was born in London, but became an American citizen and lives in the colonies now. He has for the past twenty years. Actually, he lives in the capital of the colonies, Washington DC. He earned his Ph.D. from Cambridge in philosophy and worked for MI6 out of London for a short time. However, he didn't like the politics. That's what he got for staying in an office and not being a field agent. The field is where the politics get buried, along with all of the bodies, at least most of the time. Anyway, Davie absconded permanently to the colonies. He worked as the interagency liaison for the FBI in Washington DC for a few years. I am sure the bureaucracy got to him there, too, which is probably why he left that job. However, he may still have some intelligence or Pentagon contacts, even though he is out of the spy loop. He teaches Philosophy now at a private college in Virginia besides being an author of those silly conspiracy novels. He is a busy boy. I help him with spy stuff for his books now and then." He smiled and pulled on his bushy mustache. "I can contact him and see if he is interested, he is quite a bright chap, even though he did leave his mother land!"

"Well what do you think, Ephraim? Should we get involved and have Edward call him?" Teddy asked. "It would be great fun to be involved in the game again!"

"Call him and tell him we will be his eyes and ears over here. We still have some people in our old agencies we can contact, too. Even though we are a bit slow on the legwork, we can still hear and see, at least fairly well!" Ephraim laughed. "As long as we have our coke bottle glasses and hearing aids!"

"Hell, we are slow in just about everything, Ephraim," Edward laughed. He took another sip of wine and made a toast, the seventh of the evening. He then sighed and got on the phone to make a call to DC.

"Hello."

"Davie, this is your Uncle Edward calling from your mother land. How the hell are you, old boy? And how is the weather there in the colonies?"

"Hi Uncle Edward, I'm great. It's good to hear from you! The weather is still a bit cold and rainy here, but I can feel the thaw coming and am looking forward to spring, especially the cherry blossoms! Of course, as the blossoms arrive so do the tourists. What's up uncle, you sound like you got something going on in your mustache, or have you just had too many toasts tonight?"

Edward laughed and said they had been having a few toasts. He then explained all that he had learned about the mysterious Pentagon project.

David shook his head. "Well, Uncle Edward, I must admit that is quite an interesting dilemma. One could imagine all sorts of dark and nefarious conspiracies going on there. I wonder what the Abbaye in Solesmes has to do with it? I can't really see how some monks figure into such a plot. Do you really think something new and evil is going on there other than the usual reprehensible things typical of the CIA and Pentagon?"

"We don't know for sure, Davie. My group is going to see if we can get the lowdown from some of our old spy cronies on what new American defense projects are in the making that involve three countries' intelligence agencies."

"You mean you and your two old ex-international spook buddies still get involved in wicked international plots?" David laughed.

"We haven't for some years now, but we are so damn bored! We are ready for the hunt, that's for sure. One can only drink so much wine, you know! Anyway old boy, perhaps your contacts there would have a good chance of finding what is going on, too, maybe even better than us here. You know, you being closer to the big funny-looking building and all. Do you still have some contacts?"

"Yes, I do. Do you think it wise that you guys get involved with what might be dangerous stuff again?"

"Hey Davie, we may be old, but we still like to be in the game. What the hell else do we have to do, we are too damn old to chase women anymore you know!" Edward laughed. "Anyway, I figured you still might have some contacts at the CIA or Pentagon. Also being a writer of conspiracy novels and all that, I figured you might like to take hold of something like this."

"Okay, Uncle Edward. What do you want me to do at the colony end?" he stated, knowing that his uncle loved to refer to America as the colonies.

"Right now we would like you to work on the problem of finding out what projects might be in the works at the Defense Department, especially one called, innocuously, The Pentagon Project. All of us old spooks across the ocean will pitch in and pay you a fee for your time."

"Uncle, I won't take your money, but I have to admit, the situation sounds intriguing. I'll do it just to get dirt on the CIA and Department of Defense for a new novel." He laughed. "If the novel sells it would more than meet my out-of-pocket costs. Let me write down the particulars and I'll get right on it. I have the rest of this semester and the summer off from the university to write a philosophical treatise on Kafka's works. Since I have my treatise about 65% completed already, time will be no problem. I was going to use the extra time to start another novel anyway. This will give me an incentive to go in another direction. I was going to write a conspiracy novel about South America, the Aztecs, and oil. I think one about some underground and secret furtive activities at the Pentagon might be much better."

"Well, Davie, if something big is going on at the Pentagon and involves the CIA, MI6, and Metsada, you will have plenty to write about other than oil and dead Aztecs. I'll keep in contact with you every time I get some new data and you do the same, okay?"

"Okay Uncle, let's do this mostly by computer, that will be cheaper and safer. I have a safe computer at home, a left over thing from my FBI days. I am sure you still have a safe one as well. If this is really something nefarious, we don't want to talk on phones that could be tapped. Besides, it won't cost us anything that way."

"Good idea, we have a computer in our shared office in London that is also safe," Edward answered. "I will get a pre-paid cell phone as well, just in case we need to talk the old-fashioned way. You do the same thing. Boy Davie, this is going to be just like the good old times!" He laughed excitedly.

"It was good to hear from you, Uncle Edward. I'll keep you informed with whatever I find on my end on a weekly basis, or when needed. If the Pentagon project is just a new hot dog oven for the cafeteria, I'll send you a couple of hot dogs!"

The two talked for another ten minutes about David's mother, Martha, his many cousins in England and what Edward had been doing. David found out that the Queen was knighting Edward at the end of the year. It was for his twenty-six years of meritorious service in MI5, SIS, and MI6 in the OPS bureau. He promised to be there for the big fete.

After scribbling all of the names and data on the two Assistant Directors and their agents, David sat down and looked over the messy data.

1. Marion Bartlet: 2nd Assistant Director of DIS. George Jones is an agent under her direction.
2. David Steinfeld: 3rd Assistant Director of Metsada. Meir Shavit is the Director's agent.
3. Gary Hart is a CIA agent based in the Pentagon; don't know who his boss is.
4. Some new project might exist at the Pentagon called The Pentagon Project. It appears to involve international intelligence agencies. So far, the CIA, Metsada, and MI6 seem to be involved. No one knows about the thrust of the project, what it is, or what it is all about. (Need background data on the people, as well as some data on executives in the agencies, etc. Call my favorite contact, Beverly Drew at the CIA).
5. Need to determine what civilian group could be involved. Maybe it is my favorite group, the Illuminati! Ha ha.
6. What connection does the Abbaye at Solesmes have with any of this?

David scanned the list and wondered about the possibility of an evil project being initiated in a dark room somewhere in the bawdy, baneful bowels of the Pentagon. He laughed at his use of poetic license to embellish what was probably innocent and going on in plain sight. A new highly sophisticated thousand-dollar hotdog cooker for the cafeteria was probably what this was all about.

He went to his pine-paneled kitchen to make himself some hot chocolate with thick cream and a dash of Bristol Cream Sherry, one of his favorite drinks. After heating the cream and stirring in slivers of dark Belgium chocolate in a huge mug, he grabbed his bottle of Harvey's and put in about a jigger of rum. He then took four large chocolate brownies from a cupboard and headed to his mahogany partnership desk in the library.

He started his computer, paused for a while, and started to type. *It was a cold and blustery night...* good lord, even Snoopy wouldn't use that line anymore. He chuckled to himself. He erased the line and typed, *It was night time at the Abbaye Saint-Pierre de Solesmes and some nefarious-looking men were talking in muffled tones about an ultra-surreptitious plan. The rain was pouring down in torrents as the men, with heads bent down, discussed what....*

David paused and laughed out loud again. "Jeez, what a silly start! No publisher would ever look at a book that started out like that."

He took a sip of his laced hot chocolate, took a big bite out of a brownie, and erased the sentence. He decided to forgo the start of the novel for now. He got online to look up what the Defense Department might be doing in regards to new covert projects, especially clandestine ones. When he looked up Pentagon projects for the next three hours, he didn't find any nefarious projects, just expensive ones. One project did include five thousand dollars for new hotdog cookers for the cafeteria. However, it wasn't called the Pentagon Project. He decided to call Beverly Drew at the CIA and see if she was up to a dinner date. He figured he could always get some data from her, among other things.

"Beverly, this is David. Are you up to having dinner with me Friday?"

"David? David who?" she asked sarcastically.

"David Heywood! Jeez!" he said, somewhat put out.

"Oh, *that* David! The tall lanky guy, the one that looks like Jimmy Stewart with the big brown puppy dog eyes, who I haven't heard from for over two weeks now! You brute, I thought maybe you had died and gone straight to Hell!"

David could picture her curly red hair bouncing on her head and her brown eyes flashing when she said that. He gathered up his composure. "Jeez Beverly, I have been very busy and I was out of town for over a week." He paused and figured he had better give in or he would never get anywhere. "I'm so sorry Beverly, I guess I am a brute! How about a dinner date so I can make it up to you?"

"I suppose I might as well go to dinner with you. I may be able to get rid of the rest of my boyfriends and squeeze you in for one night," she stated. "You will be paying, won't you?"

He could hear the mischief in her voice. "Jeez Beverly, now you are really starting to make me feel bad," he said feigning nervousness.

"Yeah right! Uh, wait a minute. David, is this a fact-finding date? Are you planning to hit me up for information for a new novel, is that what this is all about?" she asked in a stern voice.

"How can you say that, Beverly? Can't I just want to be with you?" he said solemnly. "Well, I *could* use a wee tiny bit of information, but that is secondary to seeing you. The data is not for a new novel, at least not yet." He felt a little bit of heat over the phone. "It's a request from my uncle in London. He and his spy friends think something clandestine is up at the Pentagon."

There was a long pause. Then she said, "Well duh, something clandestine is *always* up at the Pentagon. Anyway Davie, a free dinner is always nice... no matter whom it is with. Maybe I can discuss some things with you, too. That is as long as it doesn't jeopardize my career, like the last time you got me mixed up in that FBI mole case and I almost lost my job. Anyway, on your question, it shouldn't be too hard to find out what is going on there! I will look into it even though you have been a terrible brute!"

"Yeah, sorry about that, you are right. However, about the other thing, I made that up to you didn't I?" he said, trying to be sexy over the phone. The pause at the other end of the line indicated it hadn't worked and he sighed. "Can I pick you up around 7:30?"

"Okay. But you should know that I plan to order a huge, expensive steak with a side of spinach raviolis at some up-scale restaurant! By the way, how will I recognize you? Do you still resemble Jimmy Stewart? Do you still have that ridiculous-looking blond mustache?"

David looked at the ceiling and nodded his head. "I still look the same, don't worry."

"Davie, let's eat at that expensive little Italian café we used to go to."

He started wondering if he should have called Rosalie Perez at the Pentagon instead. She would have liked Chinese food. Chinese food is cheaper. It seemed Beverly always wanted Italian. He figured he would be in much thicker with her if he were Italian. He thought maybe he could dye his hair and mustache dark brown or black.

"That will be fine.... I'll see you at 7:30 on Friday."

"Yes, I will be waiting. I also want a bottle of that expensive Classico Chianti, too!"

"I think I can afford a couple bottles," David stated in a sexy voice. At least, he was *trying* to sound sexy, although he had no clue as to how to pull it off or whether it was working.

"I think one bottle will do, you know what happens to me when I imbibe a little too much, Davie!"

"I sure do, why do you think I mentioned two bottles!" He laughed. He wanted to hang up the phone quickly after that remark, figuring he couldn't fend off any other barbed remarks. However, Beverly had already started to say something so he kept the line open.

"But seriously David, can you give me some more details as to what you would like me to find out? If I decide to help you out of some stupid, warped sense of duty, I can have some of the data available. In that way you won't have to hem and haw all over yourself trying to get the information out of me."

David sighed heavily, then gave her all of the data he had.

"Holy crude David, that is spooky, even weirder than the things I have been into lately. I'll see what I can do. I may have to call Rosalie at the Pentagon, though. I wouldn't want you to waste your time trying to date her to get the information!" She said somewhat testily.

"Thanks, Beverly, I will owe you big time!"

"You better believe it!"

* * *

When Friday came around, David was knocking on Beverly's apartment door about 7:28.

She opened the door wearing a faded pink robe and an old scarf around her head. "Well, well if it isn't David Deadwood, or is that Heywood. To what do I owe this dubious honor?" she asked as she pulled the tattered chenille robe more snugly around her body.

David's mouth went agape. He stuttered as he stared at her in the raggedy robe and badly worn pink slippers. "Beverly, we had a dinner date tonight, you know at our Italian restaurant. Steak, two bottles of Chianti, important Pentagon information! Don't you remember?"

She stared at him for a short time then broke up and roared as she looked at the incredulous expression on his face. She stood back and removed the robe. Underneath was a dazzling mini black evening dress that fit snugly around her curvaceous body, leaving very little to the imagination. She looked beautiful and sexy, even with the well-worn pink slippers.

"Oh that date, yes, I think I remember something about that now."

David finally closed his mouth and turned red. "Dang Beverly, do I deserve all of this? Did I cause you that much grief?" he asked dubiously. "What did I really do that was so horrible?"

"That is for not calling me for two weeks after our last – er – you know, our last encounter. A girl hates to be left hanging after a tête-à-tête like we had! I thought we really had started something! You are very lucky I don't punch you right now!" She removed the scarf and put on her high heels and then tapped her foot loudly on the floor.

David glanced at the four-inch spiked heels and shivered a bit. "I am so sorry! I truly was out of town for some time, and you know I am not too bright when it comes to women. I didn't mean to indicate in any way that our last meeting was not fantastic, it was. I have to admit it was the most fantastic I ever, uh...." He stuttered and said, "I guess I am just a clod, Beverly, an unfeeling jerk! Forgive me, okay?"

"Yes, you are a stupid clod, but since you are emotionally disadvantaged and romantically lamed, I will forgive you this time. But if you ever, ever leave me hanging like that again, I'll... I'll go into your college classroom filled with all of those cute little coeds during one of your boring esoteric lectures on existentialism and tell them what a bore and cad you are!" She said that mouthful half smiling and half frowning, leaving him wondering if she was serious or not.

"Believe me, Beverly, it will never happen again. I swear on scout's honor, it will never happen again!" He held his right hand up with three fingers together.

"Do they have Boy Scouts in England?" she asked, squinting. David nodded.

"Yes, the Boy Scouts started in England."

"Okay, Davie," she whispered, changing gears to a low, sexy whisper. "Let's go get some Italian and perhaps two bottles of Chianti Classico." She took his arm and cuddled up next to him.

David turned red and smiled, almost forgetting the unromantic reason he had called her for the date in the first place.

"I can't wait to have dinner with you Beverly, and I'm definitely going to order two bottles of Chianti!"

"Okay, let's get going you naughty boy," she teased. "By the way, what were you going to say about the most fantastic something you ever had?"

David glanced at her. "I have no idea." He took her by the arm and guided her to his car, wiping the perspiration from his brow. He could see her brown eyes sparkling under her tress of auburn hair. He hoped that he would remember what he wanted to ask her. His memory always faded somewhat when he was with her. She was one beautiful woman! Her red hair and flashing brown eyes scared the hell out him sometimes, too. She was a lot of woman to handle. Actually, he thought he might be in love, ergo the reason for not calling her for so long. He wasn't sure he was ready to be in love.

Chapter Four
The Players

Heedlessly he existed, avidly
Receiving each year
The bountiful blessings
Of each blissful season
In a wasteful greedy gait,
Observing not the sun so near,
He played recklessly with
A subconscious arrogant reason,

A shadowed darkness with scythe
Then brought him death, and
In a new and bitter place,
He no longer senses or sees.
In life he seldom thought
Of his last breath,
Not realizing the reaper
Often thought of him—

The cold and undemonstrative CIA agent from the Pentagon, Gary Hart, called his boss at the office of the technical manager of InfoSec of NSA. Major General (ret.) Steven Bourne, PhD, rose slowly from his desk and closed a second door over the entry door, making the sparse utilitarian office completely sound-proof. He then switched on his speakerphone; He hated to sit down and be hemmed in by a phone held to his ear; he liked to roam when he talked.

General Bourne, 60 years of age, was a tall, squarely built man with the unmistaken bearing of a professional soldier. He had bushy brown hair graying at the temples, deep-set dark brown eyes, and a large, stern mouth. He rarely used many words when a few would do the job. One would correctly call him taciturn. Those that knew him well called him cold, calculating, and very deadly. Of course, that was behind his back.

"The plan is going well?"

"Yes, General Bourne. As you were told, Father Dumas completed inserting the devices in the two nuns successfully. The tests will begin in another day."

"Which of the targets will be first?" Bourne asked, staring at the phone sitting on his desk as though he could see Hart through it. His mind wandered. He dreamed of using the brain control system to earn his third star.

Gary Hart had been with the CIA for 23 years, and with the Pentagon under General Bourne for two years. He was a war hawk like the General. He approved of wars to solve problems, and believed that the only way the United States could ever be safe was to completely control other countries. That included controlling their leaders. He believed in accomplishing those ends either through military strategies, including wars and assassinations, or money. Bribery was always a last resort. He was a sinewy, obedient man with gray hair, a placid look, and an aloof disposition. Those that knew him well called him cold, somewhat mad, and deadly lethal. He understood his boss's reticent to converse and always attempted to fill in the gaps of his conversation. He never questioned authority and never thought about what he was assigned to do. He just did it. He was the good soldier, which is why General Bourne took him on as his personal agent.

"The one you suggested, sir," Gary answered. "The elderly of the two intelligence personnel who was originally in charge of the initiation of the animal experiments. He was the one responsible for obtaining the out-of-the-way laboratory near Le Mans. I believe, as you do, that he could be a definite problem in the future, especially since he is aware that the laboratory was blown up. I tried to make the explosion appear like an accident, but there could still be questions just because it was destroyed. He is also a politician, and they are always shooting their mouths off!"

"Yes, good choice... although the other younger scientist could be a problem as well; he would have been a good choice, too."

"Dr. Edouard Freniere, the other man involved, is the French bio-chemist of the General Directorate for External Security. He was somewhat involved in the initial animal experiments with Antoine as well. Although he had less of a role in it, he is still knowledgeable of the animal experiments. I am sure he might have some questions on the laboratory disaster as well."

The General stared abstractly out his window for a brief time at the ominous clouds accumulating high in the heavens. They added to the darkness of the other clouds far away in the mountains. He then gazed out the window to the park below, where green foliage had been produced by the May rains. He said, "Yes, I agree; they both must go. See to it!"

"I feel the same way, sir, the two scientists might also be involved not only with the RG but the President of France."

"We don't need that damn French president getting involved!"

"Yes, sir; I agree, sir! We don't need to have him getting upset over an experimental lab being blown up, or anything else either of the two might tell him about. He might just call the American President to discuss it!"

"Yes, tell Dumas that the second test will involve Dr. Edouard Freniere. If either of the men start talking there could be an investigation, which could then involve the Pentagon, and that cannot happen!"

"Yes, sir, we can't allow that to happen. Even though there is nothing left of the lab, it is still very problematic."

"A full investigation could be prompted by either of the two men."

"Then I will make Dumas aware that we need to have both of them assassinated?"

"Yes," the General answered calmly.

"Will there be anything else, sir? Do you wish to know the names of the test participants?"

"No," the General stated blandly. "The killing of the scientists in the lab, did Dumas give you any more problems on that?"

"No, I think it was cleared up when we all met at the Abbaye."

"Yes, I felt he was convinced at that time, too. Are there any scientific notes on the ongoing experiments anywhere else?"

"We don't know for sure, sir, but Dumas doesn't feel there are. He took everything from the lab. I looked through all of the files and desks before blowing it up after he left and took everything else. None of it appeared to be of any consequence. I know for sure there was nothing left after the explosion except a hole in the ground."

"This Rene Dumas, the monk, I cannot understand why he got involved in this project in the first place. Do you know?"

"No, I don't know, sir. He managed the whole project from his end. As you know, his technical corporation was personally responsible for creating the micro-miniature brain module as well as the embedding syringe."

"Yes I remember, his firm was one of the foreign corporations who received money secretly from us for their work on the computer-human interfacing devices. He was by far the lowest bidder. His bid was so low it made us wonder why he was bidding. We figured he didn't make much money on the project since the bid was so low. However, after researching his corporation's background, we found nothing awry. It was a top rated bio-technical corporation. Of course, it was he who brought the idea to the Pentagon in the first place."

"I take it that the two scientists that we plan on assassinating and their scientific groups helped design the computer and the transmitting devices?" Gary asked.

"Yes. It appears that the other scientists, other that the two who had some knowledge of the use on animals, had no idea about the actual workings of the project, so they will not have to be eliminated. Only Dumas and the two scientists have the knowledge that could be deadly if found out. Besides our group, only Dumas knew about the use of the system on humans. I would surmise that it wouldn't take the two scientists too long to determine that it *could* be used on humans. That would be especially true if we started using it."

"To get back to your other question, sir, why a monk would take part in an endeavor like this. I cannot even start to understand his involvement. It is quite odd. He might just feel deeply that something has to be done about wars. Should we look further into his background?" Gary asked the General.

"That would be wise. I'll handle it if it needs to be done," the General remarked absently.

"Very good, sir! I will be staying at the Hôtel Château Tilques until I drive to our other destination. Do you have any other instructions?"

"No. Call me immediately when you get some results. Remember: the security of America is our paramount goal."

Gary nodded and hung up his phone. The General sat back down and a side door opened. A man walked into the office and sat down in the chair in front of the General's desk. He lit an expensive Cuban HMR cigar. He was a tall, thin man with graying blond hair and a strong scent of power and arrogance. He wore a tailored gray cashmere suit and a look on his face that denoted his upbringing, lineage, wealth, and rank in the lofty domains of wealth and power. On his left hand, he wore a platinum ring. It contained a large three-carat yellow diamond, cut in the shape of a pyramid. Around the large diamond were small, perfect emeralds.

"The project appears to be going well, sir." Bourne stated.

"From what I overheard, it sounds very good, General, just make sure agent Hart keeps in close contact with the monk Dumas on the experiments. I also have some of the same questions as you and Hart do. I do wonder why a corporation executive became a monk, and then got involved in all of this. I will look into his background for you. I have some contacts that I can use in complete secrecy. Remember it is necessary not to allow any foreign nations, even our allies, except the two Directors from Israel and Britain, to know of the true use of the project. As with the use of torture at Gitmo, if this project becomes known, it could affect us and our cause negatively."

"There is no need to worry about that, sir. Besides the two French scientists, only your group, myself, Gary Hart, Father Dumas, David Steinfeld, his agent Meir Shavit, Marion Bartlet of DIS, and agent George Jones of MI6 know about the total plan."

"I suppose the involvement of England and Israel is because the project affects the use of captured terrorists at Gitmo from their nations as well as ours?"

"Yes, sir."

The tall man nodded. "Thanks to you, General, the Pentagon Project has been kept at the highest level of security and is classified black top-secret. I believe you have been able to keep this more secret than MK ULTRA, CHAOS, and even MOCKINGBIRD!"

"Yes sir, since all of the funds came from the Pentagon's black budget, no one is aware of the project, not even the Secretary of Defense and the White House."

"And even if the project is found out, I am sure you will make sure my group's identity is protected."

"Yes, sir. You can depend on that!"

"General Bourne, remember this society's elite and the intelligence agencies have always been integrated in a single, unified purpose. The nation's interests and goals are one and the same as yours and ours. We must keep it that way!"

"Yes, sir, I am aware of that."

"We need to be fully protected in this day of computer blogs, twittering, and loose information on TV. Just look at the stolen and secret Pentagon data published by Wikileaks. If the names of our group and what we were doing ever got out like that, it would be disastrous. Questions could arise that we might not be able to immediately handle. Our causes, now and in the future, could be severely compromised."

"That will not happen, sir."

"Are you sure no others know my group is involved in this project?" the tall man asked.

"No sir, only I know. Not even Hart or Dumas have that information," Bourne answered.

The tall man smiled and nodded. "Does it bother you to know that two innocent nuns are being used?"

"I selected them. They are just two nuns. And no, it does not bother me. Our cause is larger than any citizens, especially foreign ones, and in particular Catholic nuns!"

"Ah, I see; yes, the Catholics! I will be listening to the news concerning the outcome of the tests. I will contact you by the end of next week. I have to do some government transition business with the new President Elect's security team for the rest of this week and part of next week. They, of course, will know nothing of the project." He looked at the General in a benign way, glanced at his Rolex, then nodded to the General and left the same way he had entered into the room. A thick darkness covered the room and it was not from the cigar. The General looked out the window at the darkness, which was covering the stars like a shroud. He smiled.

A chauffer in a black Mercedes Benz limousine picked the tall man up when he left the Director's office and headed to a large mansion in Virginia. When he arrived at his 15-acre fenced estate, he was driven into the garage. He got out of the car after the steel reinforced garage door closed and walked to the back door. He looked into a glass square and a signal scanned across his retina. A three-inch thick steel door with a wooden façade opened and he walked inside. He sighed and put his raincoat and hat on the hat tree in the pecan wood-paneled foyer.

He walked slowly into the plush library with its highly carved and decorated plaster ceiling and floor-to-ceiling mahogany bookshelves. The bookshelves contained priceless books on world history, politics, and war tactics. All had been read thoroughly. He walked across the gray and pink marble floors. A man came out of a side door and poured him a silver-stemmed, lead crystal goblet full of a 1997 Noval Nacional Port. He then handed the tall man a Gurkha HMR cigar that had had its end clipped perfectly and lit it for him.

"Busy day, sir?" the short, muscular man dressed in a black shirt, black jacket, and dark gray pants asked.

"I guess so, Rodney, a typical one."

The tall man sat down in a plush antique green leather chair, took out a book written in French by Napoleon, and started reading. He paused for a moment to think once again about the French monk, Rene Dumas, took a puff on his cigar, frowned, then sighed and continued reading. He eventually fell into his usual fretful sleep filled with shadowy nightmares. The tall man rarely slept more than four hours a night. Most of that time was in his chair. With all of his wealth and power, he was an unhappy man. The darkness in his mind evoked fear in others and melancholy in him.

The tall man grew up in a wealthy household in upper New York. His father, Daniel J. Harper, made tens of millions in stocks, gold, and railroads in the 20's. He sold them prior to the crash in the 30's thanks to inside information. He eventually quadrupled his money, much of it in liquor and bonds. He invested in commercial real estate in the 1940's, and in technology stocks in the seventies. He sold them, once again with inside information, before the bubble burst and his money was increased again, this time fivefold. He died mysteriously in the 50's and William inherited his father's entire fortune, which was over 800 million dollars. Daniel became an international venture banker. He sold derivatives and swaps. He also loaned money to domestic and foreign corporations, even some countries, and bought commercial real estate in most of the industrialized nations. By the year 2000, he was worth over 37 billion dollars.

He never married. His true love was making money and gaining power. It was an endeavor which devoured his waking and often sleeping hours. His pursuit of money took him into the dark and nefarious corridors of extreme wealth and the powerful controllers of international societies. These places were so outré that regular citizens could not, even in their wildest speculations, understand what occurred in them. It also allowed him to become a member of an elite, powerful, and clandestine society that managed a majority of the world's power and wealth. It was a society rarely visited by even most of the wealthy. Nothing was sacred to the society or him, except amassing more power and increasing wealth. There were also very few sins that he hadn't committed more than once in his pursuit of money and power. There was also no action he wouldn't take in the future to amass more wealth and power. For him and others like him, gaining wealth through greed and sin was an obsession.

The Monk

Chapter Five
The Project is Uncovered

How amazing my joy, my grieves so few,
Since first I met that beautiful you!
Passionate times are still in view, even
Though, time left in your embrace, are few,
Each night my memories will be born anew,
A loving kindness is forever in you:

How great my joy, my grieves so few,
Since first I met that beautiful you!

David and Beverly sat down at their favorite table in the small Italian restaurant. They sat next to a large stone fireplace. He helped her to her seat and sat adjacent to her. Beverly was radiant and he couldn't figure out how such a beautiful woman could be a CIA agent who often worked undercover in evil surroundings. His mind wandered to his last activity undercover with her and smiled; that didn't seem so evil to him.

"Okay David, let's eat first and then I will tell you the data you wanted from me," she stated, looking at him knowingly.

David turned a bit red, then shrugged and opened up his menu. When the waitress appeared, he ordered two six-ounce filet mignon steaks, medium rare covered with mushrooms sautéed in Merlot, side orders of pasta with chunky marinara sauce, bowls of Minestrone soup and ravioli stuffed with cheese and spinach. He also ordered two cold Italian salads and lots of bread smothered in buttered garlic, plus two bottles of their most expensive Chianti Classico.

After they ate, drank their wine, and talked about casual things, Beverly finally sighed. "Okay David, you didn't ask me for the data right away, you win. I can't hold in my curiosity and enthusiasm about the data you requested any longer." She bent closer to him and started telling him what she had learned. "The Pentagon does have a secret project that is just called the Pentagon Project. It has no budget which means it is probably so secret it is funded by the CIA's black fund. I can't tell you about that fund or I would have to kill you!" She laughed and continued. "A CIA agent named Gary Hart was assigned three years ago to the Pentagon under the auspice of the technical manager of InfoSec of the National Security Agency, Major General Steven Bourne, Ph.D. It appears, but nothing has been proven, that they are involved heavily in the Project."

"NSA I think I understand. InfoSec... I think I've heard of it, but fill me in again?" David asked.

"Sure. The NSA and Central Security Service is an intelligence agency of the United States government, administered as part of the Department of Defense and created in 1952. It is responsible for the collection and analysis of foreign communications, and for protecting U.S. government communications and information systems. NSA's work is limited to communications intelligence, however, not human intelligence activities. By law, NSA's intelligence gathering is limited to foreign communications, but includes some domestic surveillance now as well. It has also recently been directed to develop some type of advanced computer system. I could not obtain any information on what that is all about. InfoSec is a department within the NSA responsible for the assessment of U.S. government information systems. The InfoSec process is a sophisticated and supposedly non-intrusive procedure for identifying and correcting security system weaknesses. This usually involves computers. "

"Yes, I remember a little bit about it from my Uncle Edward. NSA is a key component of the U.S. Intelligence Community, which is headed by the Director of National Intelligence. I would guess that Major General Bourne, who is the technical manager of InfoSec, works directly under him."

"Yes. NSA is the world's largest single employer of mathematicians and owns the largest group of supercomputers, which is probably why the project started there. For years, its existence was not even acknowledged by the U.S. government and, until recently, very few knew of the inner workings of the organization. That is probably another reason for the project being embedded there."

"Beverly, is that the organization that had to do with the hubbub about domestic surveillance, wire-tapping, and cyber-terrorism?"

"You got it, David, a lot of it came out in the Senate hearings."

"Yeah, I remember the Senators didn't get too much out of the Director."

"Correct, and they probably never will. Okay David, let's get to some of the juicy parts. I got some of this from our mutual friend, Rosalie Perez at the Pentagon. I had to use your name to get her to talk." Beverly looked at David with a frown and squinted her eyes. David just shrugged and smiled. She continued. "Anyway, Marion Bartlet of MI6 and David Steinfeld of Metsada met with someone from the NSA ten times during 2007 and 2008.

They met in Paris. General Bourne flew there during the same period as the meetings, so we can assume the person with whom they met was the General. The agenda is unknown because the major part of it has been kept secret, and is still being kept secret from just about everybody. Fort George G. Meade, Maryland was the location of another five meetings between participants in the states."

"Fort Meade is just about fifteen miles from here!" David stated.

"Yes, and Paris is across the ocean," Beverly said shaking her head.

"Okay, the Baltimore Sun in 2006 reported that the NSA was at risk of electrical overload because of an unsatisfactory internal electrical grid at Fort Meade to support the amount of new equipment being installed. However, this is the most important part: NSA's new technology assignment now includes the design of a new, highly sophisticated computer, which includes software as well as hardware. The type of computer or for what the programs are designed is not data that is readily available to anyone. Oh yes, and the agency contracts with private sectors, including foreign corporations in the fields of research and equipment involving computer hardware and software."

"Holy crude, it is starting to make sense now, isn't it?"

"It appears so, which means the 'Pentagon Project' is real and involves the NSA, or at least General Bourne at InfoSec, as well as MI6 and Metsada, or at least their second level Directors, Marion Bartlet and David Steinfeld."

"Did you find out anything about the Abbaye at Solesmes in France or a monk named Rene Dumas?"

"No, sorry. I couldn't find anything about the monk you asked me about. The Abbaye, of course, is a legitimate Benedictine Abbaye in Solesmes, France."

"How about the civilians or a civilian group that might be involved with the project?"

"A total blank there, once again, but Rosalie is going to keep her ear to the ground, so to speak, for any civilian group that might be involved. I will be your liaison, though; you won't need to contact her!" Beverly said, squinting her eyes at David again.

David smiled. "Okay, I won't. What about any corporations that might be receiving contracts from the NSA, are there any outside of the US?"

"You are ahead of me there David, you didn't ask about that. I just happened to find out that they contract with foreign corporations."

"Yeah, I wish that I had thought about that. Anyway, I was just thinking out loud. I have a lot of data to give to Uncle Edward thanks to you. I owe you a lot!"

"That you do, and I plan to start collecting starting tonight. Do you like scrambled eggs and bacon for breakfast?" she asked, looking so provocative that David almost choked on his wine.

He turned red and nodded enthusiastically, not trusting his ability to speak coherently. David was quite handsome, but not too debonair... he was not unlike his ego image, Jimmy Stewart.

The two drank the rest of their wine in gulps, grabbed the uncorked bottle, and headed out without dessert. Beverly said she had a very sweet dessert planned for him back at her apartment.

The two just made it into Beverly's living room before they started shedding their clothes. Beverly, wearing the least amount of clothing, pulled David's shirt off and unbuttoned his pants. In less than two minutes, the two were completely naked, kissing, and squirming on a soft shag rug in front of the fireplace. Beverly wrapped her beautiful legs around David and the two began the dance of the swans.

"Oh God, oh David, oooooh David!" she moaned.

David was so enrapt he couldn't say anything; he just simply savored the moment. It was a perfect ending to a perfect meal.

In the stillness of the evening after their dessert, David's thoughts wandered and he recalled a poem, unsure of where he'd heard or read it.

Chapter Six
The Human Tests Begin

The darkened clouds descended upon the land,
No thoughts, or understanding, nor empathy,
Within his mind existed, nor did any thought
Of compassion spin its web upon his soul.

Sister Murphy walked out of St. Cecillian's Abbaye at 7:00 PM. She got in a cab and headed toward the train station to get a TGV train to Hotel Chateau Tilques, a hotel built in 1891 on the ruins of a 17th century manor. It was three miles from Saint Omer and was where they were holding a Metanexus conference. After she reached the train station, a bus took her to the magnificent hotel with its ornamental brickwork and statuesque rooflines.

In her innocent naivety, she sighed in awe at the splendor of the hotel and then went in the front door to the lobby. Her experience of seeing the grandeur of the large lobby was breathtaking. She talked to one of the receptionists at the front desk about the conference. After she registered, she asked the girl at the desk for directions to find the session room she had signed up for. It was the one on the methodological framework for going beyond the science-religion debate. After the girl gave her a nametag and directions to the room, she started towards her destination. She had heard about the group leader, Dr. Antoine Michel, and had been inspired by his brilliance.

Sister Murphy was an ad hoc member of the inter-disciplinary group of Metanexus and was informed that the group was meeting in the large conference room at the hotel. When she reached the conference room, she sat down in the rear. The French scientist in the Direction du Renseignement Militaire Security, Antoine Michel, started speaking.

"Ladies and gentlemen," he stated in his French-accented English. "We are at the brink of a breakthrough in the interconnection between science and theology. We are at the dawn of a new age where science and theology can intersect without either contaminating the other with its convincing yet restricted ideology. We have fundamentalists on one hand who wish to discount every tenet of science in theology and scientific atheists on the other who wish to remove any element of religion from our midst. These two antithetical views must be either combined somehow or removed altogether.

"As Basarab Nicolescu has stated so eloquently, *'Modern science was born through a violent break with the ancient vision of the world. It was founded on the idea — surprising and revolutionary for that era — of a total separation between the knowing subject and reality, which was assumed to be completely independent from the subject who observed it. This break allowed science to develop independently of theology, philosophy, and culture. It was a positive act of freedom. But today, the extreme consequences of this break, incarnated by the ideology of scientism, become a potential danger of self-destruction of our species!'"*

He took a drink of water and continued, "It was William Grassie who said, *'When it comes to religious and philosophical interpretations of science, it is vital that people know the science. Good science is the precondition to any responsible religious interpretation of that science… Metanexus and others are promoting a new paradigm for teaching science, addressing the vast explosion of scientific information and technological capability in recent decades, as well as a sense of urgency in applying this knowledge in the context of growing global challenges at the crossroads of scientific knowledge, cultural clashes, and dire portents.'"*

He paused again briefly. "I know for sure that mankind is on the brink of significant and far-reaching brain research, which will enable us to understand in greater depth the implications of science and religion. In order for us to do that, we must experiment not only with how the brain functions but how the consciousness of God intervenes in that thinking."

He continued for another hour and 30 minutes and finally sat down, exhausted. Sister Murphy was enthralled and went up to discuss some fine points with the director after the session. He told her that he would be thrilled to have her visit him in his suite at the hotel in an hour to discuss the topic further. She agreed and went to one of the rooms in the lobby to have her late afternoon tea.

It was then that a message reached her inner brain and caused her to leave her half-finished tea and immediately walk outside. She went to a small shed to the back of the hotel, opened the door, and went to where a small leather case was sitting next to some garden tools. She opened the case and took out a Magnum Research Desert Eagle .44 magnum eight-shot pistol. It had a silencer on the barrel. She hid it under her habit and went back

65

into the lobby. She then headed directly to the director's room. She was walking as if in a trance. Her eyes were cloudy and vacant.

Dr. Antoine Michel was sitting in one of the pink velvet chairs next to a writing table. He was sipping a glass of 1997 Fonseca Port and smoking a Cuban Salomones cigar. When he heard the knock, he smiled and opened the door.

"Sister Murphy, it is so good to see you again! Please have a glass of Port with me. Have a seat and we will continue our discussion as soon as I get our Port." He turned around after he poured the wine and saw Sister Murphy pointing the Desert Eagle at his chest. Her eyes were glassy, as if she were not really present, but somewhere else, far away. He dropped the glasses and the bottle of Port.

"Sister, what are you doing? Why do you have a gun?!"

Before he could yell out, she fired three shots into his chest; only a subdued noise could be heard. The director fell heavily to the floor. He lay silent with vacant, questioning eyes staring at the innocent-looking nun with the benign expression on her face. She looked at him but there was no recognition of what had just taken place.

It was getting dark outside and the sky was filled with clouds saturated with dark beads of water. The clouds were starting to unload their moisture like old men ridding themselves of the weight of a long, sad winter. Lightning flashed in the mountains in the far distance and the dull roar of thunder was echoed in the valley. Only the darkness of death in the room was more foreboding. Sister Murphy calmly put the gun back inside her habit and slowly walked out of the room. There was no evidence of the evil she had perpetrated on her sweet face. She took the elevator back down to the lobby. After another signal to her brain, she silently went out the front door and got in a parked car that was waiting for her. After driving about 30 miles, she received another signal, took the gun out of her habit, and threw it into a canal as she drove by.

She continued in a daze until receiving a third signal about five minutes later. It was from a car behind her. She headed to a train station. When she arrived, she got out of the car, left it on the side of the road, walked to the depot, and got on the train. She woke up sitting in a seat on the train. She was totally unaware of how she got on the train and what she had done. She didn't even remember that she had talked to the director, let alone murdered him. She looked out the window to the pastures wet with rain and sighed; she loved to ride on trains.

The first test was a complete success; the black-robed creature with a scythe could not have been more precise. A shadow watched her. He knew that the reluctant fiend clad in holiness was unleashed in her ungodliness. Her lethal act paved the way to an unholy grave for an innocent man. *The world will never be the same,* Rene Dumas thought to himself. Moral regrets started to form muddy tracks in his brain, then a horrible blood-soaked darkness permeated his being once again. He frowned and tried to go to sleep five seats behind the nun. The railroad tracks echoed their rusty, droning message in his ears.

* * *

Later that same evening, General Bourne was sitting in his suite at The Grand Hotel de Solesmes. He was watching a French TV station. The commentator was discussing a tragic murder at the Hotel Chateau Tilques. She said that a famous French scientist, in the Direction du Renseignement Militaire Security, Dr. Antoine Michel, was murdered in cold blood in his suite. He had been the speaker at a session for Metanexus just an hour before he was murdered. There appeared to be no motive for the murder, except for the possibility of some fundamentalist Protestants or perhaps even fundamentalist Catholics opposed to what Metanexus was doing. Beyond the suspicions, there were no facts and no suspects. It was said that the director was a quiet, brilliant, and introspective man with no known enemies. The French government stated they were extremely distressed and everything in the power of the Direction du Renseignment Militaire Security would be put in place to capture the murderer. An investigation into the terrible incident had begun immediately.

General Bourne nodded and called Gary Hart. "I just heard the news on TV, the first test was very successful. Where is Sister Murphy now?"

"She is calmly taking the train back to her Abbaye with no knowledge of what she did. Father Dumas is on the train, too. The system appears to be working perfectly. All we need to do now is increase the transmitting range of the computer and it will be perfection."

"Is someone working on that procedure now?"

"Yes, the range has been modified up to two miles at this point and I believe in another week or so, we can get that up to three to five miles. We will try to use that range with Sister Adair. At this point, Father Dumas believes that the range of three miles is the maximum that can be achieved now. He believes that range can probably be expanded to a maximum distance of thousands and thousands of miles."

"Yes, we are in the process of doing more work on designing a new transmitting device as we speak."

"Yes, sir. I believe the range of three miles will be adequate for now."

"Then we will extend the range for our purposes, possibly using satellites or drones. When will the second test be staged?"

"In a few days, sir. Watch TV on Thursday night. "

"That's good, Hart, I will be watching."

"Fine, I will be watching, too," murmured the tall man as he switched off the battery-charged satellite speakerphone he had brought with him. He had received the call on his phone at the same time as the General. He had tapped into the General's phone months ago. He took out a Davidoff Zino Platinum Crown cigar, clipped off the end, and lit it with his gold lighter. The lighter was embedded with a one-carat yellow diamond cut in the shape of a pyramid and surrounded by tiny emeralds.

Gary Hart placed his phone back on the cradle. He thought to himself that Sister Mary Adair of *L'Abbaye Notre-Dame de Wisques* should be receiving a telegram tomorrow to attend the *Project Nouveau Regard* (New Outlook Project) conference in Paris in a few days. Hart and Dumas planned to fly to Paris tomorrow and stay at the Le Me'ridien Monstparnasse hotel a few miles from the hotel where the Project Nouveau would be held. This was where Dr. Edouard Freniere, the French biochemist from the General Directorate for External Security and the last outsider who was truly knowledgeable of the animal computer project, would be one of the major speakers.

Hart laughed slightly and said out loud. "And poor old Edouard will then give his last speech!"

Father Dumas and the sister had arrived at their destination. Dumas watched from the shadows while the sister got in a taxi and headed back to her Abbaye. He got in a rental car that was waiting for him. He re-adjusted the computer transmitter for the fourth time. He looked into his briefcase and took out a list of one hundred names of terrorists, which now lived in Gitmo. The list was of those the General planned to use for his Project. He frowned and put them back inside the case. He looked out a window and said to himself, "The General will be surprised and very upset to learn that I have other plans. My plans do not involve those terrorists to be released from their cells in Gitmo, under the auspices of the new President, to go back to their foreign homes. My plan is a holy plan!"

The General and his cohorts were planning for the released terrorists, once back to their terrorist camps, to engage in catastrophic military assassinations. The only thing left now was the development of a long-range transmitting device that could be utilized from a satellite and activated by a computer on the ground. The future use of such a device would revolutionize the future of wars. However, they were totally unaware that Dumas' plan would change everything. However, Dumas was not sure of anything now. His mind kept vacillating back and forth between utter darkness and light. Between piety and persecution. The two deaths of the innocent government scientists had bothered him more that he had thought they would.

The Monk

Chapter Seven
The Second Assassination

It is difficult to comprehend the human condition
Involved in man's existence, and the reasons that
Prevail in the history of mankind without the
Acknowledgment in one's life, the creation of fantasies;
That what man has done has eliminated the
Paradoxical problems of his existence.

Sister Adair was sitting in her austere alabaster cell praying when a novice brought her a letter. It was to attend the Project Nouveau Regard (New Outlook Project) conference in Paris. She was excited to be part of such a prodigious conference and was especially excited to see her old friend, Estelle Mureau. Estelle and Sister Adair both held a B.S. in Biology. They had roomed and studied together at Oxford and became lifelong friends. Estelle went on to earn her M.S. in Genetics while Mary went into the *L'Abbaye Notre-Dame de Wisques* to become a nun. Estelle was now a Ph.D. candidate in bio-chemical sciences, and an Assistant professor at the University of Paris as well as a scientific researcher. Mary was still a nun.

Mary went to her closet, took out some underclothes and a warm coat, and prepared for the trip. It was Thursday when she was taken to the TGV train station for her trip to Paris. Mary always loved to travel on the train. She enjoyed the pleasant ride and the verdant rural scenery as well as the bucolic images of sheep being herded by beautiful black and white Australian Shepherd dogs. She loved the tall mountain peaks topped with white skullcaps, the fast-moving azure streams covered with white splashes of foam bouncing off of boulders, and the copse of green trees with gray trunks lining the edges. She was also anxious to see her old friend.

When she arrived at the train station in Paris, a small bus was waiting to take her to the *Le Méridien Montparnasse*, a modern hotel located close to the Latin Quarter on the Left Bank. It was just steps away from *Saint-Germain-des-Prés*, the Luxembourg Gardens, and the Eiffel Tower which she always loved to visit.

Visiting the City of Lights was always a thrilling time for Sister Mary. She loved the excitement, the din of the vibrant humanity, and the beautiful lights at night. It was such a wonderful change from her normal cloistered existence.

Somewhat embarrassed, she took her ancient, scarred piece of luggage and headed into the plush lobby of the hotel. When she entered, she stood with her mouth agape. She gazed around and stared in amazement at the luxurious scene looming before her eyes. A dozen people were sitting in modern brown and chrome chairs in front of tan material-covered walls. They looked like huge, square pieces of shiny ecru taffy. The people were laughing, talking, dozing, or reading colorful magazines. Several people were checking in for the conference.

Sister Adair stood in line before stepping up to the check-in table set aside for conference attendees. On the agenda sheet, she recognized some of the keynote speakers and session leaders from previous Metanexus meetings. Dr. Auletta Ph.D., who specializes in science and philosophy, and Khalil Chamcham, Ph.D. and D. Philosophy from the University of Claude Bernard in Lyon, France. He was researching star formation, cosmology, and Christology. The excitement grew in her chest. She did not realize that another form of excitement, a deadly dark excitement, would soon be found there, but without her being aware. These were the circumstances which tore at Father Dumas' soul but were impossible to stop.

Sister Adair did a double-take as Dr. Edouard Freniere, a noted French biochemist of the General Directorate for External Security, was signing in as one of the speakers. Beside him were two heavyset men with short haircuts, bland dark gray suits, and incongruous-looking dark sunglasses.

Dr. Freniere spoke somewhat agitatedly. "I still don't see why I need protection. Why would the RG figure that, because Dr. Antoine Michel was murdered, I would be targeted as well? We are in totally different agencies."

The two simply shrugged, but made no hint of leaving. They kept looking suspiciously all around the lobby without talking and did not leave his side at any time.

Sister Mary Adair had heard about of the murder of Dr. Antoine Michel on the news and had called her friend, Sister Murphy, who had been at the Metanexus conference at St. Omer when it happened. Sister Murphy told Mary that she had listened to his speech. She told Sister Adair that she had no knowledge other than what was on the news about the terrible incident. She did mention that much of what happened after Dr. Michel's speech was a blur. She couldn't figure it out. In fact, she couldn't even remember getting on the train to go back to her Abbaye.

"May I help you, Sister?" the young lady at the conference

sign-in table asked, wakening Sister Adair from her thoughts.

"Oh yes, I am Sister Mary Adair of the *L'Abbaye Notre-Dame de Wisques*," she said as she stood on her tiptoes. She then showed the young lady her letter.

"Oh yes, Sister Adair, you have been signed up for several sessions and your fee has already been paid, as well as your hotel room and meals." The young, attractive lady smiled broadly.

"May I ask who paid for everything for me?" Mary asked, somewhat embarrassed as she had saved her meager earnings all year for the conference.

"Let me look at the records," the young lady said, rummaging through a stack of receipts in a small box. "Ah, here it is. Your benefactor was a Father Dumas from the *Abbaye Saint-Pierre de Solesmes*. He said it was an Alois Brunner scholarship."

"Thank you," Sister Mary said somewhat in a stupor. She had never heard of such a scholarship in the church. She did happen to know about Alois Brunner, though, since one of her aunts had married a Jew in the 1930's.

His name and background were quite esoteric, but she knew that he was a Nazi German officer, working under Adolf Eichmann. He was responsible for the assassination of over 125,000 Jews when he worked in the Central Office for Jewish Emigration in Vienna. He was eventually convicted in absentia by the French for crimes against humanity. He was said to have stated, "The Jews deserved to die. I have no regrets. If I had the chance, I would do it again...." Sister Adair shuddered at the thought and sighed as she thanked the young lady and picked up her conference folder filed with data on the sessions as well as maps and information on the surrounding area.

Sister Adair continued to the elevator and to her room on the 21st floor. As she placed her key card in the slot, she looked up and saw Dr. Freniere and his two bodyguards coming out of the elevator. He had the room across the hall from her. He smiled and nodded at Sister Mary and entered his room as his bodyguards glanced in her direction, then closed the door. She went into her room and started worrying about the nefarious scholarship. She wondered why Father Dumas had done such a thing. As she was pondering that, an agent named Gary Hart was entering a room a few doors down from hers.

When Sister Mary awakened from her dark tinged worry and looked at the room, she took in a deep breath. She gasped at the beautiful queen-sized bed with a white coverlet. Under the bed and taking up most of the tiled floor was a pale, purple-checkered rug. She felt the smooth maple desk with a glass top, which held a beautiful bouquet of lilies on top. She sat down in a comfortable, pale mauve upholstered chair next to a small table and softly caressed the fabric.

She took off her worn shoes and sighed. It had all taken her breath away. This room, though modest in tourist terms, was well beyond the amenities of her small, sterile cell at the Abbaye with a tiny cot and cold tile floors. She got up, put her luggage in the closet, and sat back down at the desk overlooking Paris far below. It was a breathtaking sight. She smiled as her eyes moved over the Paris landscape of buildings and parks and the avenues bustling with excitement. She jumped slightly when the phone rang.

"Hello."

"Sister Mary, this is Father Dumas. I am glad you arrived. Is your room adequate?"

"It is wonderful, Father. I am looking down on Paris this very moment. I thank you so much for doing all of this for me."

"Sister, it is my pleasure. I had some money left in a scholarship fund and I know how much you enjoyed the Metanexus conference last year."

"Yes I did! I was so glad when I heard that Sister Murphy had the opportunity to attend one this year."

Father Dumas paused, then said, "Yes, it is my pleasure to allow some Sisters to attend such excellent conferences. I know how much you enjoy listening to such distinguished speakers. I must say goodbye now, I have to take care of some business. I hope you enjoy the convention, and—"

"Father," Sister Mary interrupted him softly, "I hate to be rude, but why did I receive an Alois Brunner scholarship? The young lady, at the check-in desk said that was the scholarship which I received. Wasn't Brunner that terrible and infamous Nazi murderer of hundreds of thousands of Jews? Wasn't he considered the terrible black saint?"

There was a long pause again before Dumas answered. "Alois Brunner? *Non, non,* it is the Lois Drunner scholarship. The young lady got it wrong, such silly girls they have working these conferences now. Lois Drunner is a patron of our church and gives out scholarships for worthy participants to attend conferences," Dumas lied. He had no idea that Sister Mary had any knowledge of Alois Brunner. It was his attempt at irony, but it had clearly been a mistake on his part. He should not have dwelled on the irony. He would make sure he looked into his participant's background a little more closely next time, or not play such a silly game in the first place.

"Oh my goodness, I am so glad the girl got the name wrong. I am sorry I was so rude, Father, please forgive me."

"Sister, I will not give it one more thought! Well, this time I must really go. Goodbye and I hope you enjoy the conference."

"Goodbye, Father, thank you very much and God bless you."

Sister Mary sighed, then smiled as she looked out the window and down at Paris again. The city of love was framed in the window, making it look like a picture postcard.

Rene Dumas sighed and looked out the window of his own suite at the *Concorde Montparnasse,* which was ideally located on the Left Bank. It was in the Montparnasse area, a few miles from Sister Mary Adair's hotel, and well within the range of his computer transmitter. He knew that the next target, Dr. Freniere, was located right across the hall from Sister Mary. Agent Hart had made sure of that when he booked Sister Adair's room. Father Dumas thought out loud as he reflected again on the project.

"It is fortunate that the American military and the wealthy elite formed their unholy alliance many, many years ago, or things like my project could never have been created. Without the Pentagon's pro-corporate alliance, I would never have had the money to fund such a huge undertaking. But, I shall have the final laugh at their petty war-mongering and wealth-amassing goals; my aims are of a much higher nature!"

He took a sip of Port and leaned back in his chair. Blackness permeated the air of the room as he dreamed of his revenge.

After programming the computer with the Sister's instructions to take place at a certain time, Father Dumas gathered up his things and headed to the *Le Méridien Montparnasse*. He had decided to send the message and then go to her hotel. He decided not to take the chance of the transmitter being unable to reach the module in the nun's brain. If the message was not received, he could then send it again from a short distance. He questioned the idea of using Sister Adair and Sister Murphy for such evil purposes in the first place, but Bourne had insisted. He personally would have used French prostitutes for the task, but General Bourne insisted on innocuous-looking persons who would not arouse suspicion.

Dumas got in a cab and headed out to the hotel. Dark misgivings were still intruding in his mind. He also didn't like the idea of giving the computer to Hart after the assassination and heading back to his Abbaye without it, but he had no choice. Unless....

After the conference was in its final evening and Dr. Freniere had given his rousing speech on the interlinking of cosmology and religion, Hart made a phone call.

"Hello."

"Yes, is Dr. Freniere there? This is Christopher J. Corbally of the Vatican."

"Yes, Father Corbally, this is Edouard Freniere. What can I do for you?"

"Dr. Freniere, we must meet immediately, it is very urgent."

"Well, I am in the bar, Father Corbally. I am having a heavenly sherry, do you wish to talk here?"

"No, it would be better if we meet in your suite."

"Fine, I will leave shortly. I should be there in ten minutes."

"Very good, a Sister Adair will be there shortly, too; she has a message for you that I want you to hear before I arrive to discuss it." After he said that, Hart hung up his phone and laughed. He then called Sister Adair's room.

"Hello, is this Sister Adair?"

"Yes."

"Sister, this is Father Dumas, would you do me a favor?" Hart stated in a deep, gravelly voice uncannily similar to Father Dumas'.

"Yes Father, what is it?"

"Across the hall is the suite that Dr. Freniere is in. Will you watch and see when he comes up, then go to his room with a message after a little while?"

"Yes, of course, Father," Sister Mary said with some confusion. Once she had gotten the message, she hung up with an odd expression on her face.

"Who was that, Mary?" asked her friend, Estelle Mureau, who had been visiting with Sister Mary for the past few hours and of whom Dumas and Hart were unaware.

"It was Father Dumas, my benefactor. He wants me to deliver a strange message to Dr. Freniere."

"Oh, what is the message?" Estelle asked, just as a deadly message was transmitted to Sister Mary's brain from a lethal computer far away.

Sister Mary started to say something, but then her eyes glazed over and she looked right through Estelle. She walked to the door without answering her and went across the hall and knocked at Dr. Freniere's door. Estelle nodded her head and went back into Mary's room to wait for her. One of the large bodyguards opened the door. Sister Mary gave him a crushing blow to his Adam's apple and he fell to the floor. Before the other guard could take out his gun, Sister Mary dove at him, knocked him to the floor, and with a swift motion, snapped his neck. Dr. Freniere yelled and moved to the other side of the room, picked up a chair, and threw it at Sister Mary. It broke over her head, cutting her skull, but it did not stop her.

Softly, she said, "I have a message for you, Dr. Freniere. Your final day on earth is over."

He kept her at bay by holding up a small table, begging her not to kill him. She finally broke the chair in two with her fist, grabbed the doctor by the neck, and twisted it until it snapped. She then calmly walked out of the room and headed toward the elevator.

Estelle heard the commotion in the other room and looked out of the door from Mary's room. She saw Mary walking slowly toward the elevator. She called out to her as she got on the elevator, "Sister Adair, where are you going?"

Mary turned around, stared at Estelle with vacant eyes, but did not respond. Estelle frowned, made her way to the doctor's room, and glanced inside. The door was ajar, so she swung it open. When she saw the three bodies, she screamed and fainted. A maid heard her scream and ran over to help her. She looked into the room, saw the bodies, and she, too, screamed. She then ran downstairs to tell someone about what she had seen.

Fifteen minutes later, after Mary had left the hotel, she was in a car driven by Gary Hart. Estelle was still in a daze, sitting on the floor where she had fainted. The lieutenant, seeing she was in shock, handed Estelle a glass of water. She drank the water and a policeman helped her to a chair. The French policeman then began interviewing her concerning the three murders in the room across the hall.

"Can you tell me what happened, Ms. Mureau? I am Lieutenant Dubois," the short policeman said. He wore a wrinkled gray raincoat, had a large black mustache, and had a round head that was completely bald.

Estelle drank another sip of water and looked up nervously at the policeman. Tears were flowing down her cheeks. "I do not understand, Monsieur Dubois... one minute we were talking quietly, then my dear friend, Sister Mary, received a phone call."

"Do you know who it was from?" the lieutenant asked.

"Yes, she said it was from a friend and benefactor of hers, Father Dumas."

"Do you know what it was about?" he asked as he patted her hand.

"Not really, Monsieur, just that Sister Mary was to give Dr. Freniere a message of some kind. She was going to tell me but something happened."

"I see. What happened then, Ms. Mureau?"

"Right after Sister Adair hung up the phone and just as she was going to say something, she just got up without saying another word, opened the door of her room, and walked out. She went across the hallway to Dr. Freniere's room and knocked on the door. I called out to her but she didn't respond, so I went back into the room to wait for her. Several minutes later, I heard things crash and I looked out of the door. I saw Sister Mary heading slowly toward the elevator. She looked like she was in some sort of trance. I called out to her; she looked at me, but didn't respond, she just kept going. I called out again but she got on the elevator and left. When I turned around, I looked into Dr. Freniere's room, and that was when I saw three people on the floor, their necks were all twisted and their bodies were askew. They looked dead to me, and I fainted."

"How long have you known Sister Adair? That is her name isn't it? Is she a real nun?"

"Oh yes, Monsieur Dubois, I have known her since college. We roomed together at Oxford where we received our science degrees. I continued college for my Masters and Mary went into the Abbaye. She is truly a wonderful, gentle, and pious nun at *L'Abbaye Notre-Dame de Wisques*. She has been at the Abbaye for many years. Lieutenant Dubois, she is a dear, holy, and sweet lady who would never harm a fly, let alone a human being. She is a very small lady as well, barely five foot tall, and weighing only a hundred pounds. She is not strong enough to do what has been done to the huge, muscular gentlemen in the suite. There has to be some other explanation!" She sobbed. "Someone else must have come into the room and murdered the people while my friend was there."

"Hum. Has she seemed different to you lately?" the lieutenant asked.

"No, we met when she came down for tea the first day of the conference and we have been chatting every day since then. We also attended several sessions together and discussed them in either my room on the fourth floor or her room. We chatted in the evenings as well, always in her room on the twenty-first floor. We enjoyed viewing the Paris lights at night from her window; it was breathtaking.... I saw no odd behavior or any change in Mary, except after the singular phone call. After the call, she just got up and left to go to the room across the hall. Oh yes, another time was when she entered the elevator and didn't respond to me. I can't understand what happened to her!"

"You say she didn't respond to you when you called out to her and she just got on the elevator and left?"

"Yes. I was going to follow her down, but that was when I glanced in Dr. Freniere's room because the door had been left slightly ajar. I saw the three men lying on the rug; their bodies were all awry, they looked like huge, broken dolls. I fainted," she reiterated.

"What do you know about this Father Dumas?" the lieutenant asked.

"Not much. I know that he paid for Sister Mary's conference fees and her room and board. She said he is a French Monk at the *Abbaye de Solesmes* and she had known him for about two years. I don't know anything else about him."

The policemen talked to several other people on the same floor. However, most of the people were out and those that were in had been listening to the TV and had not heard anything. They eventually allowed Estelle to go back to her room after getting all the information they could about Sister Mary Adair.

They found the room that Gary Hart had been in as they looked into all of the rooms on the floor. It was empty and undisturbed. The lieutenant talked to the front desk clerk about the room. He said that it was registered to a Monsieur Arnold Vachon. Further searching revealed nothing suspicious, except for the fact that Monsieur Vachon has never been in the room.

Later on that night, after Gary Hart had driven Sister Adair to the train to take her back to her Abbaye, he called Father Dumas on a new pre-paid cell phone.

"Father Dumas, this is Hart. I placed Mary on the train a few minutes ago."

"Ah, good, she is alright? Did the job get done?"

"Yes, I heard from the concierge at the hotel that three men had been murdered. They said their necks had been snapped with great strength. Unfortunately, they are looking for Sister

Adair now. A friend of hers, an Estelle Mureau, happened to be with her when she received the signal. I was not aware anyone was in the room with her."

"Oh my dear God, did she witness Sister Adair killing the three men?"

"No, she didn't witness the murders. She had gone back into Sister Adair's room. However, she told a police lieutenant that Sister Adair received a phone call from you and was in a daze when she got up to leave the room. She said she didn't respond to her when she called out. She told the police that later, when she heard a commotion across the hall, she saw the Sister going toward the elevator. She said she called out to her, but she just got on the elevator and left. Ms. Mureau then told the police she saw the three men dead men on the floor and fainted."

"Oh dear God, my name is now attached to the murders. How can that be? I did not call her. Hart, did you call her and use my name?"

"It was a sad mistake, Father Dumas. I am sorry!"

"Well, it's too late now. This Estelle Mureau, is she an old friend of Sister Adair's?"

"Yes, from what I overheard."

"Hum, well, it could be worse, I guess. Was anything said about the conversation she had with me?"

"That I don't know," Hart answered. "I didn't hear them talking while in the room, only after they came out."

"What should I do, Monsieur Hart?"

"Drive to St. Omer and get a hotel there. I booked Sister Adair one there, too. Keep close to her and see if you can get her on another train before the police locate her. Keep me informed."

"Yes. Will you contact General Bourne?" Dumas did not say anything about keeping the computer or that he had been on his way to go the hotel where Hart was staying.

"Yes, right away. Goodbye."

Gary Hart calmly hung up his phone. He then made a call from his cell phone to General Bourne's home phone.

"General, this is Gary. The second test experiment was successful. However, there are some hitches. One of Sister Adair's friends was somewhat of a witness to the assassinations....

No, she didn't actually see Sister Mary commit the murders, but she saw her coming out of their room and then saw what had happened in the room. She has talked to the police.... Yes, they will probably be searching for Sister Adair soon. I booked her a room in a hotel in St. Omer under another name and told Dumas to go to the hotel to wait for the train and try to get her out of the area before the police come there." He didn't say anything about the phone call he had made to the sister or his using Father Dumas' name.

"We will now see if the Sister remembers anything if the police happen to capture her and question her. That is, if Dumas is not able to get her out of the area first."

"Yes, that would be the final test, I suppose. Dumas believes we should all meet in Solesmes in a few days to discuss what we should do next, possibly Friday."

"Yes, perhaps that is a good idea. I will inform the others. Do you have a place?"

"Yes, the Hotel *3 e'toiles-valle'e de la Sarthe.* You will like it, it is a fine hotel not too far from the Abbaye. Dumas suggested the hotel and said he would set up the rooms. I will send you the address and room numbers before you leave."

Hart hung up his phone and looked out of the window. He then called Dumas and told him General Bourne said it would be a good idea to meet and to book the rooms at the hotel in two days.

As Dumas got into his car, an odd smile crept over his face after verifying the meeting at the *Hotel 3 e'toiles-valle'e de la Sarthe.*

"And then, my war mongering friends, I will have no loose ends, either," he said to himself. "No one will know about the project, and then I can avenge the horrible catastrophe that occurred five years ago. The innocent dead will have their retribution."

In the distance, the mountains roared with the echo of thunder. Lightning flashes could be seen far away. It was if God was angry and was throwing giant electrical bolts at the earth. The area lit up and darkened as the thunder faded away.

* * *

Early in the morning, at about 3:00 AM, Dumas met Sister Adair standing on the platform at the train station. He had sent a message for her to get off the train instead off continuing all the way to her Abbaye. He put her in his black Mercedes Benz and headed out of the small town toward Solesmes. The computer was by his side.

He looked over at the poor, sleeping, holy nun who had committed such brutal murders and shook his head sadly. He whispered as he looked at the deep cut on her forehead. "I am so sorry, Sister. I should never have consented to use you for such an unholy deed. I hope your soul and mine never remember what we did."

Sister Adair stared at him with her vacant eyes and no expression of awareness crossed her face as he talked to her. It was as if she were gone far away from her physical body, which had been carved like a small marble statue. Only a blank mind looked out from her cloudy eyes; it was an unholy and eerie thing to behold. Part of him wished he had never embarked on the joint nefarious endeavor with the men from the Pentagon.

Then, the dark images of the horrible past events flowed into his confused brain and he was resolute once again. He stopped for some coffee, washed her wound, and placed a bandage over the gash. The sky darkened and thunder could be heard in the mountains again. It was as if God was trying to awaken him, but to no avail. His heart had hardened again, and his mind had closed. The dark side of Father Dumas had won again. The lighter side was dimming more and more each time as the pendulum seemed to swing more toward the dark side than the light side of his consciousness.

Chapter Eight
Things Get Very Serious

David pulled up in front of Beverly's apartment and got out. He could see her waving from the seventh floor balcony. He had called her every day after their last encounter. He was not going to make the same mistake again, incurring the wrath of such a beautiful woman! Especially after the elegant Italian dinner and more elegant *tête-à-tête* a week ago.

After being let into the lobby, he took the old mahogany-paneled elevator and traveled slowly up to the seventh floor. He got out and knocked at the door of room 777. He loved that, knowing how superstitious Beverly was.

Beverly met him at the door in a mini-skirt showing off her long, shapely legs. She looked suspiciously around when she opened the door and motioned for him to come into the apartment. She gave him a tentative smile and kissed him on his lips.

"Come in, David... there is a change in plans. I have ordered Chinese for tonight and we will eat here instead of going out for Italian again."

David wanted to say something sexy and cute, but the serious look on her face convinced him not to. He gave her a tentative kiss in return and went inside the room. Beverly looked surreptitiously around the hall again, then closed and locked the door quickly.

"David, I don't know how big a thing you are into, but I almost got caught delving into it!" she said somewhat nervously as she sat on the couch. David nodded and sat down beside her.

"I don't understand," David stated.

"Well, after our last date, and the new information you wanted to know, I started to snoop around using my computer at the CIA. I discovered a memo with top-secret information that was being sent from the Pentagon to the CIA. I started to copy the data and found that someone was accessing my computer. I don't know who was tracking what I was doing or why, but I thought they might know that I was accessing the memo and I logged off immediately. When I left the office that night, I felt that I was being followed. I went to my sister's place instead of going home and contacted our mutual friend at the Pentagon, probably more your friend than mine," she added as she squinted her eyes at David.

"You mean Rosalie?" David asked innocently.

"Yes, you bozo. Anyway, she said some serious things were going on not only at the Department of Defense but at the NSA as well. There were a lot of meetings being held and secret memos were drizzling onto computers like confetti at a parade. She figured the data I got on my computer was from the Pentagon and was inadvertently sent to some unauthorized computers at the CIA, like mine. Anyway, to get to the point," she took a deliberate breath, "according to the memo, a General Bourne, who is a Technical InfoSec Manager at NSA, appears to be on the hot seat for something about black funds being used for a top secret project that no one at the Pentagon appears to know much about. He was also being questioned about a top-secret memo that was accidentally sent as open email instead of top secret. The memo was probably the one I started to copy, but I shut down my computer as soon as someone tried to tap into it."

"How did Rosalie find that out about Bourne?"

"She said one of the directors of DIS in London sent the memo to Bourne and one of the directors of Metsada, a David Steinfeld. In essence, it said the Pentagon Project has worked perfectly so far... and—"

Gary interrupted her. "My God, that could be about the Pentagon Project that we've been talking about! I guess that proves the CIA agent Gary Hart works under this General Bourne at NSA!"

"She didn't say anything about a Gary Hart, but she said after the memo was inadvertently sent, some higher ups read it and contacted the director of the NSA about the memo being sent over an unclassified system. They got upset about the contents of the memo as well. Later on, a senior officer was walked out of the building beside four security types, and the scuttlebutt was that it was General Bourne."

"Marion Bartlet and David Steinfeld were names that came up on the memo, along with George Jones, Meir Shavit, and Gary Hart. We talked about those names on our last date. Something definitely is going on at the NSA, that's for sure! Now we have Major General James Bourne being detained, or whatever the CIA, NSA, or Pentagon do to their own!" David paused. "I wonder what they will do with him?"

"David, I wonder how all of these names fit in with the other name you gave me, Father Dumas of the *Abbaye de Solesmes* in France."

"Did Rosalie say anything about him?"

"No, Dumas is the one name that she had no information on. David, this is top-secret and designated for certain eyes only! That level of security is about as high a level as you can get. If we get caught, we could be in serious trouble. Rosalie could be in trouble, too, if she divulged some data to me that was *that* top secret, even if she didn't access the memo on purpose."

"Yeah, that's for sure. Was there anything else that you remembered about the memo that you started to copy?"

"Yes, but I am not sure if it is important or not."

"What was it?"

"The memo said something about some animal test being successful. And an old building on the outskirts of Solesmes, a few miles from Le Mans, that was blown up a few weeks ago."

"Hum, nothing else? Nothing about what the test was all about?"

"No. Do you think the blown up building is related to the tests discussed and the Pentagon Project?"

"I have no idea, Beverly, but I need to contact my Uncle Edward tonight after I get back to my apartment and my safe computer."

The two discussed the situation for another fifteen minutes and then there was a knock on the door. Beverly looked at David and took out her Sig Sauer 229, a .445-caliber semi-automatic pistol. She placed it behind her back as she went to answer the door. David slipped around the back of the door with a large vase and waited.

"Yes?" Beverly asked.

"Chinese food, hot and ready, miss!" a voice answered.

She relaxed, but still kept the pistol behind her back as she opened the door. Standing in the door holding onto a large red container of food was a small, smiling Oriental man. "That will be $34.15, please," he said with a heavy accent.

Beverly stepped back and said, "Darling, will you please pay the man while I go into the kitchen and get the warm Sake?"

* * *

In another part of the world in another time zone, a man was making a phone call.

"Teddy, this is Ephraim. I have received some critical information from Claude. We all need to get together immediately. Will you contact Edward?"

"Yes, I'll have us meet at my house this time."

"No, this time let's meet at the office, it will be more secure!"

"Hum, this sounds mysterious! I'll call you back when I get him and have a specific time to meet."

"Yes, fine," Ephraim said and hung up the phone without commenting further.

Teddy finally got ahold of Edward at his club. "Edward, Teddy here. We have to meet immediately. Claude gave Ephraim some critical information that needs to be discussed as soon as possible."

"Okay, I'll go home right away and meet you there."

"No, Ephraim said we should meet at the office because it will be more secure."

"Now why would he say that?"

"I have no idea, but he wants us to meet at the office."

"Okay, I'll be able to be there in about a half hour."

"Good, I'll call Ephraim back and tell him. We will see you soon."

Edward got on his computer and phoned Davie. The phone rang four times and the answering machine came on. "You have reached Dr. Heywood, please leave a number and I will call you back when I get home. Thank you."

Edward sighed in frustration. He left a message. "Davie, it's your Uncle Edward here. Contact me on your computer as soon as you get this. Something critical is happening!"

* * *

After discussing the information contained in the top-secret memo, David and Beverly ate their delicious Chinese dinner. After dinner, they had a wonderful *tête-à-tête* American-style dessert. Beverly got up from the bed after about an hour and stretched her beautiful, lithe, and naked body. David grinned, grabbed her, and pulled her back into bed.

"You know, you are more delicious than Chinese or even Italian food!" David laughed. "You are even more delicious than a chocolate dessert!"

Getting back into bed, she rolled on top of him. "My next maneuver, my shy little professor, will top that! Even a chateaubriand steak sautéed in a 1959 Grand Puy Lacoste with Shitake mushrooms will never satisfy you again," she purred.

David moaned as she performed her magic, doing things he had only ever dreamed about.

* * *

David got home late that night, savoring the evening in his mind over and over again. He got out of his cab, went up to the front door, and punched in a set of numbers. The heavy door opened and he walked into the lobby of his apartment building. He took out his keycard and placed it in a slot and the elevator opened. Two other persons were already in the elevator waiting. He jerked when he saw the men and paused. The two men wore dark glasses, dull, dark-gray overcoats over wool suits, and had short haircuts. He knew immediately who they were, but not why they were there. The men took out pistols as he entered the elevator. David stared at the Browning high-powered 9 x 19, 10-shot pistol one man was holding and the Colt Anaconda .44 magnum six-shot long-barreled gun the other was holding. He put his hands nervously over his head.

"Put your damn hands down, Dr. Heywood, and close the elevator door," the older of the two stated as he looked cautiously around the room before the elevator door closed. They put their guns away and the younger man stared coldly at David.

"What did I do to get the CIA on my case?" David asked calmly.

"We will ask the questions, Heywood," the older man stated as he pushed the stop button on the elevator between the fifth and sixth floor.

"What were you doing at Beverly Drew's apartment tonight?"

"We had a date. We had Chinese brought in, and the rest is confidential," he said, turning a little pink.

The young man smiled slightly then looked at the older man and brought back the steely frown. The older man moved his lips in an odd way and then nodded. "Are you involved with her on something concerning the CIA?"

"Er, no, I am simply teaching my philosophy classes, starting a new novel, and having a date with my girlfriend. Ah, that's what this is all about, isn't it?" he asked innocently.

"What?" the older man asked.

"The novel, the CIA is wondering if my new novel is going to reveal some new things about the CIA again like my last one did. They want to have their stories all lined up for the press ahead of time this time!"

"Are you writing a novel about the CIA?"

"Well, actually I haven't started my latest novel yet, but yes. I will tell you also, this elevator activity is certainly going to come into it somewhere!" David stated as he smiled. "I take it you haven't read my last novel that concerned the CIA?"

The two men looked at each other and shook their heads back and forth. The elder of the two men frowned.

"Don't get to delving too deeply into things, Heywood; it might not be healthy. We will be watching you, just so you won't have to wonder about it."

"Why would you waste your time watching a philosophy professor? We are all superfluous, you know."

The two agents talked to David until they were supposedly satisfied, at which point they both nodded their heads. The older agent then punched the elevator button to the lobby. When it landed at the lobby and they got out, the younger of the two men turned around.

"Be very careful, Dr. Heywood."

David nodded and then just hummed, trying to stay calm. After the elevator door closed, he stood quietly as it crept slowly up to his floor. When he got to his apartment door, he found that he was shaking. He placed his key card in the slot three times before he could get the door opened.

He looked down and felt along the bottom of the door. The small thread that had been attached to the bottom of the door and carpet was missing, letting him know that the CIA or whoever they were had been in his apartment before accosting him in the elevator. He got used to placing a thread under his door while he was working for the FBI and never got out of the habit. He went from room to room and saw that several things that others probably wouldn't have noticed were out of place. He then looked everywhere for listening devices. He found five. One was in his computer and one under his bed (he figured that one was so the agency could get their kicks out of whatever activity took place there). Of the other three, one was in the phone machine, one in the overhead light fixture, and one in the air vent. He removed them and put them in a drawer for the time being.

He then noticed that he had several messages on his machine. Two were from students, both girls, who needed help with their essay on Camus. One was from his cleaner reminding him to pick up his dark suit, and another was from the bookstore telling him an esoteric book on the life of Kafka, shipped from Germany, was in. The last message was from his Uncle Edward.

"Damn, I hope they put in the bugs *after* my uncle called!" he stated out loud. He knew they would not have the time to determine the password and decode the message from his safe computer.

He called Beverly immediately on his cell phone outside his room in the hall, just in case he had missed a bug. He told her what had happened in the elevator.

"Bev, you had better check for bugs in your apartment as well. We are definitely under their surveillance now."

"I don't like this, David. I am a trustworthy agent, and I certainly don't understand how some stupid memo that inadvertently ended up on my computer got there. Jeez, I didn't even have time to read it. I am sure that is what this is all about." That was, of course, for the benefit of anyone who might be listening in to their conversation from some bug in her apartment. However, she had already talked it over with David, so the cat was already out of the bag.

The two talked for another three minutes about innocuous things then said goodnight and hung up their phones. Beverly immediately checked the phone and all throughout her apartment for bugs, but she found none. She knew that just as soon as she was out of the apartment, some would be placed in many innocuous places. She planned to check under the bed first the next time she came home. She didn't want her agency listening to her and David.

David went back to his room and disengaged all but one of the bugs so they couldn't hear anything other than what he wanted them to hear. He placed the bug in the kitchen, which was a room sealed off from the rest of his apartment. He opened his computer, inspected for sophisticated spy files, and erased a program the CIA had put in, in an innocuous-looking file. He sighed and started typing.

He told his uncle about the encounter with the CIA and the bugs all over his apartment. He also told him all about what he had learned from Beverly and Rosalie, including the removal of a man from the NSA building, which he figured to be General Bourne. A message came back immediately.

"Davie, that is critical data. I hope that they placed the bugs after I called, too. Anyway, we can't do anything about it now, old boy. I also have some news for you. Ephraim's nephew Claude in the *Renseignements Généraux* relayed a conversation between General Bourne and a Benedictine Monk named Rene Dumas. Dumas is the one no one can find anything about.

"Anyway Davie, there have been four murders now. Actually, they have been officially labeled as assassinations. One took place at a Metanexus Conference at the *Hotel Chateau Tilques*. It was a French scientist in the *Direction du Renseignement Militaire Security* named Dr. Antoine Michel. There were also three more murders at the *Project Nouveau Regard* conference. Those assassinations took place at *Le*

Méridien Montparnasse, a modern hotel in downtown Paris. There were no witnesses to the first murder. Dr. Antoine Michel was shot at point blank range but there was no noise reported. None of the occupants in the adjoining rooms said they heard anything. The authorities figured the gun had a silencer, ergo the label 'assassinations' instead of 'murders.'

"The second murders of Dr. Edouard Freniere, the French biochemist of the General Directorate for External Security, and two other men, took place in another hotel and this time there was a witness. Lieutenant Dubois said that the two other men that were murdered, along with Dr. Freniere, were probably bodyguards. It appears someone had an inclination, for some reason, that the doctor was in line to be assassinated.

"Anyway, about the witness; a participant at the conference named Estelle Mureau stated that a long-time and dear friend of hers, Sister Mary Adair of the *L'Abbaye Notre-Dame de Wisques,* got a call from a Father Dumas. She told Lieutenant Dubois of the Paris police that Sister Mary left the room to give a message to Dr. Freniere. She told the lieutenant that after she heard a commotion next door she looked out of the door and saw Sister Adair walk to and get on the elevator without saying a word to her. She also said, it appeared she had a cut on her forehead, for it was bleeding. She described the Sister as being in a daze and her eyes appearing vacant. She then noticed, when she turned around to go back into the room, that there were three bodies in the room across the hall where Sister Adair had gone to deliver a message. I guess she fainted after that."

David sent a message back immediately.

"Uncle Edward, I can't believe what has happened. Why would anyone assassinate two French scientists? And the name Dumas, could that be the same Dumas that came up in the conversation Claude overheard with Bartlet and Steinfeld?"

A reply came back.

"We figure it must be the same Dumas, and we found out that there is a monk named Rene Dumas at the *Abbaye Saint-Pierre de Solesmes*. We gave that information to Dubois as well, since he has been so forthcoming with data to us. "

David sent another message.

"Why would Dr. Freniere have bodyguards?"

The reply came back immediately.

"It is believed that the top brass in the intelligence agencies felt that since Dr. Antoine Michel was assassinated, there might be a connection between him and Dr. Freniere. We are looking into that assumption right now to see if there was something going on that connects the two. We haven't been able to find out anything yet. We do have a connection between Sister Mary Adair and Father Dumas now, however. We also have a connection between Dumas, Bartlet, Steinfeld, and Bourne. We gave that data to Lieutenant Dubois and our contacts in Metsada, CIA, and DIS as well. Also, when the police went to find Sister Adair to talk to her, she was gone.

"David, be careful, if the CIA is looking into your actions because of your connection with Beverly and the memo, someone else may be as well. Those people could be the ones that are responsible for the assassinations."

David shook his head and poured himself a stiff Gin and Tonic. He sat down in front of his Ben Franklin to think. He decided to put the data down on a list. He needed things to be organized.

1. Four murders: Dr.Antoine Michel, Dr. Freniere, Directors in French intelligence agencies, and two bodyguards. (Were the two doctors connected in some single enterprise? Could it be the Pentagon Project?)

2. How are Sister Adair and Father Dumas connected? Was there more to it that just giving her a scholarship for the conference? (Who is Father Dumas? Where is Sister Adair?)

3. Was the man taken away in handcuffs General Bourne? What is the connection between Bourne, Bartlet, Steinfeld, and Father Dumas? (Are they connected to the secret project at the Pentagon mentioned in the memo that we have been investigating?)

4. Are the two murdered men from the two different French intelligence agencies connected to Father Dumas and the others? (Does the connection also have to do with the Pentagon Project? How?)

5. What were the tests Claude Lambert mentioned to Ephraim that took place between General Bourne and Dumas? (Where did they take place?)
6. What does the explosion of a laboratory on the outskirts of Le Mans have to do with the case? (Who would be looking into the explosion?)

David finally put his pen down, sighed, and went to his kitchen to get some hot chocolate with cream before going to bed. This time he placed a jigger of Brandy in it instead of rum to make sure he slept. He also made sure he gave Beverly a call before he retired. He was not going to make the same mistake twice with the beautiful and sexy Beverly!

"Hello," her sleepy voice stated.

"Hello, beautiful lady. I just thought I would call to wish you a wonderful sleep and say thank you for the magnificent dessert."

"My goodness David, you certainly are responsive now. I should have raised hell with you years ago!" She laughed. "I wish you were here, my feet are cold! Besides, you could have some more dessert with me," she stated coyly as she hung up the phone, leaving David in a dither. He got up, poured some sherry in a glass this time, and drank it all in one gulp. By the time an hour passed, he was sound asleep, dreaming of desserts.

Chapter Nine
A New Plan Unfolds

The vibrations in his mind shook by the
Thunder of his actions, no longer allowing
Him to experience the goodness of life,
In reality, his sorrows have made him dead
Since the throngs of Vengeance echoed in
The day of his grief, they now lie buried
Deep inside the rot of his decaying mind—

Teddy, Edward, and Ephraim were sitting in their safe, spacious office on the top floor of an old hotel. It was one of the perks given to Edward by the prime minister when he left the agency. The office was located on the top floor and had access to the roof of the building as well as the building next door.

This particular meeting took place after the murder of Dr. Edouard Freniere at *Le Méridien Montparnasse* in Paris, the taking of General Bourne of NSA in Washington DC by NSA officials, and the disappearance of Sister Adair. Edward had just logged off of his computer after his conversation with his nephew, David. Things had been happening at an explosive rate, yet nothing was overtly evident.

"My God, Edward, we have more data than we used to possess to destroy a whole army, yet we still don't know what is actually going on in this case. What is the latest on Father Dumas from Lieutenant Dubois?" Teddy asked as he shook his head.

"Well," Edward began, "according to the Paris police and the RG working together, Father Dumas is a real monk and is now missing from the *Abbaye de Solesmes*. According to the abbot, he left a few days ago and has not returned to the Abbaye. Lieutenant Dubois did find another connection between Dumas and another sister. It seems a Sister Murphy of St. Cecillian's Abbaye was also an acquaintance of Father Dumas. It also just happens that she attended a conference of Metanexus three miles from Saint Omer at the Hotel Chateau Tilqucs."

"Wasn't that the hotel where Dr. Antoine Michel was assassinated?" Ephraim asked.

"You got it. Two nuns who know Father Dumas and two assassinations of directors of French intelligence agencies attending conferences that the two sisters attended. It is somewhat beyond coincidence, don't you think? Now the question is, where is Dumas, where are the sisters, and what did the two directors have in common?"

"And, what does all of this have to do with the Pentagon Project?"

"And, why would a monk and two nuns be murdering French directors in the first place? I better call Claude."

"Bonjur, ceci Claude peut-il j'est-el vous aider?"

"Claude, it is Ephraim, can you talk?"

"Ah, yes Uncle Ephraim, I am safe. I am sure you have heard of the entire goings on from Lieutenant Dubois. He contacted me as well. I believe I am now somewhat up to date. What can I do for you?"

Ephraim gave all of the information the group had so far, including the information Davie has just given him. He then asked Claude what the two French Directors might have in common.

Claude took all of the data down on a notepad and whistled. "This is a lot of excellent information, Uncle Ephraim. On your question, I had heard the two were involved in a secretly funded project that had to do with computers and animals. However, outside that small bit of data, I have nothing. The initial funding for the project, according to one agent here, may have come from the United States, possibly the American's Pentagon. Beyond that, he didn't know anything more, either.

"As I listened now to the new information you gave me, I think you may be right. Maybe all of the people we are looking into are involved in some way in what is called the Pentagon Project? What does such a project have to do with assassinations, though? How or why a French Benedictine monk and two French Benedictine sisters would be involved in such a secret project, or assassinations, is beyond my imagination. If they are the assassins, the question takes on a more confusing and evil hue! I will see what more I can find out about it and will call you back when I get the information."

"Yes, please do Claude, it could be extremely important."

"What do you think this weird scenario is all about, Uncle Ephraim?"

"I don't know, Claude, but it can't be good."

After the conversation, Ephraim looked at his two chums and shook his head. "Well, we were right to ask. Claude believes that the two directors were involved in a research project involving computers and animals. It may have been funded by the United States Department of Defense, but he didn't know for sure. It is my guess that it is the one and same secret Pentagon Project that was funded by black funds so that no one would know about it."

"Yeah, which probably makes it untraceable at this point!" Teddy responded.

"Hum, let's see... Bourne may possibly be in custody, Sisters Murphy and Adair along with Father Dumas are missing. What about Bartlet, Steinfeld, and their agents? Where are they now?" Ephraim asked.

"Let me call my contact at DIS," Edward stated.

"I'll call mine at Metsada," Ephraim added.

After about five minutes, the three sat looking at each other and shaking their heads.

"Bartlet is missing," Edward said, "and there are hundreds of DIS agents looking for her as we speak."

"Steinfeldt is missing, too; the Metsada is going crazy," Ephraim stated as he shook his head. "What about Bourne's agent, Gary Hart, anything on him?"

Edward nodded. "I found out that he does work under Bourne and has been called in for discussions, but my contact didn't know why. That kind of clinches the fact that Bourne was the one taken into custody. However, Hart is nowhere to be found either, but he is not considered missing, just out of touch."

"Typical of the CIA!" Teddy commented.

* * *

In the *Hotel 3E'toiles-vall'ee de la Sarth* in Solesmes, Father Dumas was sitting in a luxury suite with Sisters Adair and Murphy. Gary Hart was present.

"Why are we being kept here against our will, Father Dumas? What is happening? I don't understand why you are doing this." Sister Adair spoke while Sister Murphy cried softly. They were no longer under control of the computer and felt fearful.

"You two are in terrible danger, Sister. I am simply trying to keep you out of harm's way. Mr. Hart here is a CIA agent and has informed me that there is a conspiracy to murder you both. That is why you have a cut on your forehead, Sister."

"What? How could that be? Why would anyone want to murder us? We have done nothing wrong!" Sister Adair's eyes pooled. "I don't remember getting the cut on my head, either... dear God, what is happening to me?"

"We are just simple nuns!" Sister Murphy stated, wiping a tear from her eye. "Why would anyone want to harm us?"

There was a knock at the door and Gary looked through the keyhole. "It is Director Bartlet, she is with George Jones."

"Ah, yes. Gary, let them in while I go to the other room for a moment."

Dumas left and went to his computer, where he typed in some instructions before going back to the other room.

He told Sister Murphy that she should go with him to allow the others to talk in private for a while. When they left, Sister Murphy asked why Sister Adair hadn't come with them. He told her that Sister Adair needed to tell the others about her experience in Paris. After Gary had opened the room for Marion and George, his cell phone rang. He said he had to take the call and went outside so he could get better reception. Marion and George sat down to wait for Gary and Dumas. They casually looked over at Sister Adair. They noticed her vacant eyes and then a look of fear crossed Marion's face.

"My God, George, shoot her... shoot her quick," Marion whispered urgently. "She is programmed to kill us!"

When she said that, George took out his gun but Sister Adair knocked it out of his hand and was on him immediately. The two struggled and Sister Adair flung George to the floor. He grabbed a chair and hit her over the head. In a split second, Sister Adair grabbed him and snapped his neck. She then turned to Marion, who had grabbed the gun. She shot the nun in the chest, but Sister Adair swung her fist and hit Marion's arm and the gun flew to the floor. Marion started to run out of the room to the hall but was pulled back in by her hair. Marion grabbed a large vase and slammed it over Sister Adair's head but it didn't faze her. Sister Adair then grabbed Marion by the neck and snapped it in one quick jerk.

Sister Murphy was filled with fear as she heard the breaking of furniture and the vase in the other room. Father Dumas then typed in some instructions and she went limp. He looked into the other room and saw that Gary had come back and was about to enter the room. Dumas hurriedly typed some more instructions into the computer. Sister Adair looked up at Gary as he entered the room.

Hart looked around the room at the carnage and shook his head.

"What the hell has happened here?" he yelled. "What is going on? Where is Dumas?" He then looked over at the nun and watched as Sister Adair walked slowly toward him. Dumas watched from the bedroom door.

"Dumas what the hell are you doing? Have you gone crazy?" he yelled as he took out his gun and shot Sister Adair three times in her chest.

Sister Adair jerked each time but kept coming. She grabbed the gun out of his hand and threw it out the window. When it hit the pavement many stories below, it discharged. The explosion was heard by all of those in the area. Sister Adair grabbed Hart as he started to run out the door. He hit her in the face, kicked her, and grabbed her by her neck, but her strength was beyond his capability to overpower. She grabbed him and pulled him back into the room. She clutched the agent by the neck and snapped it. He fell to the floor with a frown and vacant eyes. Dumas looked into the room, sighed, and then went back to the computer. He typed in some more instructions. Both of the sisters were now docile, but both were still under the spell of the computer. Sister Adair however, looked at Dumas with an odd expression on her sweet face. Then she fell over and died, still looking at Dumas with her sad, puzzled, and uncomprehending eyes.

Dumas stared at Sister Adair, shook his head violently, and crossed his chest a number of times. Tears formed in his eyes and bled down his cheeks as his dark thoughts started consuming him. He sadly grabbed the computer case and the arm of Sister Murphy, who was still in a trance. Together, they fled the room and went down to the lobby in the elevator. They left the hotel and got in his car just as four police cars pulled up to the hotel with red lights flashing like crazy dervishes. Lieutenant Dubois, along with other agents from the RG, rushed into the hotel while some policemen talked to people in front of the hotel who had heard a gun hit the pavement and discharge.

Rene Dumas sadly watched from his Mercedes as he slowly drove away. His mind was swinging back and forth between hatred and self-incrimination. His eyes were filled with dark tears as he shook his head and gazed at the vacant-eyed nun next to him. He sighed and pushed down on the accelerator to escape the lethal scene and his deadly thoughts.

"Agent Roux, the desk clerk said they are supposed to be in room 567. Let's go," Lieutenant Dubois yelled in French as he headed to the elevator.

When they arrived, the door to the room was open. Just inside the open door was a woman who an RG agent identified as Marion Bartlet, 2nd Assistant Director of MI6.

"My God, Agent Roux, are you sure?" Dubois asked.

"Yes, I have met her several times. The man over there is her agent and personal bodyguard, George Jones."

"What about the other man and the nun?"

"I do not know. What a horrible, horrible mess. It looks like all but the nun had their necks snapped. She was shot once in the chest with a smaller fire arm and three times in the chest with a large caliber pistol." As he said that, one of the policemen rushed into the room with a gun in a plastic bag.

"Lieutenant, we found this gun on the pavement below, a lady said it fell from up here and discharged when it hit the pavement. It discharged on impact. We retrieved the bullet as well; it was lodged in a tree trunk."

The RG agent took the gun and looked at it. "It's a Smith & Wesson .44 magnum six-shot pistol with a long barrel. I believe that is a favorite of some of the CIA agents in America. It looks like the caliber that shot the nun. One bullet from that gun would kill a horse. I don't understand why she needed to be shot four times. We need to find the others that were here! They must have killed the men and the nun."

The lieutenant got on the phone and called Claude Lambert.

"Agent Lambert, we have a serious problem." He spoke to Claude for about three minutes, then clicked off his cell phone.

"Well gentlemen," he stated to his policemen, "let's get to work! Go over this room with a fine-tooth comb. Don't miss a thread or a crumb! We have to get to the bottom of this. Talk to the maids and the occupants of the rooms on this floor. See if they can remember who was here!"

"Ephraim, this is Claude. I have some more information for you, and it isn't good! Marion Bartlett of DIS, her bodyguard, and a nun are dead. They have been assassinated."

"Oh my God, are you sure it was Marion Bartlet of DIS?"

"Yes, and her bodyguard, agent George Jones, as well. Both of their necks were snapped."

"Wasn't that like the murder of the French Scientist and his two bodyguards?"

"Yes, Uncle Ephraim, and there was also the body of a CIA agent. I would guess it is Gary Hart, and a nun named Sister Adair."

"Wasn't she the nun that was at the hotel where one of the assassinations took place?"

"Yes, that is correct Uncle, she is the one the police were searching for on a train from Paris to St. Omer. She is the one that never showed up, along with the monk, Dumas. She was suspected of assassinating Dr. Edouard Freniere. This time, she was shot in the chest once with a small caliber pistol and three times with a .44 caliber gun. She might have killed the others before she died."

"That proves the monk may have something to do with the assassinations! ... What? I see.... Okay, we have some more data for you too, Claude. We received some data from Edward's nephew. I will give you that now." After another three minutes, Ephraim flipped his cell phone shut and looked at Edward and Teddy.

"Things are happening awfully fast—too fast! Marion Bartlet, her agent George Jones, the CIA agent Gary Hart, and Sister Adair were all found dead in a suite at the *Hotel 3E 'toiles-vall'ee de la Sarth* in Solesmes. Claude believes that Dumas, the monk from the Abbaye in Solesmes, could have been involved in the assassinations. But why would a monk be involved in murdering a director of intelligence and a nun, for God's sake, or anyone for that matter?"

"How were they killed, Ephraim?" Edward asked.

"Bartlet, Jones, and Hart all had their necks snapped like a stick, they were broken in two, actually. Sister Adair was shot in the chest four times. Three times was with what they think was the CIA agent's gun. The other one was a smaller caliber pistol, which belonged to George Jones, Marion Bartlet's agent. They will know for sure after a ballistics test."

"They had snapped necks, huh? That's the same way Dr. Freniere and his bodyguards were assassinated. I wonder if Sister Adair murdered them as well?"

"That seems highly suspect," Edward stated. "She is a very small woman with seemingly little strength. The whole thing is unbelievable. Besides, what would be her reasoning? What would a nun have against scientists and intelligence agents? It makes no sense at all. Of course, her even being with the others is beyond reason or logic."

"Well I have seen small female Metsada agents take huge men apart in a minute," Ephraim stated.

"Yes, but they have been conditioned and trained to do such things, and they have reasons as well," Teddy replied.

Edward sent a message to his nephew, told him all about the latest situation, and asked him to come to London as soon as possible. The ex-spies then looked at each other and shook their heads as Edward opened a bottle of wine.

"We still have David Bourne, David Steinfeld, and his bodyguard, Metsada agent Meir Shavit, as well as Father Dumas to contend with," Edward stated solemnly. He then looked at his friends. "And, we still might have a group of civilians that we haven't even identified."

"And they are all missing, except Bourne who is in custody," Teddy commented.

Edward's computer started playing Moon River. He got a little red, smiled, and punched a key. A message from David appeared on the screen.

"Uncle Edward, I just received your message. It is all so unbelievable! Why would a nun assassinate anyone? If she is as small as you say, how could she do what they say she did? Anyway, I have some new data, too. General Bourne was in custody, but he is now missing. He escaped somehow, from solitary confinement in a federal lockdown facility. My contact tells me most of the officials in the NSA feel it was an inside high-level escape, planned by someone with a tremendous amount of clout. They are looking into it as we speak. One of the guards at the facility who was being held for questioning was found dead the day after. I will take the first plane to London tonight. I should see you sometime tomorrow afternoon! I think there may be another player or players in all of this mess and at a very high level. I wish I knew what this was all about!"

Edward told the other two ex-spies about the last thing David had told him, looked at them, made a toast, and took a drink of wine. The others followed suit. This went on for several hours, and a third bottle appeared and was opened.

David looked at the note with the questions he had written before. He read the items and murmured to himself. Item number one appeared to be partially answered. The two murdered French scientists were involved in an animal-computer experimental laboratory. Item number two concerning the connection between Father Dumas and Sister Adair seemed to be affirmative as well. Dumas and Sister Adair knew each other and were now known to have been connected. Item number three appeared to be true also. It was Bourne, and it appeared that the others were also involved in the Pentagon Project, whatever that was. Item number four, the connection between Dumas and the French scientists, appeared to be true as well. Item number five remained a question. However, they probably had to do with the assassinations somehow. Item number six was answered to some extent; the two assassinated directors appeared to have been involved together in animal experiments, which might have taken place at the facility that was blown up.

* * *

Edward looked at the others after drinking his fourth glass of wine. "David says that General Bourne escaped from lockup.

It is felt that this was a high-level plot. David will be here tomorrow. I think we all need to go to France when he gets here, what do you say?"

"Hell yes, I have all of my medicine, what could happen?" Teddy laughed.

"I'll call Claude and tell him, maybe we can all get together in Paris. It will be like old times." Ephraim laughed. "Like old times with the exception of seducing beautiful women and staying up all night drinking!"

"Yeah right, Ephraim, when did you ever seduce beautiful women?"

The three old spies looked at each other and roared so hard they started coughing. They then made another toast to seducing beautiful women and drank more wine.

"Teddy, don't you have a contact at the Vatican? Maybe he knows something about this monk fellow, Father Dumas."

"Yes I do, he is Bishop Brian Fitzgerald, one of my second cousins. He is in charge of the Holy Literature and the Vatican library. I don't know why I didn't think of getting hold of him before... old age I suppose!" He laughed. He then dialed a number and was connected to the library.

"Yes, may I help you?" a raspy Irish voice asked.

"Yes, I need to talk with Bishop Fitzgerald."

"Speaking, who is calling?"

"Father Brian, it's your cousin, Teddy Dell."

"Well my goodness sakes me boy, I haven't heard from you for over four months now. How have you been, Teddy? Still thinking of leaving that Anglican Church and becoming a real Catholic?" He laughed. "Is that why you are calling?"

"No, Father Brian, I'm still sticking with the Anglican church for now. But I am still a sinner!" He laughed. "I called, not about religion but about a religious. Do you have any knowledge of a Father Rene Dumas, a monk at the *Abbaye Saint-Pierre de Solesmes*?"

"Hum, that name does sound somewhat familiar, Teddy. Wasn't he the president of a French firm before becoming a monk? Ah yes, I think he was and the name of his corporation was the *Informatique Humaines, Inc.*"

"That would be Human Computer Technology, Inc.?"

"Yes. It seems he granted the Vatican two million dollars when he was allowed to become a monk at the *Abbaye Saint-Pierre de Solesmes*. He also gave the Abbaye another two million. If I remember, he was 45 when he entered the Abbaye. That was four or five years ago. I felt that was quite late for a person to become a religious, let alone become a monk. However, in the Catholic Church, money has a very loud voice!" He laughed.

"Father Brian, do you have any knowledge of what his firm did and where they are located?"

"No, I'm sorry, Teddy. I don't know what the firm did. I do remember that the plant was not too far from Paris, though. Let's see, if my brain is correct in its recall of such memories, I think it was located somewhere near Le Mans. That is about 250 kilometers from Paris."

"Thank you, Father Brian. Have you heard anything else about him?"

"No, sorry Teddy, but I can ask a few people here, someone probably knows more about him than I do."

"Great, I'll give you my new phone number. Thank you, Father Brian, take care!"

"You too, Teddy... and Teddy, when you are ready to convert," he chuckled, "I will be your representative. Come by and see me sometime soon, even if you don't leave that other church!"

"Thank you, Father Brian, I'll think about converting next year, but I will come to see you before that," Teddy laughed. With that, they hung up their phones.

"Okay guys, Father Brian believes that, at one time, Dumas was the President of a company. The firm was called *Informatique Humaines, Inc.,* which is Human Computer Technology, Inc. in English."

"If it is located near Le Mans that makes sense. If I am not mistaken, it was near Le Mans where the news said a laboratory of some kind burned down or was blown up some time ago. I wonder if there is a connection there?"

"Things are getting interesting, my fellow spies. It is feeling like old times again, except my arthritis is acting up!"

Edward laughed. "We might as well get our reservations to Paris all set up now. Davie should be here tomorrow and we can all fly to Le Mans."

Ephraim nodded. "I'll contact Claude and Lieutenant Dubois and let them know that we will all be arriving in Paris tomorrow! Now let's have another toast!"

Teddy smiled and poured the glasses full of the beautiful red claret. He made a toast and they all took sips and sighed.

*   *   *

Rene Dumas and Sister Murphy were speeding toward Le Mans in his Mercedes Benz. Sister Murphy was still under the influence of the computer and was asleep. The green hills and little valleys of the beautiful French countryside passed by like in a dream. The streams that he crossed several times were dark cerulean and looked cold. Dumas stopped to pick up three female hitchhikers who looked cold standing by the side of the road; one of the girls was German, one was Italian, and the other was American.

"*Jeunes dames de bon afernoon ou etes vous allant?*" Father Dumas asked, thinking the girls were French.

One of the girls, who was actually Italian, smiled. "*Stiamo and ando vedere it Abbaye in Solesmes!*"

Father Dumas smiled and said in Italian, "*Molto buon, sono un Monaco al Abbaye!*"

The German girl nodded her head. "*Nehmen sie uns zu der Abbaye?*"

Dumas nodded. "*Selbstverstandlich, aber ich musse zuerst einen Umweg nehmen.*"

The comely American girl named Lucy giggled and stated with her eyes wide, "You guys are speaking in so many darn languages at once I can't understand hardly any of it. What is going on?"

The girls laughed and the German girl, Anna, said, "Lucy, he asked where we were going and we said to the Abbaye at Solesmes. He then said he was a monk and lived there."

Cristiana, the Italian girl, then spoke up. "He then said he would take us there and give us a personal tour, but he had a detour to take first."

"That is cool," Lucy stated with a large smile. "I am freezing and that Mercedes looks nice and warm."

Dumas smiled, let the girls into the back seat, and continued driving toward his corporation.

"What is wrong with the sister, Father Dumas?" Lucy asked as she noticed the nun was sound asleep in the front seat and hadn't awakened.

"She is very tired, she has had a very trying day. Sleep will do her good. You should try to get some sleep, too. I have a little errand to run before we go to my Abbaye. It should not take more than a few hours or so after I finish my business. There are some crackers and cheese in the side of the door, please have some."

Dumas arrived at his old firm, the *Informatique Humaines, Inc.,* in the evening. The place was empty of personnel since he had let them all go after the devices were completed for the Pentagon and he had joined the Abbaye. The front of the glass and metal building shone an eerie yellowish-orange as the last rays of the sun reflected off of the two-story array of tall glass windows. He parked his car and went inside; the girls were all asleep.

He collected hundreds of the micro-miniature devices to be embedded into brains. He gathered over five dozen of the miniature embedding devices along with a gallon of a newly created, highly effective and concentrated ether derivative. After placing plastic explosives with timers all around the building, he got back in the car. The timers were set for thirty-six hours, or if someone came too close to the building prior to that time, they would trip a wire and the building would explode within about 30 seconds.

The sun had gone down and only a small, thin line of dull pink remained below dark, ominous clouds on the horizon. The cobblestone driveway was now a grayish-pink turning dark gray and the tall trees along the outside of the building appeared like ghostly figures.

He sighed as he looked back at his building. He opened the back door and sprayed the backseat with the ether derivative. The girls moved slightly but did not wake up from their sleep. He looked at the darkening sky, sighed, and shrugged his shoulders as another dark sky emerged in his brain.

He took out one of the metal syringes used to insert the micro-miniature chips and inserted the devices into the base of each of the girls' necks. He put the large suitcases of the other devices in the trunk of the car. After about five miles, he turned to the west and headed towards the *Abbaye de Solesmes*. It was now dark and rain-filled clouds were forming in the north, a harbinger of a new spring storm. Soon the clouds would be releasing their sorrows and God would be throwing his bolts of electricity at the damp earth.

* * *

He thought back to his three nephews in America and what had happened to them years ago. He shuddered as he remembered the phone call from the Boston police telling him they had all committed suicide, as had their mother, his beloved sister. That was after she found her children dead and the reason behind their suicides. He couldn't believe what had happened and it had turned his stomach and mind inside out. He had thrown up until there was nothing left in his stomach.

He followed the situation for a year and found that nothing had been done to bring justice to the perpetrators who had sexually abused his nephews. He kept every scrap of information on them, and as his mind slowly clouded over with a nefarious and deadly darkness, he had formed his plan. The plan was one that would repay evil with what he rationalized as holy justice.

He used the war-minded directors in the intelligence agencies in America, Britain, and Israel to support the project, and the Pentagon to furnish the money for the project. It would eventually be called the Pentagon Project. The people he had contacted became enthused about the project and how it could alter how future wars would be managed. However, his personal plan had nothing to do with their inane wars; it had to do with his revenge, retribution, and retaliation for sins. He would use the people in the Pentagon to help further his personal plan while they believed he was helping them with their plans.

* * *

He arrived back at the Abbaye in the early hours of the morning, after driving for hours. He slipped the four women carefully through the entrance court into the long and narrow Abbaye church itself. He looked down the aisle under the tall ecru-colored ceilings, sculpted idols with cold marble eyes staring out at him from all sides. In his mind, they had harsh and thunderous accusations carved on their marble mouths.

He glanced at the beautiful, colorful lead glass windows of the nativity. Their beauty was now hidden by the lack of sunlight in the church as well as in his mind. He then glanced at the Crucifixion and the Last Supper with tears in his eyes and shook his head sadly, then angrily. "How could they? How could they dare?" he asked the four by his side. He looked to the right hand side of the nave and saw the solid stone statute of Saint Peter, the patron saint of the monastery. "How could He have allowed it? Why could God not intervene, in their sins?" He mumbled almost incoherently as he led the four women forward to the first transept with its beautifully sculpted groups called *Les Saints de Solesmes*.

Unknown sculptors had carved all the saints. Their identities had been destroyed during the revolution, just as his was being destroyed by the avenging angel within him. He stared down the center to the monks' choir where he had first become engaged with the beautiful Gregorian Chants. He shuddered. He looked to the southern transept dedicated to the entombment of Our Lord and shook his head angrily.

"How could it be possible?" he murmured. He walked with the four to the northern transept dedicated to Our Lady, where the tests of his design were first discussed after the completion of the animal tests. This time he shook his head despondently. He then walked back to the tomb of Our Lord. It was the most famous carving of all of the 250 depictions of the scene, which were all over France today.

He gazed sadly at one of the figures, one that seemed out of place. He had been told it might be Jean d'Armagnac, Lord of Sable. He wondered how that happened. He assumed it was probably because he donated a house on the isle of Sable called the *Logis de Solesmes* to the monks in 1365, serving as their place of refuge.

It seemed money and power had eventually overpowered everything, even faith and the pious religious. He figured it was similar to what happened in contemporary church life now. Money and power was the force behind the Pentagon Project as well. He looked back at the southern transept and glanced first at the upper then at the lower scene. Above was the triumph of Mary, and on the upper right the virgin of the Apocalypse. He had made this particular Mary his idol of prayer, for she had to do with destruction, as did he.

He traveled with the four to the monks' choir, the major addition to the end of the church in 1864 by Dom Gue'ranger, and looked down the side aisle with the beautiful tall wooden benches. This was where the monks stood resolutely and sang the Gregorian Chants that filled the church with its mystic and enchanting tones, tonal prayers of love and piety.

"Why did this happen?" he angrily murmured as he glanced up at the roof vaulting that was initiated at the time Columbus was sailing for the new world. Dumas thought about the thorn – believed to be from the Crown of Thorns from the head of Christ – which was exposed only once a year at Easter. He shook his head violently. "How could they do it, those scarlet ogres of the Lord, those nefarious traitors of all religious precepts?"

The marble-eyed sculptures stared down at him with their pious accusations and empty answers. He had tried to understand the whole tragedy as explained by Dom Philippe Dupont, the abbatiate. However, he could not fathom the depth of it, not even after many honest attempts over the past years. It was pointless to question it now that the deadly process had settled in his mind. Many lives had been lost, all as part of the plan to avenge his tragedy. He was now the avenging angel, the soldier at the side of Mary of the Apocalypse. He knew that only she could understand, even though at times he couldn't understand it himself.

The dazed females stood by his side, unable to see the beauty, the darkness of the evil, the light of the piety, or the tragedy of what was taking place in the mind of the monk. They were also unaware of their future part in the sad drama of the avenging angel that would continue to unfold. His mind's neural networks had become chaotic, just as the renowned physicist Pranab K. Das had once explained could happen to the mind of man.

The only other person who might have been able to explain his dark dilemma was Arnold Lebeuf, Doctor of the EHESS, who wrote the *Cosmology of Love Madness*. Arnold Lebeuf believed that the violent rupture in the mind between holy piety and the quest for blood revenge existed between the two entities' reality and non-reality. The reality was that some men who had become religious had also become mad, and in their madness had created the shadowy evil that plagued their brains. Their dysfunctional brains, confronted with a dark obsession, could have caused them to destroy the children of God. The non-reality was that their superiors did not see them as mad, but simply as sinners who must be forgiven as God forgave all sinners.

On the human level, the consequences of their carnal knowledge of subjective reality had not only been tolerated but also accepted by their superiors as a simple, meaningless, sinful fantasy, a mistake of passions. On the spiritual level, the pedophile priests of which were spoken had committed a massacre of tiny souls on a scale beyond that of the fall of the archangel from heaven.

They had created an uncivilized and unholy world where small souls were held in abject terror of their behaviors, behaviors which would permeate little minds and souls for all eternity. They had created a mysterious quantum space-time break, which would eventually affect the consciousness of all humanity. He, Rene Dumas, had to stop the madness. He had to be God's avenging angel. It was up to him alone to destroy the cause of the rift between God and man, between the religious and those small children who perceived the holy relationship as pure only to become their victims. He had to demystify the unholy behaviors by destroying at least three men who had become insane and tried to destroy the children of God. In this case, the children of God were his nephews and sister.

Dumas glanced over at the innocent women in his midst, bent his head down, and sobbed. The four females stared at him with vacuous eyes, unable to soothe him or understand his dichotomous predicament. He continued sobbing until his mind was filled with the sorrow that fills all of those who search for justice and mercy by using evil as their avenging tool. He could never love those who committed such evil upon the innocents as directed by his superiors and his God. He was a man lost between good and evil, between the darkness and the light. He was a man traveling alone in madness.

Chapter Ten
A Pause in the Avenging Storm

Within his disquiet, there is a subconscious
Awakening to the reflection of evil, which
He has embraced and yet does not understand.
He is no longer aware of the universe nor
The havoc his manic search for vengeance
Has wrought upon his mind

General Bourne looked at the tall, distinguished man and asked, "How did someone know I was involved and how did you get me out?"

"To the first question, General, I have no answer, but I am aware that some intelligence communities are rife with unauthorized communications going back and forth overseas. Even the Pentagon Project is in the light to some extent, and it's raising quite a bit of nervous interest now. Of course, there is no data in any file concerning the ramifications and goals of the project, so we are safe for now and the project is almost completed, except for the final phase. The development of the new long-range transmitter is almost complete and one of our men is in Gitmo awaiting the signal for the release of the prisoners. We will send the embedding devices when those dates are determined. However, for the second question, I have many contacts in various places who owe me tremendous favors. Your escape was just one of the paybacks."

"How many of us who knew of the project are left?"

"I believe only you, David Steinfeld, Meir Shavit, Dumas and my group. The others are all dead. The laboratory and the scientists who carried out the preliminary tests are dead. The two French Intelligence scientists, Dr. Edouard Freniere and Dr. Antoine Michel – who were initially involved with the computer-animal project – are also dead, assassinated by Sisters Murphy and Adair. We accomplished that and destroyed the laboratory, but the others, including Marion Bartlet and her bodyguard George Jones, and your agent Gary Hart, were all assassinated by Dumas' holy assassins. Unfortunately, the intelligence communities of America, Britain, and Israel are ubiquitous now with activity and communications in regards to these events. The Pentagon Project will be under increased scrutiny from now on. However, since it was paid for by black budget funds and no one is aware of the aims of the project, it should remain invisible for a while. Regardless of all of this scrutiny, we must still remain resolute in our goals." The tall man spoke solemnly.

"Since the laboratory was blown up and most of the others are dead, that means the only data on the project is held mostly by your group and Dumas now," the General asked rhetorically.

"Yes that is true, but our plan has been sabotaged by that crazed monk, and it might fail if we cannot retrieve the data, computer, and devices from him somehow. The new president is likely to free the terrorists from Gitmo within a short time after he gets into office, if Congress allows him to do so. If they don't, we will have to force an escape. I have heard that the Senate and Congress may stop his actions to free the prisoners and we must be prepared to act quickly if that happens. We will know sometime after his swearing-in if Congress will vote to free the prisoners.

"We are putting pressure on many key legislators of both parties to vote for his proposal right now, but I have heard some of them will not comply. We need to get to about a hundred of the hard-core Gitmo prisoners so we can inoculate them before they make it back to their respective terrorist bases. Under our control, the freed terrorists will be the most effective assassins in the history of the world. They will even be more skillful and brave than the Nizaris', a sect of Shi'a Islam founded in the 11th century. Where the Nizaris' used fear and violence, our assassins use calm, superhuman strength, a total lack of fear, deadly determination, and a complete lack of a guilty conscience. The Islamic Jihad will crumble into tiny pieces and it will take at least 50 years for them to build up their terrorist armies again. That is if the prisoners are freed so we can send the assassins embedded with the devices back to their various terrorist camps. We cannot allow our plan to fail! The security of America is dependent on our success. We know for sure that three of the terrorists at Gitmo are from the Al Takfir Wal Hijra, the extreme extension of the Saudi Arabia's Wahabbi group. Just think what those assassins could do to their group!"

The General nodded and looked out the window of the jet. As dark clouds spewed their liquid and electricity upon the plane he nervously asked, "Where are we now?"

"We are heading over the ocean to Paris. We will then go to the Le Mans area where Dumas' firm is located. If we do not find him there, we will go back to the Abbaye at Solesmes. He has to be at one of those places or in some hotel nearby. I can't see him at a hotel though, not now anyway. He must know by now that we are aware of what he has done and will be after him. He will go underground and will be on guard. Besides, he must be aware that the RG, French Police, CIA, DIS, and MI6 are all looking for him now. There must be intelligence agents tripping all over themselves trying to find out who he is and where he is."

"Yes, I know sir, and we have to find him first or the plan is dead and the terrorists win," the General whispered as he looked out at the darkness filled with bolts of lightning, and clouds engulfing the plane.

*   *   *

It was raining violently, the thunder was as deafening as a huge waterfall, and the lightning intermittently exploded the sky into flares of light amid the darkness. At the Abbaye, Dumas and the four women stood silent in the northern transept where Our Lady was entombed. Dumas looked around to make sure no monks were walking in the area and then went back to the rear of the sculpted tomb.

He listened to the Gregorian chants wafting from the monks' choir like beautiful, intoxicating perfume. The sounds of the chants were only interrupted by the muted roars of thunder echoing through the thick walls of the Abbaye. He paused and shook his head to clear his mind of the dark clouds filled with violent images and pushed on a small, slightly extended marble tile. The tomb slowly moved aside to reveal a set of steep and narrow marble stairs in the rear of the tomb. He took the four women and led them down the steps.

He was thankful that he had taken care of Father Adamo Diego Giotto when he was 97 and in his last days on earth. Father Giotto was the last one who knew of the secret stairway hidden below the sacred, carved tomb. He died at the age of 98 a year later, and Father Dumas was one of the very few he told about the stairway below the sacred tomb. The only other living person who knew of the stairway was Monsignor Riley, now 87. He had dementia and was being taken care of at the Vatican. No one listened to him when, at times, he ranted about secret stairways in the Abbaye, especially one located to the rear of a sacred tomb.

Dumas took a torch from the side of the hallway and lit it before he led the way down the narrow stairs to a room at the end. A larger room contained three smaller rooms with low alabaster ceilings, leading away along a small hall to the rear. Two of the rooms were austere sleeping cells with rope cots. The third was a tiny, ancient, but functional bathroom. On the walls of the hall of the large room, twenty golden candleholders with large tapers hung silently, looking like holy specters.

Dumas lit some of the candles and sent the women to one of the other rooms containing four cots. The women lay down on their cots and went to sleep. Dumas looked at their innocent faces and moaned sadly. He paused for a short time, but recriminations once again started to flood his mind. Then, as the tears ran down his cheeks, the dark images of his sister and her children intruded into the neural pathways of his brain and he stiffened.

He went back to the main room, set his computer down on a mahogany table, and opened a large bag. He could barely hear the rain now and the initial roar of the thunder was almost forgotten. He took out various cheeses, several types of crackers, apples, hard bread, and a bottle of wine. He uncorked the wine and poured a large glass full of the purple liquid. He held the glass up to a picture frame containing images of his nephews and sister and drank fully of the wine.

"You will be avenged, my lovely children, my dear sister. Your deaths will not be in vain, it will be soon." He placed his head in his hands and sobbed uncontrollably until he became exhausted. He eventually fell into a dark, twisted, nightmarish sleep depicting hideous ogres in robes devouring small, innocent children.

* * *

The corporation jet circled and then landed on the landing strip at ORLY. The moon was high and shone dimly through the dark clouds that were vanishing to the south like swirling black omens of the past. The General and the tall man walked down the ramp to the wet pavement, got into a limousine, and left. The car headed west toward Le Mans and clearer skies.

The General poured himself a glass of 25-year-old bourbon and placed one ice cube in it. He swirled the liquid around for a short time, then took a large swallow. The tall man turned his head and placed a pillow against the door. Bourne turned and looked out the window, watching the rain turning to a soft shower as the darker clouds and the roar of the lightning faded to the south.

He wondered about the wealth and power of the man beside him who was now sleeping fretfully. He didn't really know too much about the man, nor at this point did he care to. He finished his drink, took another pillow, leaned against the other door, and went to sleep.

As the two men slept, the rain continued to decrease. The lightning bolts no longer came down to the earth with a brilliant, terrifying, evil vengeance... unlike the firing neurons in the mind of a dark monk hundreds of miles away.

Chapter Eleven
A New Plan Takes Form

Within his torn mind, he finds no peace,
He is flying, yet cannot soar above the
Lowly earth, which holds him prisoner in
Its darkness, he cannot find comfort nor
Solace in his actions, nor his lonely quest,
His voice of reason has faded, his
Self-hate has grown, and he feeds upon his
Sorrow. He despises his life, but abhors the
Existence of the life of the others with whom
He is consumed.

It was morning and the spring rains had abated for a short time. Some ominous clouds with dark, flat bottoms still hung silently over the mountains in the far distance, but the sun was peeking out through small cracks in the clouds. The air smelled of fertile, damp soil and freshness.

The 747 landed at the Heathrow airport in London with a series of soft bumps. The last bump woke David Heywood. He looked out the foggy window and saw three cars: a black sedan, a blue and white police car, and an old brown sedan. He figured the older sedan belonged to the old spies and the black one to some new ones. The blue and white had red lights spinning like gaudy birds dancing in fire on top. He grabbed his overhead bag and walked down the ramp. Uncle Edward emerged from the brown sedan, a policeman came out of the blue and white, and a man in a gray overcoat emerged from the black sedan.

"Uncle Edward."

"Hello, Davie, how was the flight?" Edward asked as he took David's bag and placed it in the brown sedan.

"Great, Uncle Edward. Why the other vehicles?"

"Oh, that is Lieutenant Dubois in the police car. Ephraim's nephew, Claude Lambert from RG, is in the black sedan; we have all been working together on the case. Davie, it is like the old times, I feel 20 years younger!"

The two men came over and shook hands with David. "It's good to meet you, David," Claude stated as he shook his hand. "Ephraim says that Edward talks about you all the time. He says he thinks you are a genius."

Edward smiled, nodded his head, and shrugged his shoulders. Claude laughed.

Ephraim and Teddy shook hands with David and told him his feet, as well as his brain, would be invaluable to them. David stated he probably did have better feet but didn't know about his brain. Lieutenant Dubois came up to David and told him how important some of the information he had discovered was to the case.

"Where are we now on the case, Lieutenant? Do we know where Dumas is located?"

"We are not sure, but he is probably somewhere in Solesmes or near Le Mans. The police recently went to the Abbaye of Solesmes, but did not find Father Dumas or the nun there. Your information on General Bourne escaping was very helpful; it gave us some insight into how high up the food chain the plot originated. It told us that the General had to have had some very high-level inside help. What is your take on the Pentagon Project now?"

"Well, I think it has to do with super assassins, that's for sure. But I don't know how a small nun who has been shot four times in the chest can still snap the neck of a very large, strong, and qualified CIA agent. Unless some drug had been introduced into the person's blood stream, it doesn't make any logical sense. Did you get a reading from the coroner on Sister Adair, Lieutenant?"

"I just got the package before Edward called me and asked me to meet you," Claude interjected. "It's in the front seat of my car." He ran back to the black sedan, reached in, and took out the package. He looked at the analysis sheet on her blood and handed it to the lieutenant.

"My God, look at the level of Phencyclidine in her system... it is unbelievably high!" Lieutenant Dubois exclaimed in disbelief. "You were right, David, something had been injected into the nun's system."

"That makes sense, Lieutenant. It would take something like PCP for her to still function after being shot in the chest, especially if she was shot three times with a .44 caliber slug. I wonder if she was the one who snapped the necks of the three, or if it was someone else? However, we had a case recently reported where a thief jumped out of a five-story building, broke both legs, and still ran off. He was captured, but only because he kept falling down. We know that Phencyclidine makes the person extremely strong as well as immune to pain. It took four policeman to hold the thief down, and that was after accidentally breaking one of his arms as well."

"Anything else, Lieutenant?" Teddy asked.

"Yes, but I don't understand what it is. An extremely tiny, miniaturized device was found in the mid-brain of the nun who was shot. They said it was an electronic module of some kind."

"Let me see that report, Lieutenant Dubois," said Claude.

"So that's what it is!" Claude exclaimed after looking over the report for a moment.

"That's what, Claude?" Ephraim asked.

"There was a project going on in France that was top secret. I couldn't talk about it before, it was for specific eyes only. Dr. Edouard Freniere and the French scientist Dr. Antoine Michel were involved in a joint project with a French firm. It had to do with computer-controlled animal experiments concerning animal behavior. I think now that they were probably involved with the Pentagon Project. It appears from the autopsy of Sister Adair that the original animal modules that interfaced their brain with a highly sophisticated program in a computer has been micro-miniaturized and used on humans."

David nodded his head. "The firm that developed the micro-miniature device was probably Rene Dumas' company."

"Yes, that might be correct, David. Anyway, the module the two French intelligence scientists were involved with had to do with embedding a receiving module into the brain of animals to control their behavior through a special computer program. Instructions were transmitted at a specific frequency from the computer to the module in the animal's brain. The RG could not find much more data on the project, including its goals or its test outcomes. We didn't interfere or look into it that much since scientists are always doing tests on animals for a multitude of reasons. We found notes in a hidden safe in the home office of Dr. Antoine Michel after he was assassinated, though; those notes concerned the animal tests. We also found data about a laboratory near Le Mans where the testing took place during the past two years. It looks like the laboratory where he and Dr. Freniere had research scientists working on animal-computer experiments could have been the one that was blown up. That fact was hushed up because RG was still looking into it at the time. All we have now are some notes and some internal memos concerning the mutual interaction between the French Doctors Freniere and

Michel and the Pentagon Project. The basics of the experiments and the general goal of using a sophisticated computer to control the behavior of animals, or possibly in this case humans, is all we have. There was no technical or scientific data of any type found in his notes, and no plan detailing how they were to be ultimately used."

"I think we need to go to Dumas' firm in Le Mans, gentlemen!" Edward stated.

The RG agent Lambert made a phone call, then he and the Lieutenant went over to where David and the others were waiting.

"Gentlemen, we have our agency's Cessna Citation X available," Claude exclaimed. "It is an eight-seat plane that can cruise at 590 miles per hour. I called ahead and it's fueled and ready to fly us to Le Mans. There will be a car waiting for us at an airport in Le Mans, a private airport a few miles from Dumas' firm."

The ex-spies and David got into the brown sedan and followed Lambert and the lieutenant to a private airport a few miles outside of London.

"The action is getting exciting!" the three old spies commented in unison as they lifted their hands in a mock toast.

*   *   *

Rene Dumas lifted his head from the table where he had fallen into a fretful, shadowy sleep filled with dark nightmares and images of sinful popes and saints. He visualized in his brain an image of Pope Urban II smashing the brains of small children who he considered heretics. He then saw the pope and his bishops marching off to the Crusades with thousands of small, bloodied children marching in front of their horses to protect them. He was totally unaware that the Abbaye had been filled with police searching for him while he was in a deep sleep. Even when he was finally half awake, he could only hear faint voices and footsteps treading softly like mice over the marble ceiling as he struggled to awake from nightmare terrors.

He finally became fully awake, heaved a sigh, leaned forward in his chair, ate a few more crackers and some cheese, and had a few sips of wine as he thought about his quandary. He finally got up, woke up the four women, instructed the three girls to change back to their street clothes, and had them eat the rest of the crackers, bread, and cheese before going back up the stairs to the tomb.

After making sure no one was around, he pushed the tomb back to its original configuration, took the four women to the nave, and sat them down in pews. He then went to his laptop computer, punched in some instructions to the brains of the women, gazed at them sadly for a short time, and left.

Lucy was the first to become conscious. She looked over at Anna.

"Anna wake up! We must have gotten here early and fallen asleep. My gosh, look at this place!"

Anna woke up and looked at Cristiana, who was now awake, stretching and yawning. The three girls looked at the nun who was just waking up.

Sister Murphy looked startled as she looked up at the vaulted ceilings and the niches with the carved statues and frowned. "How did I get here?" she asked.

The three girls shrugged.

"We don't know, Sister," Lucy said. "We don't know how we got here, either. The last thing we remember was being picked up by a monk on our way to this Abbaye."

The nun looked perplexed, then looked at the girls and said, "It must have been Father Dumas who brought us here."

Anna nodded her head. "Yes, the man said he was a monk at this Abbaye and would bring us here and even give us a personal tour."

Cristiana looked at the others as she rubbed her eyes. "I don't remember taking any tour."

Sister Murphy sighed. "Well children, I will take you on a tour, and then we will visit my Abbaye and I will take you on a tour of that Abbaye as well."

* * *

It was early in the morning the following day and the rain had finally stopped. The air was brisk and fresh, but still had the feeling of returning showers. Father Dumas had been driving from the Abbaye at Solesmes to a private airport near the outskirts of Le Mans. He had called ahead and his Cessna CJ3 was fueled and waiting for him. A man in a blue uniform came up to him when he arrived and spoke to him in French.

"Monsieur Dumas, it is good to see you again, it has been some time since you have flown your CJ3. Company business, sir?"

"Yes Jean, I have some important business to take care of in Rome. You have filed my flight plan for me?"

"Yes sir, the Rome Fiumicino airport, as instructed."

"Very good, Jean."

Rene Dumas got inside his CJ3 Cessna, ran through a series of checks, then taxied on the tarmac and increased his speed. In a matter of minutes, he was soaring above the Le Mans area and heading toward Rome. He communicated to the airport to have a black Berlingo Citroën ready for him when he landed.

After a short time, he changed direction toward Lyon and began thinking about the onerous yet exhilarating task ahead of him. He had learned some vital information when he contacted a friend of his at the Vatican. He was going there now to follow up on the information. He put the plane on autopilot, laid his head back on the seat, and closed his eyes in contemplation.

Chapter Twelve
Reasons Become Clearer

The storms are raging longer in this place,
Spring is colder than normal this year,
If the darkness continues, even the sun
Of summer will be colder and damper, and
More dreary.

"Uncle Edward, did you ever contact anyone at the Vatican to inquire about Father Dumas?" David asked as the plane soared along from Paris to Le Mans.

"Yes, Davie, but I didn't learn too much, just that he was indeed a monk at the *Abbaye de Solesmes* and entered into the priesthood only about four or five years ago at the age of 45. He was described as a gloomy monk, but a dutiful recluse who spent the majority of his time alone in his cell or singing Gregorian chants with the choir. He seldom talked to any of the other monks. However, the present Abbatiate Dom Dupont said he talked to him many times about cardinal sins and forgiveness, especially of priests who had committed extremely sinful behavior while being priests. He said Father Dumas had a difficult time understanding the Catholic Church or the Vatican's behavior in forgiving priests with horrible and dark behaviors. Abbatiate Dupont said he felt Father Dumas had some terrible and grievous sins that he had a hard time believing could ever be forgiven."

David wrinkled his brow and then shook his head. "I can understand the Pentagon, NSA, and the CIA getting involved with this human computer thing, even the assassinations, but why a Benedictine monk, why nuns, why especially one Rene Dumas? There has to be some underlying reason that we don't understand. He has to be involved in something different than the plans of the others. But, what it is, that's the question, and why?"

"Well, prior to becoming a monk, he was the president of a company that delved into computer things."

"It still doesn't make sense, Uncle Edward. He certainly doesn't need the money as a monk. There has to be another deeper reason. Then there are the assassinations. It is hard to believe that he or nuns could be involved in such repulsive and evil behaviors. Those types of behaviors are antithetical to all Catholic moral precepts."

"I am afraid all the evidence points to his being the one," Claude explained. "I, as a Catholic, have a very hard time with that assumption as well."

"Maybe he is insane," Ephraim stated as he looked at the others.

"Perhaps that is so, yes..." Lieutenant Dubois commented as he shook his head. "It is much harder to catch an insane criminal than a sane one, the insane one never has a reason for their behavior that corresponds to common logic. It is always something different than we think! Yes, Ephraim you may have hit the, er, *ongle sur la tete*."

The Cessna banked and headed down to the cities below. Before them, green pastures lay basking in the pale orange morning sun, partially hidden by white gleaming clouds. Things were clean and glistening after the cleansing rain. The countryside was spotted with hundreds of small white cottages, verdant valleys, and small rills that meandered about the landscape like a blue snake. Suddenly the city of Le Mans came into view and the plane headed down toward a private airport miles below.

As it circled to land, David thought about what Ephraim had said and murmured, "Even if insane, what could be his goal for using a device which controls a person's mind? More importantly, why engage in assassinations after becoming a monk? Why couldn't he accomplish his goal just being a crazy president of a corporation and not as a religious?"

Teddy overhearing David's murmurings and said, "David, you are right; those are the questions we need to think about!"

When the Cessna landed, the six got out and walked to a large Citroën sedan. They got in and the car headed to Dumas' firm, *Informatique Humaines, Inc.*

The six relaxed and watched the beautiful scenery speed by as the Citroën traveled along the smooth ebony road. Lazy sheep were meandering along ancient trails of verdant green. Sheepdogs were herding the sheep with communications from a whistle that a man in tattered clothing held to his lips.

David thought about the sheep and the dog, then about humans who could be similarly controlled by a computer. He shuddered in disgust. "The ultimate weapon," he said aloud.

"What did you say, Davie?" Edward asked.

"Uh, I was thinking about the sheep, and a dog controlled by a whistle, then about humans being controlled by a computer and said that would probably be the ultimate weapon."

"Yes, perhaps that is what some of those in the intelligence agencies thought as well. That could be a valid military reason for such a nefarious and far-reaching project. One must go back to the 11th century and the charismatic leader named Hasan I-Sabbah to see what the Nizaris assassins did. Then one can look at the Fidais, a dagger-wielding bunch of killers; they would assassinate anyone at the urging of a Grand Master. Just think of such a Grand Master who could control others through mind control on a massive scale! It is ominous and quite scary."

"First torture, now using humans as assassins without their knowledge, what has America come to?" David lamented.

"Pretty much what it has always been I am afraid, Davie," Ephraim stated sadly. "Those on the outside never get to see or hear of the evil inner workings of their governments, or I should say, the persons in power in the governments. Only those in the service of their governments, like we used to be, really know what is going on. Sometimes it is definitely not a pretty sight! Most civilians would cringe if they really knew about what goes on at the hands of their leaders."

Claude nodded. "Just think if the police could insert something into the brains of criminals. I wonder what could happen if the tens of thousands of those incarcerated in prisons, or the terrorists in your American Gitmo, were freed with brain modules embedded in their brains? One could surmise what could happen if they were sent back to their gang-infested ghettos or terrorist organizations with instructions from a computer to assassinate the criminal leaders or terrorist leaders in their organizations. A weapon like that could be the ultimate doomsday weapon. Such an awesome weapon would be hard to turn down, regardless of the moral imperatives against it! Sometimes those in power can only see the end and neglect to see the means, but evil means are usually what contaminates the moral fiber of a person, or a nation."

David then said, "Especially after the CIA and Pentagon have been using torture already to achieve their goals. Man's abnormal and hideous acts seem to become normal when he keeps doing them over and over again. Familiarity does not promote contempt; it promotes familiarity and then acceptance. Millions of American citizens condoned the torture of terrorists in Gitmo when it was spun to look like it was used to protect their fat, pathetic little hides."

Lieutenant Dubois nodded. "That acceptance through familiarity theory is true, look at the historical behavior of the serial killer. The more he kills, the more compulsive or obsessive he becomes, and the easier it becomes! Finally, in the end, the more desirable it becomes. It is the same with bad habits; the more you experience them the easier they become, that is what addiction is all about. Look at smoking for example, of course that is an addiction based on the need for nicotine, but the behavioral principle remains somewhat the same. Alcoholism falls into that category, too."

Ephraim nodded sadly. "Yes, my friends, just look at the Holocaust; millions of Jews were murdered, experimented upon, tortured, and abased. The end justified the means in the minds of the Nazis. Even though most of the German citizens said they did not know anything about what was happening, many did and said nothing about it. Their moral reasoning had been desensitized."

"David, you are probably right about Dumas, but it must take a person with no conscience to consider such a horrible abuse of another human being. Either that or he is truly insane," Claude remarked.

"Ephraim," Lieutenant Dubois began, "do you think it is possible that greed or some other powerful need can become such an overwhelming obsession that the mind will excuse any moral argument against abnormal, unethical, or even criminal behavior being used to obtain it? What if that behavior helps the person reach ideological goals deemed to be necessary, valuable, or even holy in the person's mind?"

David nodded. "We can see that mentality in those greedy bankers who caused our recession. The end, gaining tremendous wealth, justified everything they did."

"I wonder if evil behaviors in the seeking of wealth could be such an obsession?" Edward mused.

David grinned. "Well, that is the holy mantra of Ayn Rand as well as the Illuminati."

Edward shook his head and smiled.

Ephraim looked at the others. "I wonder if wealth-seeking behaviors influenced the Germans to start out just desiring the Jews' riches and their wealth, and that desire eventually led to the mass murdering of the Jews? Perhaps a wealth obsession might affect some who seek wealth above all else." Ephraim shook his head sadly. "God, I hope that is not what is happening to our societies. That type of wealth-seeking behavior does appear to have led to the financial collapse."

Teddy nodded. "Yes, it does seem it was the obsession of greed that led to the behaviors of the bankers and the corporation leaders on Wall Street that caused the downfall."

"That it is true. Look at the actions of Enron executives, investment bank executives, and all the others in the banking industry. They have almost destroyed America and the world with their obsession for the amassing of wealth and their risky wealth-seeking behaviors. Look at Madoff! It was reported that he even bilked his own family out of millions, let alone the 40 or 50 billion he took from others who trusted him and relied on him for sage advice."

David looked at Ephraim. "Ayn Rand's philosophy and the tenets of the Illuminati, an organization most think is mythical, has wealth and the obtaining of wealth placed above all else. That was what her novel *Man and Superman* was all about. The organization claims that no behavior to obtain wealth can ever be considered wrong or sinful. It all appears to fit the current pattern. Perhaps those in control of the military industrial complex are of that same mindset, and have been for years and years. Just look at the series of wars that we have had over the short history of the United States. Remember, it was President Eisenhower who warned Americans to be aware of the power of the military-industrial complex in their midst. He may have been deadly accurate. The system may have bred monsters with no consciences. Or perhaps the people who come to power value wealth-seeking behaviors, regardless of how heinous, above all else, including human life."

"You are saying, David, that there might be a group of civilians who helped mastermind the human-computer project at the Pentagon for the purpose of gaining wealth and power, while the military complex acquiesced in order to gain military superiority and power?"

"I'm just saying that it does seem to make more sense looking at it that way. Anyway, what still doesn't make any sense at all is Father Dumas' part in all of this and the assassinations of some of those who were probably part of the project in the first place. What are their goals? And do they differ from the other two groups?"

"Perhaps Dumas was part of the project in the beginning for a personal goal, not the goals of the others, not for purposes of amassing wealth and power or military superiority," Teddy remarked.

Lieutenant Dubois' cell phone rang.

"Hello... yes... yes... I see, and three other girls as well? ... Yes, what? ... Yes, have them contact me immediately... yes, thank you."

He looked at the others in the car. "Gentlemen, we have a break in the case. Three young girls on vacation and Sister Murphy have been found. Father Morel of the *Abbaye de Solesmes* found them in the nave early this morning just as the monks were going to start their chanting. He contacted his cousin, Sergeant Lavigne in one of the Paris precincts, and told him three girls and Sister Murphy were found. They were okay but had large lapses in their memories. However, their stories all related to Father Dumas. The sergeant contacted the local police and they contacted the RG. The four have been taken to a hospital in Solesmes to be checked for the devices."

"That is wonderful news, but why would Dumas leave Sister Murphy and the three girls if he was going to use them to achieve some personal goal?" Teddy asked.

David nodded his head. "Maybe his conscience kicked in and he decided not to use any more innocents. Maybe he figured that the three girls and Sister Murphy might die like Sister Adair."

"Hm, that means he might be on his way someplace to finish his self-ordained task, whatever it is, himself. He might also consider finding some unholy persons to fulfill his goal. Gentlemen, I doubt if he is here at his firm." The Citroën pulled up to a large glass and steel structure in the center of acres of grass, bushes, and trees.

A huge sign with the name *Informatique Humaines, Inc.* stood to one side of the road as the Citroën drove up to the building. The car, unbeknownst to those inside, ran over a wire as they drove up the driveway. The six men got out of the car and started to approach the huge building.

Just as they got near, a huge explosion erupted from within the building. Yellow and red flames shot out from the broken glass like colored confetti and the building burst into a blazing inferno. The men ducked behind their cars as splinters of glass flew at them like crystal bullets. Widows blew out and then other explosions shattered their ears as they continued ducking behind their cars. Within five minutes, there was nothing left of the building but bent steel rods sticking out of glowing metal ashes. They all formed a red webbed canopy of molten steel that looked like a ruined ancient cathedral. There was nothing left now but a pile of ashes and broken glass.

"Good God!" Edward exclaimed. "Dumas must have set up a system to blow up his own building."

"I would say he doesn't plan on coming back," Teddy said as he nodded. "He must have been here recently and placed timed explosives or some kind of trip device."

Lieutenant Dubois' cell phone rang again.

"Yes.... What? When? ... You have the destination? ... Yes, thank you."

He shook his head and looked at the others. "Damn it! Gentlemen, we need to fly to Rome immediately!" Dubois exclaimed. "Dumas filed a flight plan to a private airport just outside the Vatican. He left about two hours ago."

"Did you find out anything new about Dumas?" David asked.

Claude shook his head. "We didn't find out much that hasn't already been discussed.... I can't comment too much on his personal sins or the sins of others. He might have become involved in the project as the president of a company that delved into such things, and it somehow affected his mind later... I just don't know."

"As I stated before, he is probably insane!" Ephraim stated as he looked at the others. They all nodded their heads.

David and his five cohorts had the driver speed to where the Cessna was parked and ready to go. They jumped out of the car, raced to the plane, and yelled to the pilot who was smoking a cigarette beside the hangar. Within about ten minutes, they were soaring toward Italy.

Claude called out to the pilot. "Did you by any chance take the opportunity to fuel up?"

"Yes sir, I always do. It is RG protocol. One never knows when plans change and I need to fly someplace immediately." He smiled.

"David, do you have a hint as to why Dumas is flying to Rome?"

"No but it has to be pretty significant." Just as he said that, his cell phone rang.

"Yes... yes, this is David Heywood.... Hi Beverly, this is a pleasant surprise.... You found out some information on Rene Dumas? That is wonderful news, shoot!"

When he clicked his cell phone off after listening and taking notes, he stared out the window for a moment. His mind seemed to be lost in the murky vapor of the darkening clouds.

"What's up, Davie?" Edward asked. "You look like someone slugged you in the stomach."

"I just learned the reason why Rene Dumas is doing all of this. His nephews and sister are the reasons!"

"I don't understand, David," the lieutenant said.

"Rene's three young nephews were molested by two Catholic priests from the Boston Diocese. The bishop, instead of turning them in to the authorities, sent the priests overseas."

"Oh my God," Ephraim exclaimed.

"That is not the worst of it. The three nephews committed suicide. It seems the two priests told them they were evil little children."

"Now I know why I am an agnostic," Teddy exclaimed in disgust.

"There is more. Rene's sister went to the bishop to plead her case, and he told her she had to forgive the priests. That is

139

what Christ would want. He also told her the children did a sinful thing by committing suicide, which could affect their souls in Purgatory. She got so angered and upset that she hit him with a vase, cutting his head. The police were called, she was arrested for assault and battery and was put in a cell for arraignment... she hung herself in the cell that same night."

"Oh my God," Lieutenant Dubois and Claude muttered in mutual revulsion.

"No wonder the man flipped. I think I would, too!" stated Claude. "And I'm a good Catholic in spite of all the crap that has been going on lately. I sometimes wonder why things so horrible keep happening to the little innocents. It is enough to test one's faith."

"I personally never understood how the Boston bishop or the other bishops in America got away with what they did," commented Teddy.

"Me neither, Teddy," Lieutenant Dubois replied. "In my world what they did is called aiding and abetting, and whoever does that is guilty of the same crime as the one he abets. They should all have been arrested and tried as felons!"

"I believe some of the powers that be at the Vatican removed the bishop and brought him along with some other bishops and pedophile priests to Rome," David stated sadly.

"It seems to me that I heard that the Boston bishop is now the head of one of the major churches in the Vatican," Teddy commented in a disgusted manner.

"Well that is vile," Ephraim stated,. "I would say we now know where Dumas is heading. He is heading to the Vatican to assassinate the pedophile priests and probably the bishop. However, this time he does not have an assassination machine, it is just him alone." Ephraim was starting to sense in his mind a dim empathy for the monk for the loss of his nephews and sister.

"He is alone now but he may plan to stop somewhere and pick up some less innocent persons to be his assassins," Claude commented. "As mad as he has become, he may still not be able to commit murder personally."

The others nodded their heads and thought about the terrible possibility of more murders. The heavens started to cloud up again and they saw eerie flashes of light and heard the roaring of thunder in the north again.

Chapter Thirteen
Father Dumas's New Assassins

A private Lear jet was ten miles from its destination in France when the pilot received an urgent message. He gave the satellite phone to the co-pilot to take back to the cabin.

"Sir, there is a communication for you," the co-pilot stated as he arrived at the sitting area and handed the phone to the tall man.

The tall man took the phone and sat back down in his seat. "Yes."

"This is agent Barnes, sir, I have some important information for you."

"Go ahead, Barnes."

For the next few minutes, the tall man shook his head while he listened. When he got through, he gave the phone back to the co-pilot and looked out the window at the approaching storm.

"What is it, sir?" General Bourne asked.

"I now have the reason why Dumas betrayed us. He was never in support of the project for military goals in the first place. He was setting up a personal plan of murder and revenge. I believe he is going to the Vatican to assassinate two priests and possibly the ex-Boston Bishop Daze." He then explained the information to the general who shook his head.

"I would kill the bastards too, sir. If we ever do get ahold of the devices and computer, maybe we can assassinate a few thousand Catholic priests and many bishops along the way. I never did like that weird cultist church with all of its stupid gaudy god idols anyway." The General snarled, showing his teeth. "I can't see why they still depict Christ nailed to a cross, either. God, I am glad I'm a fundamentalist Baptist."

"Well, that is not our concern, General. Control your emotions. Ours is a more noble aim: we are going to wipe out the Islamic terrorists once and for all!" He didn't mention to the General that it was primarily to create massive wealth for himself and his group by creating wars and selling trillions of dollars in arms to the governments involved.

"I am not sure that is at all possible, just assassinating a few Islamic leaders here and there. It would be like killing a street gang leader, as soon as he is dead another one pops up to take his place. The same thing happens to drug lords, look at Mexico and the drug gangs... kill one leader and another takes his place. Just look at the assassinations of dictators in the past, after the tyrant is assassinated and the coup is over, one of the coup leaders becomes the dictator, then in time, another tyrant. Then, in time, it all starts over again. And what about the African nations, what a bloody mess they have there. It is all cyclical in nature! The only way to stop the recurrence of modern terrorism is to destroy the countries that have terrorists and every one of the ignorant citizens that could become future terrorists. I believe we need to use atomic bombs to destroy Islamic nations with terrorists. The devastation must be so substantial that there will be an existential fear to be a terrorist and then there will be no people wishing to be terrorists left, at least not for many generations. Just look at Japan, they surrendered immediately and have never been a threat since."

"Don't you feel that would just lead to more retaliation by other Islamic nations, General?"

"Possibly, but if they do, we could use atomic bombs to destroy them as well, and so on until all of the Islamic terrorists nations have been destroyed. That is the only way to end terrorism for generations to come. We have enough atomic bombs stockpiled to bomb every nation in the rest of the world a thousand times over. It is not just the terrorists who are to blame; it is also the Muslim citizens who, in their stupidity or naivety, harbor them. It is also those who allow the terrorists to use their homes as hideouts or caches for their weapons. What gets me is they complain about getting shot by coalition forces and there they are having supper with terrorists and militants who are responsible for ten times the number of civilian casualties. What the hell are they thinking? What do they expect? Those people are so damn stupid and illogical it makes me crazy. As long as you have breeding grounds for poverty, ignorance, and radical ideology, you will have terrorists. Just look at those who are complicit in what the Hamas terrorists are doing. They watch the missiles being fired into Israel from their yards, and then yell and scream when Israel shoots back and destroys their homes. Their whole attitudes and behaviors are crazy illogical."

"I prefer not to use atomic bombs, General, we could end up being bombed ourselves. We might even get bombed by one of our present allies who don't trust us anymore. They might believe that if we can use atomic bombs on some Islamic nations, we would not hesitate to use it on them if sometime in the future we have a disagreement. That is what caused the cold war. Russia believed we would bomb them next. Remember, only the United States, so far, has ever used the atomic bomb on another country. Dropping more atomic bombs would create a war not just between Arabian nations and us, but it might also create a war between North Korea, Iran, Russia, China, and us. It might even possibly include India and Pakistan. No... the human assassination project is our best bet, or just conventional high-density bombs. We can always obtain thousands of the terrorists' own people who can be used as assassins."

After telling the pilot to change his flight plan and fly to Rome, the tall man sat back and rested his head on the back of his seat. "Ours is a very noble and awesome responsibility, General; we must succeed to insure the safety of America. What would the little people do without us? They would have no jobs in our corporations. They wouldn't be able to afford a house, a fancy little SUV, or a speedboat. They wouldn't be able to go to the mall and buy things. They especially wouldn't be safe, and they would certainly have no future. The elite are the saviors of the world, General, always have been, always will be." He sighed. "If only the stupid little people had the intelligence to see that. The ultra Conservatives understand that reasoning. What the hell is wrong with the Democrats? Why do they always fight against our goals and strive to give our hard-earned tax money to the illegal, poor, lazy, and ignorant!"

"I don't know, sir, I am just a military man, not a philosopher. My job is to follow orders to the best of my ability, but I do understand why Dumas would want to murder the bishop and the priests. It reminds me of the novel *The Death of the Archbishop*... he was a son of a bitch, too, and the Zuni Indians took care of him by throwing him over a cliff! Maybe we should get rid of the whole damn Catholic Church and all the priests. The church is nothing but a damn anathema to religion anyway. God

I am glad I am a fundamentalist Baptist and know the answers to what God is all about!"

The jet droned on as the tall man and the general became lost in their own thoughts, hundreds of miles apart from each other. They were still about an hour and half from Rome.

* * *

David's group was two hours away from Rome. Each of the men in the plane had their own private thoughts, some were even hoping a little bit that Dumas would succeed before he was caught.

Lieutenant Dubois' cell phone rang.

"Yes, this is Dubois.... What? ... Thank you, I will inform the others."

"What is it, Lieutenant?" Ephraim asked.

"One of my men just called. He said the doctor told him the three girls and Sister Murphy all had microchips embedded in their mid-brains. He didn't know how to get them out at this stage and therefore had to leave them there. He will keep them at the hospital until they can get a brain surgeon to look into the situation. You were correct... they were computer-controlled humans like Sister Adair. They also found extremely highly concentrated doses of PCP in 25 micro-millimeter capsules there as well."

"That is why Sister Adair could still snap the neck of her targets even with bullets in her chest," The Lieutenant exclaimed mostly to himself. "Now the question is, will Dumas use other humans less objectionable to his sense of morality to assassinate the bishop and the priests, or will he do it himself?"

"I need to alert the Rome Police and the RG agents in Rome that Bishop Daze is to be the target of an assassination and give them Father Dumas' physical description." Claude got on his cell phone and started making calls.

* * *

147

Dumas' small Cessna had flown to the ocean instead of going over the Alps. Flying over the Alps was a feat his little plane could not maneuver. He had headed instead toward Marseille across the Iles d'Hyeres and then toward Italy. He was now about 25 miles from Rome and planning his move to assassinate the bishop. Before he killed him, however, he would find out where the two Catholic priests were based and take care of them later.

He looked out the window of his Cessna. The view below was of bucolic, verdant pastures filled with sheep, soft rolling hills of green, and miles of grape vines. His thoughts traveled to the past, back to his nephews and sister. John Paul age seven, Adrien age six, and Rene age seven, who was named after him. He could see images of their innocent little faces in his mind.

They were all exceptionally sensitive souls, much like his sister, Chantal. They had moved to Boston with Henri, Chantal's husband, who had been hired as a supervising manager for an engineering company there. Just six years after they arrived, Henri had a heart attack and died. Chantal and the nephews turned to their church, Saint Mary of the Sorrows in Boston, for compassion and solace. Less than six months after that, the nephews came in one day sobbing. They told Chantal that they were horrible children and were the reason their father died. When asked about it, they said Father O' Brion and Father Ducane, the Irish Catholic priests that had taken them under their wings, said so. Later during the following month, Chantal found out from the children that the two priests had repeatedly sexually molested them. A few weeks later, Chantal found the children dead in their bedrooms. They had overdosed on sleeping pills. There was a note asking their mother to forgive them for the terrible sins they committed against the holy priests.

She called the police and told them of the children's confessions and showed them the note. The police looked into the matter for a week and then found out that when they asked to interview the priests, the bishop had sent the two to other parishes outside of the United States before they could be arraigned. The police told Chantal that their hands were tied since the priests were gone.

She went to the church and confronted the bishop, who told her unsympathetically that it was the Christian thing to forgive them as the church forgave them. When she told the bishop that her children had committed suicide, he told her they must have had other problems for them to do something so dire that it could damn their souls.

Chantal lost her temper and hit the Bishop in the face with a vase. It cut a large gash in his left cheek, broke his nose, and the force knocked him to the floor. He called security and they notified the police. The security guard held her to the ground until the police came and took the sobbing woman away. The bishop filed charges against her for assault and battery. Later that night in her undersized cell where she was being held prior to being arraigned in the morning, she hung herself with a scarlet scarf another inmate had smuggled in.

Rene Dumas remembered when he came to America and took the bodies back to France where he buried them. Unfortunately, not all of his sorrow nor any of his anger were buried with them. The anger eventually grew into an intense and uncontrolled black hatred. His mind could not handle the pain and he had a serious breakdown. It was close to that time when he devised his plan. He told an official in NSA that he had an idea for a military weapon. A year later, he contacted General Bourne with the computer-brain control system. Later, there was a call for corporations to aid in developing a plan to control the behavior of animals by ESB via short-range computer transmissions. His company won the bid for part of the project and he was on his way to forming his plan of revenge. He knew he would win the bid, for his bid was significantly lower than any other corporation could ever afford.

*   *   *

It was a few hours later, after the sad dark memories had left his brain, that Dumas landed in a small private airport a few miles from the Vatican.

He went to an infamous red light area of Rome and saw what he had hoped to see. He smiled as he filled the syringes and asked some young women to get in his Mercedes Benz. The young, pretty, but hardened prostitutes with skimpy skirts and low-cut blouses climbed into the back seat, giggling.

"Are you looking for a big party?" One of the girls laughed.

"Do you know what you want us to do for you, signore?" the youngest of the girls asked as she leaned over the seat and rubbed Dumas' shoulder.

"Oh yes, ladies, I know exactly what I want you to do for me!" he stated as he looked at the giggling girls in the back seat. Their skirts were up above their thighs now and they were already taking off their blouses, exposing their ample breasts.

Dumas looked in the mirror, grimaced, and pushed a button. The doors locked and a dark glass pane went up between the front and back seat. The last thing the girls heard was a strange hiss and then darkness. Dumas had his new assassins, and this time they were not innocents – they were sinners.

Chapter Fourteen
The Bishop Leaves the Vatican

Will the devil hide secretly in the shadows,
Unseen in the vagueness of his wanderings
Or will he make an error, which will bring him
Into the light of holy justice, and a cease
to more murders.

Claude contacted the Assistant Director of the *Renseignements Généraux*, who in turn contacted the Rome Police and the Vatican security concerning the assassination threat to the bishop. He also gave them the cell phone numbers of Lieutenant Dubois and Claude Lambert and said they should be contacted if things arose that they couldn't handle.

* * *

"Yes, sir, thank you for the information," the overweight Vatican policeman in charge of security stated nervously. He then wiped his brow, looked at the other security guard, and said uneasily, "We have a verified threat to assassinate Bishop Daze, Alphonse."

The guard crossed himself and asked, "What should we do, Antoine?"

"We must alert the Vatican religious on duty, it is their call. I'll call Bishop Malloy."

Brother George, a bitter small-framed religious with a cane and a crooked leg overheard the communication between the Vatican Police and the RG. He left immediately.

Bishop Malloy stood shaking his head after putting down the telephone. He looked up at the small, out of breath man who had just entered his office. "Brother George, I just got some dreadful news. There has been an assassination threat against Bishop Daze."

"I am amazed it took this long, Father," the small bishop's aide said coldly.

The bishop didn't pick up the iciness of the brother's attitude, just the words.

"Yes, Brother George, I suppose you are right! I am sure there are many who would like to assassinate all of the pedophile priests and the bishops in the Diocese of the United States who harbored them. However, that is not the way to solve the problem, as you and I know. That is not the way of the Church or of our Lord Jesus. We must always forgive sinners in the name of Christ, when others scream justice we must give mercy. Forgiveness is the way of the church. It is not man's responsibility to judge others, that onus belongs only to God.

"We are aware, Brother George, that all humans sin. All men and woman are susceptible to bad, even evil behavior, but Christ loves them all and it is our duty to forgive them as well. It is our duty to try to guide them back to the Word, not condemn them. Christ did not condemn the girl at the fountain or the prostitutes, did He?" The bishop looked firmly at the frowning brother, then sighed as he turned and looked at the large gold figure of Christ on the cross above his desk. "We must notify the religious powers in charge to see what they wish to be done." He dialed a number and waited.

Brother George mumbled under his breath, "Render unto Caesar those things that belong to Caesar and to God those things that belong to God! Man's law belongs to man, not God. The predators should have been given to the police and charged for their crimes, not protected."

The Archbishop Deschamps answered the phone and listened to the information.

"What did you say?" he asked, shocked. "I must not have heard you correctly!"

"I am afraid you heard me correctly, Father Deschamps. I have received verified information that Bishop Daze has been targeted for assassination here at the Vatican. It was an RG agent who notified his Italian office. They just called our security a few minutes ago, and they in turn just called me. Yes sir, I agree he must be moved, but where?"

"The *Abbaye Sainte Marie De Maumont* in France, they are shut down for some restoration repairs for a few months. There will be no guests there."

"That is the one in the northwest of Paris, not too far from Bordeaux?"

"Yes."

"When?"

"Immediately."

"I'll see that it gets done, Father. I will use our private plane to fly him there."

"Thank you. I will notify Bishop Daze to pack to leave immediately."

Brother George listened in on the conversation and then went to his tiny cell and made a phone call.

"He is going to be moved to the *Abbaye Sainte Marie De Maumont* in France immediately. They will fly him there from Rome. He should be there in about four hours."

"Did they mention anything about the other two?"

"No, but I found out where they are, Father!" the small crooked man said excitedly.

"Wonderful, Brother George! Where?"

"The same Abbaye, Father Dumas, the same Abbaye!"

"That is magnificent news, Brother George, thanks be to God... now I can get all three at once. Thank you, Brother, I owe you!"

"No, Father Dumas, I owe you. My nephew was molested by the same priests and I was injured by a sadistic priest when I was a child; that is why I am crippled."

"I am so sorry, Brother George. When did the problems with your nephew start?"

"About four months ago, Father. It was when he and his mother were living in Angoulême, just 30 kilometers from the *Abbaye Sainte Marie De Maumont*. My sister, Marie, worked there as a cook when they had large numbers of people at a retreat. Danny, only nine years old, went with her from time to time. The two new Irish priests from America taught him English when he was there. They both molested him every time he went there, too. He told my sister what was happening after a few months, but she would not believe him and even punished him for telling lies about the priests. Deviant, sick animals never change their evil behavior. They deserve to die, Father Dumas."

"Yes, Brother George, they do deserve to die; and they shall, I promise you! Your nephew and my loved ones will be avenged!"

Father Dumas and his ladies, now under the influence of his computer, left the hotel in Rome in the gloomy darkness of the night after they had changed into religious habits. The devices had been embedded into their brains and basic instructions had been delivered to them prior to going to the airport to fly back to France and Angoulême.

Father Dumas took two of them with him and placed the other two in a cab to go to a hotel in Rome to await further instructions. He had programmed the two to go to the hotel in the heart of Rome near the Vatican museums. He booked the two into a specific room, with deadly instructions to accomplish their tasks.

The other two counterfeit nuns, no longer saddled with their impious behaviors of prostitution, sat sedately in the back of the plane with cloudy eyes and glazed stares as Father Dumas took the same flight path he had before, except this time, he did not register a flight plan. About three and a half hours later, he set his Cessna down in a small private airport near Angoulême. He and the counterfeit nuns left the airport in a rented car. They drove to the train depot and got on the Paris-Bordeaux train line to the *Abbaye Sainte Marie De Maumont*.

After arriving at the train station, Dumas hired a small car and drove to the Abbaye. A half hour later, he stopped near the edge of the Abbaye among a copse of trees and let the nuns out. He then reprogrammed each one as they silently walked down the pasture toward the *Abbaye Sainte Marie De Maumont*. He smiled in anticipation of the three deaths. He planned to watch as Bishop Daze and his two depraved priests died in front of him after he told them what they had done to his loved ones. He made a phone call before he made his way back to the front of the church.

"General Bourne, this is Dumas. I imagine by now that you are just about in Rome. I just wanted you to know that I plan to sell the devices and computer back to you, since I will have achieved my goals in a short time."

The general wrinkled his brow and stated angrily, "Why in the hell did you betray us, Dumas? We gave you tens of millions of dollars for the research as well as our total support! My God man, all of this was your idea in the first place!" He never questioned how Dumas knew he would be flying to Rome, a lapse in his military mind that would prove to be a fatal error on his part.

"I had a grave personal task to perform, General, it took precedence over anything else in my life. You will still have the devices to achieve your military goals and I will have money to live out the rest of my life in leisure."

"How much, Dumas?"

"Only two million Euros."

The General put his hand over the phone and quickly discussed the offer with the tall man who was gazing calmly at him.

After a minute, the tall man nodded. The General spoke.

"Yes, Dumas, we will meet your demand. Where can we meet?"

"Go to the hotel at this address after you arrive in Rome. I will be there later. Have the money with you," Dumas said calmly.

The general took down the address and hung up the phone. "He said he will meet us at the Hotel Arcangelo, room 217."

"Contact David Steinfeld and Meir Shavit to meet us there too, General. They are in another hotel in that same area." Then the tall man squinted his eyes and said, "That hotel is named after the statue at the Castel Sant'Angelo. It is the Angel who put an end to the Black Death at the end of 500 A. D. I am not sure I appreciate the irony of Father Dumas, if it is irony."

The tall man gave the address of a bank nearby to the cabbie, then Bourne and the tall man sat in the back of the cab silently, each in their own unspoken worlds. When they reached the bank, the tall man got out and went inside. In less than 20 minutes, he came out of the bank with a metal case and got in the cab again. The general nodded, gave the cabbie the hotel destination, and they were off again.

The Cabbie looked at the two men and said in broken English, "The Hotel Arcangelo is very nice hotel, and very reasonable for being attractive one. The rooms beautiful, you enjoy to stay there."

Neither the general nor the tall man were listening to the man's prattle, they just nodded their heads. The cabbie went on talking in broken English as if they had responded excitedly. He continued talking about the hotel and the area until he pulled up to the old ecru-colored brick building.

The tall man handed the driver some bills and he and the general headed into the old lobby as the cab drove off. They didn't pay any attention to a nun sitting in a chair in front of a lattice reading a magazine, and another sitting in a settee across the way watching a TV screen. The nuns both looked up as the men entered and recognized the general immediately from the instructions in their brains.

The two men headed up the stairs to their room. David Steinfeld and Meir Shavit arrived a short time later and went up to the same room. David knocked at the door as Meir looked around with his hand on the butt of his pistol. The general got up and looked through the peephole. He opened the door and nodded to the two as they entered. David looked at the tall man and introduced himself. The tall man nodded but did not give him his name. Meir looked at him suspiciously, then sat down in a chair. His hand was still on the butt of his pistol inside his jacket.

"What is this all about, General?" David asked.

The General sighed and answered, "Father Dumas has double crossed us. He has the computer and the devices and will not give them back to us until he achieves his personal goal."

"Which is?"

"We aren't totally sure but it looks like he plans to assassinate a bishop and two priests at the Vatican."

"What? Why?"

The tall man stopped the direction of the conversation and said, "It's a long story and quite irrelevant at this point. What he wants after he finishes his task is two million Euros for the computer system. The money is what is in this metal case. He will be bringing the computer and the devices over when he is through with his personal task. Now, I must go make an important call. I will be back in an hour or so. If he comes before I get back, shoot him and take the computer and devices, but show him the money first to get him to relax."

About ten minutes later, a nun knocked at the door. The general looked through the peephole again and gave a startled look. He opened the door slightly and looked at the nun. "What can I do for you, Sister? Ah, is Father Dumas with you?"

"No, but he gave me instructions as to what to do," she stated quietly.

The general opened the door to let her inside. "Do you have the computer and devices with you?"

The prostitute dressed as a nun stared blankly at the men as she entered into the room. She took out a Rossi short-barrel pistol and aimed it at the general.

"What the hell are you doing? What is going on?" He then noticed the glazed look in the nun's vacant eyes and immediately knew what was happening.

He dove at her, knocking her against the bed before she could fire. Meir took out his gun and fired into the nun's back. She jerked from the impact, then snarled and fired her pistol and shot him in the middle of the forehead. She kicked at the general as he tried to wrestle the gun from her hand by breaking her wrist. However, because of her added strength, he could not get the gun from her hand.

David picked up Weir's gun and shot the nun again. She jerked and kicked the general in the stomach, knocking him to the floor. She moved the pistol to her good hand and fired at David. He bent over as the shot went into his chest. After a few more minutes of struggle with the general who had tried to subdue her again, the gun went off and he saw a red blotch forming on the front of the nun's habit next to the two other blotches. He stopped beating her and got up assuming she would fall over dead. Instead of falling down, however, she kicked him in the head, grabbed the gun that had been dropped on the mauve carpet, and started shooting at him.

The general felt the bullets tear into his body and he fell back on top of the writing table with an incredulous look on his face. His weight broke the thin wooden legs of the desk and he fell awkwardly to the floor. He looked up at the nun, who was bleeding from her chest, and started to get up. She aimed the gun at his head and shot him one final time in the middle of the forehead. His eyes went expressionless as life flowed quickly out of his body.

The nun bent down, took the metal case filled with money, and walked slowly and unsteadily out of the door, bleeding from her chest. She headed to room 213, threw the case inside on the floor, then after closing and locking the door, started down the stairs. Half way down, she stumbled and fell the rest of the way. When she reached the bottom of the stairs, landing on the lobby floor with a thud, she was dead. Women screamed and people fled from the lobby.

The tall man, who had been talking on a telephone in the lobby, looked over at the nun's body. He went over to where it lay supine, with legs and arms askew on the red carpet. At that moment, a crowd started to gather in the lobby. He looked around for the metal case but saw that she didn't have it with her. The manager called security and the police as the tall man quietly headed upstairs to room 217.

When he arrived, he saw the bodies of the general, David Steinfeld, and Meir Shavit, but no metal case and no computer. He searched all over the room but to no avail. He then went back down to the lobby in the elevator. At the same time, a nun came up from the lobby using the stairs and approached room 213. She opened the door with a card key and went inside.

The tall man walked unhurriedly out the front door as the Italian police were running inside. He hailed a cab and left. He knew that now only his group and Dumas knew of the computer and the brain modules. He also knew he had to leave the area or he could be assassinated next.

The nun calmly walked out the rear door and down the back stairs after retrieving the metal case in room 213. The policeman standing watch there saw her open the door to the outside, but simply bowed.

"Hello, Sister," he said as he crossed himself and allowed her to go by him.

*　*　*

Near the Vatican, Claude put down his cell phone and looked at David, Edward, and Ephraim. "General Bourne is dead, so is David Steinfeld and Meir Shavit. They were all shot, some in the head, others in the heart or chest. "

"My God, that makes ten assassinations now and we know that Dumas is after Bishop Daze and two priests as well," Edward said as he shook his head. "Did they find the assassin?"

Claude nodded. "Yes, a woman in a nun's habit. She had been shot through the chest three times, once at close range; she also had bruises all over her body and had a broken wrist."

"Claude, why did you say a woman in a nun's habit, and not a nun?"

"Because underneath the habit, she wore the clothes of an Italian prostitute," Claude replied.

"Dumas is using Italian prostitutes in place of nuns?" David asked.

"It appears so. I need to contact the Italian police to see if any other prostitutes are missing."

"Claude, that could take weeks."

"I don't think so, Ephraim. Dumas probably went to the red light area around the Vatican. I am sure if some are missing, the police that work in that area or the other girls will know." He picked up the phone and dialed a number, explaining the situation to the policeman on the other end.

"I will assign Sergente Alfonso Rossi to the task of accounting for the prostitutes, he has an undercover policewoman in that area. She will know about all of the girls there. I should have the data shortly."

"Thank you, Lieutenant Ricci, you have been a great help."

"*Non un problems, Claude, resta in contatto.*"

"Yes I will, and keep me informed too. Bye," Claude said as he hung up the phone.

* * *

The tall man, after talking to a secret contact in the Vatican, took a cab back to the airport in Rome. He got on his private jet and headed to France with the *Abbaye Sainte Marie De Maumont* as his destination. He knew from his contact at the

Vatican that the two priests were there and the bishop was being flown there. He figured that Dumas would be going there to murder them, which also meant the computer and the devices would be somewhere nearby.

He wasn't sure where his two million Euros were now, nor did he really care. He figured he could shoot Dumas and then only he and his group, and one very high-level person at the Pentagon would know of the project.

He reached inside a compartment under his seat and took out two pistols. One was a stainless steel Smith & Wesson .44 Magnum six-shot pistol, the other was a .32 caliber automatic Derringer pistol. It was only four inches long and he had an ankle holster for it. He put the guns in their respective holsters, put extra ammunition in a leather sack in his suit pocket, sat back, and frowned.

He watched the landscape fly by as the plane left the Italian shore and headed toward France over the dark cerulean ocean. He sipped on 38-year-old Duncan Taylor Auld Blend malt whisky and smoked a Ghurka HMR cigar. He had made a real buy on the box of precious cigars... a box was normally $10,000, and he bought it for only $9,300.

His mind wandered to the use he and the secret powers within the Pentagon would put to the assassins. He smiled as his mind drifted to dreams of achieving his goals of amassing more wealth and power.

First, we will assassinate the Islamic leaders who are against America, he thought to himself, *then the terrorist leaders and left-leaning dictators. Finally, we will assassinate any opposition in America or the rest of the world to our goals for a stronger and more militarily powerful United States of America.* He finally fell asleep with his sinister dreams surrounding him. His Gurka cigar was smoldering in an ashtray, its sweet aroma filling the cabin in a feeble attempt to overwhelm the stench of evil.

The tall man, William J. Harper, was one of those children people forgot about, even if they were in the same room. He displayed a complete lack of emotion about everything, and was rarely worried, excited, or annoyed about anything. The toys he liked were boring, his questions – when he had any, which was seldom – were boring. All in all, he was not a memorable child.

In his teens, he was gangly and still boring with a long face, big ears, and no personality. He never had much to say about anything because not many things ever excited him. He did excel in his business classes, was a success learning economics, and was a good student in mathematics. He had little interest in much of anything else. He didn't care for girls or jocks. To this day, he still didn't care much for women, or men, but he had since learned to tolerate them for his own purposes.

His father was extremely wealthy, divorced his mother when William was ten, and had little time for William. A nanny raised him from ten years of age until he was 16. She was strict and at times cruel. When he complained to his father, he was told to suck it up and be a man. In that atmosphere, he had learned to be devious, self-reliant, and noncommittal about everything. That attitude fit in well with his boring demeanor and reluctance to talk much.

In his senior year in a private, preppy eastern high school, he found that students were always in need of money for dates or liquor, condoms, drugs, or something else he considered stupid. He loaned them money at a high interest rate. When he first started, a few of the jocks refused to pay him back. He hired a couple of dropouts from the public high school to collect the money and rough up the boys. They did; the two boys ended up in the hospital. From then on, no one refused to pay him back the money they had borrowed. It taught him a lot about money and more about the use of power.

He went to Yale and graduated in Economics. He joined the skull and crossbones, and with his inherited money and new contacts, eventually became a venture capitalist and then an international banker. He was now in his late fifties and worth about thirty billion dollars, but still boring. He knew that he would be successful attaining his new, loftier goals if he could get his hands on the computer and the other devices. It would probably double his worth and increase his power over others tenfold. That was his sole motivation.

* * *

Claude looked at the others after his conversation with Bishop Malloy.

"Damn it!" he exclaimed. "Well gentlemen, we need to fly back to France. I just learned that Bishop Daze is being taken to the *Abbaye Sainte Marie De Maumont* and the two priests he harbored in America are there as well. Dumas will probably be going there to assassinate them all."

"I can understand the part about taking revenge on the priests and the bishop," Edward said, shaking his head. "That is logical, although immoral and quite psychotic. What I can't comprehend is why he assassinated all of the spy types, including General Bourne and the rest."

"He probably thinks Bourne and the others were the only ones left who knew about the project and what the computer and brain devices can do," David answered. "He surely doesn't know we all know about the project."

"Yes, thank goodness or we might all be assassinated as well. By now he should be aware that hundreds know about him and his damn computer. He does seem to have a logical neural thread missing in his brain. He probably doesn't know that we now know the exact use of his assassins, and that he is on his way to another Abbaye to assassinate a bishop and two priests."

"I wonder if his final goal is just to get rid of the bishop and the two priests, or if he has other plans as well?" David wondered as he shook his head. "He certainly got rid of all of those in the agencies who knew about the Pentagon Project for some reason. Why would he even give a damn who knew about the system if his primary goal was just to assassinate the bishop and the two priests?"

"That line of reasoning makes me think in circles, Davie. It was much easier for me to go down the narrow route, you know, his only goal was to assassinate the bishop and the priests and the others were just accidental... or perhaps part of his ruse!" Edward shook his head.

"Well, maybe we will find out in France at the *Abbaye Sainte Marie De Maumont*. We need to fly there immediately," Claude stated.

Chapter Fifteen
The Abbaye Sainte Marie de Maumont

How contemptible you are as you slash your
Soul so it can no longer soar in the Heaven
Surrounded by His love, how deplorable your
Bloody hands, which cut short the lives of
So many humans! You are but a parasite upon
The earth.

Sister Joan-Baptiste picked up the phone. The man on the other end spoke in a gravely French voice.

"Sister Baptiste, this is Father Dumas from the *Abbaye Saint-Pierre de Solesmes*. We met at the meeting of the Metanexus Global Network conference this year."

"Oh yes, Father Dumas! How are you?"

"Very well, thank you, Sister Baptiste. I hope you are well, too. Ah, Sister, I have a request. I know you are not taking anyone at the Abbaye because of your renovations there, but two nuns are coming to visit your Abbaye to study your texts on the French ecclesiastic Cardinal Pierre de Bérulle. They are Benedictines from the congregation of Subiaco and follow the rule of Saint Benoît de Nursie. They are aware that you have some wonderful historical texts on the founder of the French Oratory at the Abbaye and wish to study and copy some of the papers you have. Would that be alright with you?"

"Oh, that will be fine, Father. They can also stay with us; we always have extra rooms for the religious. We do have many of Cardinal Pierre de Bérulle's spiritual writings on the Catholic Reformation. However, many believe his influence was based less on his writings than on his individual relationships, his political actions, and his beliefs advanced through his followers. We have some data on them as well."

"That is wonderful, Sister, he certainly had an impact on his contemporaries. The sisters should be arriving soon. I will be there in a half hour or so myself. Uh... could you put up with us for a couple of nights?"

"Oh yes, of course Father Dumas. As I said, we always have several rooms that are available for the religious. We will also be having another very important guest arriving soon and we have two resident priests as well, they from America. We will be having dinner at 8:00, will you all join us?"

"You are so gracious, Sister, I would enjoy that immensely."

After hanging up, he sat down and reprogrammed the two assassins. He frowned when he was finished, got out of his car, and after taking the laptop computer out, placed it in an attaché case. He started his walk through the verdant countryside to the

Abbaye in the near distance. He shivered with an outraged anticipation as he thought forward to seeing his hated nemeses. He had decided to shoot the two predators himself and have the false nuns assassinate the bishop while he watched and laughed. That was why he re-programmed their brains with new instructions.

The two prostitutes dressed as nuns had their brains adjusted to the new messages as they approached the front door of the Abbaye. Sister Joan-Baptiste opened the door and, with a big smile, welcomed the nuns into the Abbaye. The two stood like pale ghosts in their ebony black habits, stared at her with cold, vacant eyes, then moved silently like specters through the massive door and into the hallway. The Sister felt an unrecognizable malevolent gust of air go by her as the nuns passed. She shivered involuntarily. She looked at the two nuns and asked if they would like to be shown to their rooms. They did not answer. They simply nodded as they looked at her with vacant eyes.

After leading the odd nuns to their cell, she watched as they went in and sat on their cots, becoming immobile. They stared at her again with inexplicable and expressionless eyes. She shivered again, hesitated for a moment, and then closed the door.

As she walked back to her room, she felt a tiredness envelop her as if she had been out in the snow for too long. A feeling of deep sleep leading toward death beckoned her. She had the feeling of deep evil overcoming her being. She slumped on her hard cot and then slid to her knees and looked up at the silver Christ on his polished mahogany cross. With an inexplicable uncertainty, she started praying in soft whispers.

Her prayers were interrupted after about ten minutes upon hearing the brass clapper hitting the sides of the bell at the entrance to the Abbaye. She slowly rose and shook her head, trying to obliterate the desperate tiredness in her soul and the vague evil feelings in her head. She walked slowly to the front door and opened it, hoping she would not encounter any more vacant staring eyes.

"Oh... is that you, Father Dumas? Please come inside," she said, relieved.

167

"Thank you, Sister Joan-Baptiste, it is nice to see you again."

Father Dumas was dressed in a black cassock with the hood over his head. He appeared to her like a shadowy apparition. She shivered once again and gave him a diminutive smile as she opened the door wider. He walked past her and she experienced a scent of dark evil fluttering past her for the second time, just as it had when she met the two nuns. She shook her head to clear her mind. Dumas pulled the hood off of his head, bowed, and smiled broadly, instantly extinguishing the sinister spell.

He clapped his hands together. "My, it is getting awfully chilly outside! You get colder winds here than in Solesmes!"

"Yes, it does seem that is true especially in the evenings and at night, Father. The air is quite crisp during those times, our microclimates in this area are quite different from those in Solesmes. May I show you to your room?"

"Yes, thank you Sister. By the way, did the two nuns from the congregation of Subiaco arrive?"

Sister hesitated a moment then whispered, "Yes they did, Father... uh, they are somewhat strange."

"How so, Sister?" he asked, looking at her suspiciously.

"They seem distracted and far way and did not communicate!"

"Oh, I can imagine they are quite out of their normal world being here. Remember, Sister, their Benedictine order follows the rule of St. Benedict of Nursia. They live a very strict coenobitical life structured around the eight offices of the day. I am sure they are totally out of rhythm without their routine and are feeling somewhat lost."

"Oh my goodness, that must be it. I am so sorry if I seemed out of sorts over it, Father Dumas. Please let me show you to your room right away. I will also start getting some of the materials for the sisters. The two other American priests have rooms just down the hall from yours. I am sure you will enjoy talking to them. They have wonderful stories to tell. They have been here for almost a year now."

Dumas smiled. "That will be wonderful, sister, I am looking forward to meeting them. I am especially interested in listening to their stories. Are they in now?"

"No, they are still out in the garden picking vegetables for dinner at 8:00 tonight. They should be back around 5:30. You will be able to meet them at dinner though, as well as our newest guest. Oh Father, I am so excited. I am not supposed to tell anyone, but since I know you, I feel it would be all right to tell you. Bishop Daze from the Vatican will be here for dinner and a long stay. He is being motored down from Angoulême after flying in from the Vatican right now."

"My, that is truly very exciting, Sister. I am sure the two sisters will be especially interested in meeting him. Where are the rest of the sisters in the Abbaye?"

"I sent most of them on a pilgrimage to *L'Abbaye Notre-Dame de Wisques* for a few weeks. I felt that until the major portion of the repairs are completed, they would not be needed. Since we do not have any people attending retreats now, there is little for them to do here. I felt they could use a little vacation from their normal duties. They have worked so hard these last ten months, with all of the retreats we have had. The only ones left are Sister Ursala, my right hand who helps me with everything, and Sister Marie, who is very old and unable to travel."

"Ah, I see, at least the restoration process gives you a break from all of the hustle and bustle of retreat work. I am sure you are quite busy when you have people on retreat."

"Yes Father, that is true, but I enjoy it. Ah, here we are, your room is the one on the right."

"Thank you, Sister. I believe I will take a short walk before dinner. Maybe I will visit your garden; I have heard it is one of the finest of all the Abbayes. Perhaps I can engage the American priests in conversation as well."

Sister Baptiste smiled, gave Father Dumas the directions to the garden, and left. He immediately walked outside the back door, found the telephone wires, and clipped them. He then went back into his room, took the gun with the silencer from its case, gathered one of the sisters, wrinkled his brow, and headed out toward the garden.

* * *

The tall man's private jet arrived near 8:00 that evening at a small private airport near Champniers and the pilot awoke the only passenger.

"Sir, we have landed."

"Yes I see, thank you. Keep the plane fueled and ready to leave on a moment's notice."

After watching the plane disappear around the corner to get fuel, the tall man walked to the small office to the left of the hangar. He saw a man at a desk and approached him.

"I require a cab or a rental car."

The man answered in French. "I am sorry, sir, there are no cabs. They are at the festival in Angoulême, and most of the good rentals have all been leased this morning. I do have a 1988 Citroën which is in fair shape, and it is only 30 Euros a day."

"Well, I must have a car," the tall man stated in American-accented French. "I suppose the old Citroën will have to do."

The tall man paid, nodded, and left the office with the keys in his hand. He shook his head as he looked at the old, dented sedan and slumped uncomfortably on the cold plastic seat. It had a tear in the seat patched with duct tape. He shook his head in disgust. He looked out at the dark clouds forming in the east, sighed, and headed to the RN10. He dialed a number on his cell phone as he drove.

"Yes, I have arrived. I should be able to get to the Abbaye around a quarter to nine. That should be in about 40 minutes, more or less."

* * *

At about 8:30 that evening, Claude Lambert and his group landed at the airport in Angoulême. They had repeatedly tried to contact the Abbaye, but the phone was out. There was a black sedan from the RG waiting for them. Claude got out of the plane and approached the female agent who was standing by the car.

"I'm Claude Lambert," he stated in French.

170

"Yes, Monsieur, I am agent Claire Rousseau. I was sent from Bordeaux to take you to the Abbaye. How was your trip?"

"Fine, I hope we are not too late."

"We should be there by 9:30 or so. Is there a deadline? No one told me about the situation."

Claude and his group got in the car and Claude said, "The ex-bishop of Boston, Bishop Daze, is going to be assassinated. I was unable to contact anyone at the Abbaye, their phones appear to be down. The faster you can drive there, the better."

The agent shook her head and pushed the accelerator to the floor. The Citroën leaped and then smoothed out to about 140 kilometers per hour as it sped toward the Abbaye.

* * *

Two hours earlier, Father Dumas had been walking with the false sister toward the enormous vegetable garden, which took up over two acres of space. He saw two priests laughing as they walked up a pine-laden path from the garden with baskets of vegetables.

Father Dumas approached the two and smiled.

"You must be the American priests Sister Joan-Baptiste told me about. If I am not mistaken, you are Father O' Brion and you must be Father Duncane."

The two priests stopped laughing and stood deathly still with their baskets by their sides. They had uncomfortable looks on their ashen faces.

"Uh, yes... who are you, Father, and who is the sister beside you?" The short, flabby one, called Father O' Brion, asked. "How did you know our names? We are called Father Donald and Father Murry here. Are you from the Vatican? Did Bishop Daze send you?"

"No, but that is of no consequence, Father. However, the bishop is on his way, he will be here soon I am told. I am Father Rene Dumas." He then looked at the two priests with cold eyes. "My sister's name was Chantal Vachon and her children's names were John Paul, Adrien, and Rene who was named after me. Do you remember them?"

The tall weedy-looking Father Duncane sneered. "No we don't, and what has that got to do with anything, Father Dumas? I don't remember those names, or yours. Now please step aside, we need to take the vegetables to the Abbaye to be prepared for dinner."

Father Dumas stood in their way, blocking the path. "My sister, Chantal, and her children attended Our Lady of Triumph Catholic Church located on Arlington Street in Boston. I believe, Father Duncane, that you were the pastor and Father O' Brion, you were the assistant pastor there for many years. You are Marist Fathers, I believe."

Father Duncane started to get angry. "What do you know about Our Lady of Triumph, and want do you want?"

Father Dumas took out his pistol with the silencer and gave it to the sister. She pointed it at the two. They both turned ashen and dropped their baskets of vegetables, spilling them on the gravel path.

"I want to tell you two deviant pervert priests a little story, so I want you to sit down on the rocks over there and listen very closely."

The two priests were pale as ghosts and sweat was appearing on their wrinkled brows.

When Father Dumas got through with his story about the molestation of his nephews and their suicides as well as the suicide of his sister, both priests were ashen white and shaking. They begged Father Dumas to forgive them. He told them forgiveness was for the Lord and vengeance was for him.

The two were wild-eyed now, trembling and sweating. Copious tears were running down their cheeks. They begged the sister to forgive them, but she simply gazed at them with vacant eyes. Dumas ordered them to get on their knees and pray. They got on their knees and begged the sister not to hurt them. Father Dumas stood in front of them shaking his head, then typed some instructions into his computer and moved to the side.

The sister, with a benign look in her eyes, fired a shot into the forehead of each of the priests as they stood wide-eyed, begging her again not to shoot. In a few seconds, the two predator priests fell on their faces with holes in their foreheads. Dumas turned them over to see their faces again. Their eyes were vacant, but their faces still showed fear. He dragged them behind some bushes so they were out of sight, picked up the vegetables, put some of them in a basket, told the sister to return to the Abbaye, and left. His mind was reeling with moral indignation, then he snapped and pure evil took over his being... and he sneered.

He reached the Abbaye just as the bishop's private car arrived about 100 meters from the entrance. He watched as the two nuns' brains recognized the bishop's face as they walked out the front door.

A bodyguard and a chauffeur got out of the car and were accosted immediately by the nuns. At first, the guards would not fight the nuns, but after several deadly blows to their heads and bodies, they were forced to fight back to protect themselves. One bodyguard finally took out his gun and fired repeatedly at the two nuns. The bullets tore into them, leaving blood flowing down their black habits, but they kept charging until the two men were subdued and their necks were snapped.

The bishop's eyes were wide with terror and his mouth was dry as he watched the terrible scene unfolding in front of his eyes. He was so terrified that he was unable to scream. The only thing that came out of his mouth was a horrible gurgle. The false nuns turned toward him, staring at him with vacant eyes, and he knew instantly that they were his assassins. He dropped to his knees and started begging for mercy.

"Who are you and why do you want to kill me?" he screamed. "Please don't kill me! I will do anything for you!"

Father Dumas walked around the car. "They are going to kill you, my dear Bishop, because you shielded your pervert priests! You are a sadistic monster! You will die because you are as guilty as your sick priests and deserve to die."

He watched as the nuns approached the bishop. Dumas watched the bishop's face as the nuns grabbed him. He tried to fight back, but was no match for the superior strength of the women. One of them snapped his neck.

The nuns looked at Dumas with uncomprehending eyes and fell to the ground, dead from their bullet wounds. He took one last look at the bishop and walked back to his rental car. After about five minutes, he heard screaming and knew Sister Baptiste had found the bodies of the nuns, the bishop, and the two men.

He placed the computer on the passenger seat and headed toward his airplane at the airport. It was about 8:30 in the evening and the moon was sending cold beams of silver across the highway. His mind was flashing frantically back and forth between satisfaction and guilt. He had 30 kilometers to drive to his plane and then to his other destination. Every mile would be an increasing strain on his sanity. He thought he would feel gratified, even joyful about the deaths of the priests and the bishop, but now he only felt a horrible gut-wrenching guilt and black grief.

As he headed to the airport on RN10, he passed an old Citroën sedan speeding toward the Abbaye. Just as he neared Angoulême, a dark sedan passed him with red lights flaming on the roof. It was going over 140 kilometers per hour. He sighed with tears running down his cheeks.

"Too late, too late, the deed of justice has been done. It is all over; my nephews and sister have been avenged, and I am destined toward hell." He then shook his head violently, frowned, and sobbed.

Later on with no tears left, his mind cleared and he wondered how they knew to go to the Abbaye. He realized that they had to have left to go to the Abbaye before Sister Baptiste could have called. He then realized in his muddled brain that he was a hunted man. He stopped, took off his black Cassock, and threw it out of the car. It lay on the ground like a battered, torn soul rustling in the wind, looking like a terrible dark specter.

He accelerated as dark images of the priests' bodies and the bishop's terror-stricken face kept traveling back and forth across his thoughts. His mind was being torn apart and guilt was ripping at his soul. Icy tears started flowing down his cheeks once more. This was all at a time when he should have been rejoicing and celebrating. His eyes were red and swollen, his soul rendered to burning parts. He looked up toward the heavens and said out loud, "I now know why you said vengeance is mine. Mortal man does not have the ability to withstand it. Dear God, please forgive me."

Chapter Sixteen
The Bishop is Dead

With the bitterness of vengeance and death
Weighing upon his soul, death's architect
Reaches out to heaven for solace, knowing
The horrors of his sickness, he now must
Atone or die. Yet, who, on this earth, can atone, and
Be forgiven for the darkest of sins?

The tall man sped into the lot and saw Sister Baptiste and another Nun on their knees sobbing next to a long black car. He walked over to her.

"What happened here, Sister? Who caused this horrible thing?"

"Oh, monsieur!" she cried out. "The bishop has been assassinated... it was the two nuns lying on the ground over there." She sobbed and pointing to the bodies. "They also murdered the two guards." She cried as she crossed herself over and over again. The other nun simply stared in disbelief and prayed as tears streamed down her cheeks.

"Is there anyone else here?" the tall man asked.

"Yes, two American priests, they have been here for some time. They were out at the gardens picking vegetables. I don't know where they are now. Father Dumas was here, too, but he has gone. I don't know where he went!"

The tall man frowned and nodded. He then went back to his car and left without another word.

After he had gone about five miles up RN10, a black sedan with red lights flashing like dervishes sped past him in the opposite direction at about 170 kilometers per hour. He frowned and pushed the accelerator down. The old Citroën rattled and trembled when it hit over 90 kilometers per hour.

He dialed a number on his mobile phone.

"I got there too late. The bishop is dead, probably the two priests as well, but I did not see them. They were not near the Bishop. The monk was not at the Abbaye either, so I left. Dumas still has the computer and devices and I have no idea where he has gone. I am heading down RN10 to the airport now. Also, a very curious thing just happened a few miles back. As I was about five miles from the Abbaye, a black sedan filled with about five people, mostly older men, sped passed me going over 160 or 170 kilometers per hour. Someone else must know about the assassinations and Dumas. That could also mean they might know something about the project, and that would be extremely unfortunate for us. Can you check with some of the other intelligence agencies and find out? ... Yes, good.... What? No, I have no idea where Dumas is going now. Does he have other plans? No idea.... Yes, I will be heading back to Paris and will stay there for a while."

* * *

The black sedan with Claude and his group arrived at the Abbaye about 30 minutes later and saw the nuns still standing by a long black limo. They got out and went over to her.

Claude asked in French, "Sister, what happened here?"

"Are you the police?" she asked tearfully as she tugged at her habit and dabbed at red, swollen eyes.

"Yes, Sister, we tried to call you earlier but your phone was down."

"Oh my... the nuns must have cut the phone lines, they are responsible for this horrible, evil act. Why would nuns do something so evil like this? Have they gone mad?"

"That could be true, Sister," David said in English as he tried to comfort the nun.

Edward looked over the carnage and shook his head. "These guards have been beaten to death, Ephraim. Their necks have been snapped just like some of the others. I am sure the two nuns were programmed assassins."

Ephraim shook his head and asked Sister Baptiste a question. "Sister, are there two other priests living here?"

"Yes, Father Donald and Father Murry, but I have not seen them since they went to gather vegetables from the garden. Father Dumas was here, too, he went to talk to the priests."
The men exchanged glances.

"Which way is the garden, Sister?"

Sister pointed her shaking finger to a wide path. "It is down the path about two hundred meters. What's going on?"

Ephraim shook his head and motioned to David. They both headed down the path as Claude and Teddy questioned the sisters. Within moments they came upon one overturned basket of vegetables. They continued for a few more meters down a gravel path.

David spotted two bodies in the bushes. "Ephraim, over here."

The two looked at the bodies, resembling huge rag dolls dressed up like priests.

"Well, David, I guess Dumas found his pedophile priests. They were killed execution style, too! He must have killed them personally. Now that the deviate priests and the bishop are dead, I wonder what Dumas is planning to do? I wonder if the chaos is over."

"I don't know, Ephraim. I thought that this would possibly be the end of all the horror. However, if the killing of the priests and the bishop was the end of his bloodlust-driven terror, I am sure he would have stayed here and waited for someone to come and take him away. Since he didn't, I have a feeling he has something else in mind."

"Yeah, and now we are back to square one!" David stated as he shook his head.

After they all assembled back in the Abbaye, Edward came up to David. "I had a feeling the two were dead," he stated. "Davie, we are certain the two nuns were not nuns, they had gaudy street clothes underneath their habits. They were probably Italian prostitutes. They also have the tell-tale tiny red dots at the base of their skulls."

Teddy walked over and said, "I have sent for the coroner and an ambulance to remove the bodies. What a mess. The guards were literally beaten to death by the two women, even though the women had been shot in their chests multiple times."

"I found out from Sister Baptiste that a tall man came upon the scene soon after the assassination. He asked some questions and left immediately without doing anything. She said she'd had a telephone call from him before. She said he is someone very important."

"He just left? He didn't do anything or try to contact the police?" David asked.

"Nope, Sister Baptiste just said he asked her about what happened and when he was told that Father Dumas had gone, he left immediately."

"Hm, I wonder...?" David mused.

"What, Davie?" Edward asked.

"I think that we ought to check on planes leaving the area at both private and public airports. The person may be one of the secret civilian group, and we may get lucky."

"Yes, good idea. I'll ask Claude to get on it immediately."

About 40 minutes after Claude and his group arrived at the Abbaye, the tall man was getting aboard a private jet heading toward Paris. A call was received.

"Yes?"

"We have the information that you asked for from our contact at RG. It seems an RG agent named Claude Lambert and some retired ex-agents are involved in finding out about the Pentagon Project and in trying to find a monk named Dumas. They apparently knew about Bourne and the others who were assassinated as well. We think one of the older agents has a contact at Metsada, which means the Israelis know about the project and Dumas as well."

"Hm, do you see that as a problem?" the tall man asked.

"We are not sure as of yet. However, if they are also looking into the project, they probably already know too much; that could be a definite problem! We will take care of the problem as if it is a national security crisis before things get worse. We will have to shut down all intelligence agencies in regards to the project."

"Yes, very good idea. I will look into it when I get to Paris, I have some contacts within the RG as well." He hung up the phone.

The tall man frowned, poured himself some aged whiskey in a glass with an ice cube, and lit a Ghurka HMR cigar. He leaned his head back in his seat... his mind contained dark thoughts. The plane droned on, as did the tall man's mind.

"There are probably many in the intelligence community who know about Dumas now," he thought aloud to himself as he sipped his whiskey. "I wonder how many have true knowledge of the project? I hope not many, since Dumas eliminated most of them except some of our Pentagon people! However, it pays to be careful. Shutting down all of the agencies' activities looking into the project is necessary regardless of the consequences."

* * *

Claude and his group, after the coroner and ambulance arrived at the Abbaye to take the bodies away, were on their way back to the airport and their plane. He answered his cell phone. "Yes. What? Yes, he is here."

Claude handed the phone to Ephraim. "Hm, yes Danny, that confirms many of our assumptions about the matter. What? Damn, really? ... Hm, now that is frustrating. If we decide to continue, can we still rely on data from you from time to time? ... Okay, call me once you do. Thank you, Danny. Bye."

"What is it, Ephraim?"

"Claude... this thing is really big!" he stated.

"How big?" Edward asked.

"Probably too damn big for us poor old duffers to remain involved... yeah right!" He laughed.

"Damn I knew it, it is gigantic isn't it, Ephraim?" Teddy asked excitedly.

Ephraim shook his head and frowned. "That was my nephew, Danny, from Mossad. He has been informed that someone at the highest levels at the Pentagon ordered all action related to the Pentagon Project, Father Dumas, and the assassinations be suspended by all allied intelligence agencies immediately."

"How were they informed?" David asked.

"The Director of Mossad as well as the RG and MI6 have all been informed by a top black secret memo from the Pentagon to cease and desist immediately. That means that everything we were looking into is now off base!"

As the group was heatedly discussing the new situation, another call came in to the plane.

"Yes?" Ephraim shook his head and sighed. "Yes, we were told about it, too, Lieutenant Dubois.... Do we plan to follow the instructions? Hm, well, do you?"

"Yes, I have to!" the Lieutenant replied angrily. "I am an official in the government and must obey the damn edict. I don't like it. I have murders committed in my city that I need to solve.

I sure as hell can't do that now since I was told by my superiors to stop my investigation into the assassinations."

"I am sorry, that is terrible. However, to answer your question.... Our little group is debating that right now. We are not bound by any edict from anyone as far as we know. We are free citizens and can do what we want.... Yes, I guess some agency might try to stop us by using the argument that we are hindering an official international investigation, but I don't think it would hold. I also don't think they would do that because it would open up a can of worms concerning the secret project. On the other hand, they might decide the whole thing, including the project, is so damn critical and of such importance to national security, that we could be deemed expendable if we got in the way. If our interference started to become a big problem, they might decide to erase us! That of course would mean we could be assassinated by our own governments."

"Are you saying that some intelligence agencies might try to assassinate your group?" Dubois asked angrily.

"Yes, Lieutenant, if they knew who we were. However, I don't think anyone does so far. You haven't related our names to anyone, have you?"

"No, I don't like to share my data gathering sources with anyone, not even my own men. I don't believe anyone here in France knows of you except Claude and I don't think he has told anyone in his agency."

They all looked at Claude and he nodded his head.

The Lieutenant spoke up. "Does that mean you may continue looking into the matter?"

"Yes, we might just do that. If we stay on the case, would you like to be kept informed of our progress?"

The Lieutenant answered excitedly. "But of course, my dear friend, I hate to have unsolved murders on my watch!" He then laughed. "We will have to set up some clandestine system of communication. I am sure even my personal police cell phone will be tapped soon. I am out of the office now, but when I left I saw some guys in dark suits and skinny ties coming in the front door with dark glasses and suitcases. I am sure they were from the *Renseignements Généraux*. My boss, I am sure, does what he is told by his superiors." He paused and laughed again. "I myself am a little shady in that area sometimes... Well, perhaps often!"

Ephraim laughed. "We are too, Lieutenant Dubois, and cranky too! We don't like anyone telling us what to do at our ages! Claude does not plan to stop either, but he will have to do everything underground. Since he hasn't told any of his superiors the names of our group, we are safe at this end, at least for the time being. I am sure, though, that he will be questioned about us."

Claude nodded his head and wrinkled his brow as he put his finger across his neck.

The phone conversation continued for a few more minutes before Ephraim covered the mouth piece. He turned to the others. "I think we all need to vote on this. If we continue, it could get messy and might even get dangerous. I think it must be a vote of 100% for us to continue."

"I call for the vote! All in favor raise their hands!" David looked around and saw that everyone had their hands raised as high as they could get them.

Ephraim uncovered the phone and told the lieutenant what they had decided.

"Okay, since your group is in and Claude is in, I will continue as well. That is even though my superiors will tell me to cease and desist and I could get fired if I don't. I will buy a prepaid cell phone to keep with me just for our communications. I'll put my official cell phone on my desk so they can put a bug in it. I will keep my ear to what is going on around here, too. Do you think maybe I need a code name?"

"Yes, how about nosey?" Claude laughed.

"So be it, and your group will be the OD, for old duffers!" He laughed.

When the group started talking again, Ephraim's cell phone rang. "Yes.... What? My God... thank you, Danny, yes, we will be extra careful. Bye!"

Ephraim looked at the group. "Danny gave me information that a small Cessna left about an hour before a jet left Angoulême, they were both heading toward Paris."

"Well don't let us die of heart attacks, who was on the planes?"

"The Cessna was flown by Dumas. The private jet, which took off after he left, contained one William J. Harper. He is President and CEO of Armament, Inc. and a special friend of the Secretary of Defense. He is worth about 85 billion dollars and has subsidiaries all over the world, some of their names are not even known. He is also the CEO of Black Warriors, a security company that has billions of dollars' worth of security contracts with France, England, Germany, and the United States. His brother-in-law is a US Senator, and his nephew is a member of Congress. But here is the most nefarious part, he has been linked to the JASON Society, a somewhat mysterious scientific group."

"Isn't the JASON group an independent scientific advisory group that provides consulting services to the U.S. government on matters of defense science and technology?" David asked. "It seems to me that the JASONS hold the highest and most restrictive security clearances in the nation. They are given the protocol rank of rear admiral when they visit or travel aboard naval ships. They can't be the bad guys."

"Well, maybe that JASON Society is not the same as this JASON group," Edward said, looking at David and shrugging his shoulders. "The JASON Society, I believe, is composed of scientific scholars. It was President Eisenhower who commissioned the secret society in the 60's. I think it was under the leadership of the Director of Central Intelligence."

"Wasn't Dr. Henry Kissenger once the leader of their scientific efforts looking into UFO's?"

"I don't know, Uncle Edward, sounds a little like a conspiracy theory to me!" David laughed. "Now that is right down my alley!"

"David, when I was in the spy business I heard that JASON guided America's most important security decisions, working behind the scenes in complete secrecy," Ephraim stated. "Even their funding was secured in the office of the Director, Defense Research & Engineering, not the regular Pentagon budget. Some have even said they have a secret black fund at the

Pentagon in the tens of billions of dollars that not even your Congress has knowledge of or access to."

Teddy had been quiet up to this point. "I wonder if the secret civilian group at the Pentagon is the JASON group?"

"My God, Teddy, that could be it! JASON might run the human-computer interface project at the Pentagon. I'll bet Dumas' company was given a contract to help design part of it. However, from what we have learned, he had his own reasons for doing it. The killing of the directors and intelligence agents may have been to lessen the number of people who knew about the project, but I can't understand why that would be important to the others, especially Dumas. He must have other reasons that are beyond us. JASON and the Pentagon probably wanted to use the assassins for war purposes, maybe Dumas didn't want that to happen."

"If JASON is part of the Pentagon Project, William J. Harper is involved!" David exclaimed. "He is a bigwig in JASON. Wow, we could be in deep you-know-what if we get caught messing with JASON!"

"Well we all have to die sometime!" Claude exclaimed, nodding his head and shrugging his shoulders.

"Well we three are too damn old now so it won't make much difference to us!" Teddy replied then shrugged his shoulders and laughed. "I think I'll go get a bottle of wine, I think we need a toast!"

"I keep wondering why Dumas continues to be involved in the project if his main goal was to get his revenge on the bishop and the pedophile priests," Claude commented. "That goal has been achieved. Why wouldn't he simply destroy the computer and control devices so that no one could get hold of them after he completed his revenge?"

"Perhaps his new goals are worthy ones... you know, to achieve justice for wrongs on all the innocents." Edward stated. "He might also want to atone for his own sins. Perhaps he wants to destroy those who started the project for the purpose of stopping wars! Which means he might know about the JASON group and plans to destroy them, or at least their project goals."

"I don't know about that line of reasoning, Uncle Edward, he sounds like he just may have a few screws loose to me," David remarked. "He has to be psychotic to murder people in cold blood even to achieve moral goals. I mean, that is the ultimate ironic religious hypocrisy."

"It sounds like a person who disposes a despot with high moral reasons in a country only to become just like him when he possesses wealth and power. We have seen a lot of that lately, especially in Africa and Asia. However, I don't think they profess to be doing it for religious and moral purposes.... Well, on second thought maybe they do at the start," Claude added.

David spoke up. "Maybe the human mind has not evolved adequately enough for peace. Maybe that is the reason why brains can be manipulated and controlled so easily in the first place. If man's brain were innately wired for moral purposes, how could they really be controlled for evil purposes?"

"I don't know, Davie, but you may have a point," Edward said. "It has been said that someone under the control of a hypnotist will never do something against his or her own moral subconscious. Maybe the hypnotic control is initiated in the higher lobes of the brain and the computer control is initiated in the middle brain, you know in the Limbic system. Isn't that the ancient emotional part of the brain? Maybe the mid-brain has not evolved, maybe it is not moral... perhaps only the lobes are."

"Well, what did the coroner that found the first device embedded into the brain of the sister say?" David asked.

Claude spoke up. "He said the device was in the Limbic system, close to the Hypothalamus."

"Well there you go!" Teddy commented. "The hypothetical argument makes sense then, doesn't it?"

"Perhaps if the hypnotist's words go only to the higher lobes and not the mid-brain, but if they don't, then it is still moot," Ephraim stated.

Edward spoke up. "Gentlemen, all of this chatter is quite interesting, but we need to get to Paris as soon as possible. I think we need to dispense with the moral and scientific assumptions and get onto some solid stuff, like finding Dumas!"

The group looked at him, nodded their heads in agreement, and drank a toast.

* * *

Rene Dumas was near Troyes and heading towards ORLY. The last woman, who was no longer in her habit but dressed in basic street clothes, was still asleep. He knew that someone from the JASON Group was following him, but he had a plan that was driving his brain.

He called the ORLY and contacted a car rental agency. He used his own name to order a new Citroën and casually mentioned he would be going to Paris and would be staying at *Le Meridien Montparnasse*. He knew the tall man would probably be asking the different car agencies about him. He smiled and continued to ORLY.

The tall man landed at ORLY and, as suspected, went to various car agencies to determine if a man named Dumas had rented a car. The third agency proved to be the correct one. The young lady at the desk remembered talking to Dumas on the phone and that he said he would be driving to Paris. When he arrived to pick up his car, he had told her that they could pick up the car at the hotel tomorrow. William Harper smiled, rented a Citroën, and headed to Paris. He pulled out his cell phone and made a call.

"I have located Dumas.... Yes, I should have the computer, two million Euros, and the devices in my hands in less than four hours.... Yes, I will. Will you be coming to Paris, Henry? I see.... Yes, we can discuss what we need to do with the project at that time.... Goodbye."

The tall man lit a Ghurka HMR and pulled in the sweet smoke. He tensed as he thought of the short, dark-complected man with whom he had just spoken. Henry was a Saudi by birth but had been in the United States for 20 years and was an American citizen. Hani, which he changed to Henry, and Hamid, which he changed to Hammer, was his name.

Henry Hammer was a multi-billionaire shipping magnate and owned a dozen oil liners as well as oil fields in Saudi Arabia.

He became a member of the JASON group eight years ago. The JASON group now had five foreign members, all billionaires, all Muslims. William was bothered by the new intention they had brought so very carefully into the group's goals, as well as their religion. Henry Hammer, now number four in the JASON group, especially had ideas with which he had serious misgivings. Of course, he didn't like any foreign blood regardless of their wealth. His upbringing was part of his soul.

*   *   *

Dumas and the beautiful young lady entered the lobby. He ordered a family room and signed for it. He placed the money on the desk, smiled, and filled out a registration card with a large signature. The lady beside him stared out at the lobby with vacant eyes. The young lady behind the marble-topped registration desk stared at the pair quizzicaly. He smiled, shook his wrist, winked, and picked up his attaché case and computer. He then took the keys from the front desk clerk and headed up to the ninth floor. When he opened the door, he sat down at the desk and re-programmed the young lady's brain. She took out a Glock with a silencer and put it behind her as she sat down to wait. Her eyes were uncomprehending and stared out at nothing. Only dark instructional images that had been placed in her brain were active now.

Dumas poured a glass of sherry, took a long sip, and sat down across from the young lady. He looked at her vacant expression, closed his eyes, shook his head sadly, and sighed. "What do I do now, God? I have sinned by taking lives. I have allowed the avenging angel inside my damaged soul to take over my being and she has taken over my mind. What do I have but darkness and death to keep me company from now on?"

He crossed himself and stared out the window at the beautiful city of Paris, the city of dreams and lovers, far below. It was a city filled with life and lightness, not darkness and thoughts of death like in his sad and lonely mind. He sighed and thought about the JASON group and the girl who sat in a trance across from him.

He had just received a call from the tall man about a compromise. The new direction for the computer-human project that had formed in his brain could be accomplished now. Would it bring his soul back, though? Could anything atone for the taking of lives of others, even if not innocent?

His mind wandered to and fro through the dark corridors of his past, attempting to write a new chapter in his shadowy existence. He nodded as the thoughts rambled ever faster in his brain and the new strategy coalesced. He sipped his drink and smiled. *Perhaps... perhaps*, he thought.

Chapter Seventeen
The Deadly Meeting

Can anyone grasp the full impact
Of the turmoil, the terrible despair, or
The dark restlessness of these times, can
They even understand the impact
Of such evil actions, greed, and vengeance?

The tall man from JASON drove into the lot of *Le Meridien Montparnasse* and parked. He looked up at the tall skyscraper. It was the type of hotel that he liked: huge, modern, and expensive. He smiled and went into the lobby.

"*Est-ce qu'ou monsieur, jepeux vous aider? La jeune dame au bureau demande',*" the desk clerk asked.

"Yes, a friend of mine, Rene Dumas, asked me to get a room beside his. Can you do that for me?" the tall man asked in broken American-accented French.

The young lady wrinkled her nose slightly at his American accent. She then nodded, had him register, and said Dumas would be in room 913. It was one of the family rooms. His room would be 918, a classic room. She asked if he wanted her to page Mr. Dumas and he said no, he knew he was coming. He smiled slightly at the young lady, grabbed his attaché case, and headed to the elevator.

When he arrived at the ninth floor he looked around, found room 913, hesitated for a moment, and went to room 918. He used his key card and went inside. He smiled as he looked at the king sized bed and ample space. Sitting down in one of the soft light mauve cushioned chairs, he placed his attaché on top of the writing desk. He took out a Glock .45 and made sure that it was loaded. He decided to get a drink before seeing Dumas and called for room service.

"I would like a bourbon and water please. I want the best bourbon you have, and some aged cheese and crackers as well. Yes, room 918, thank you."

After he finished his drink, cheese, and crackers, he picked up his attaché and left the room. He walked to room 913 and knocked on the door. When the door opened, he took a deep breath and walked in. A short, dark-complected man a few feet down the hallway in room 915 watched him go into the room and smiled.

When William pushed the door open, he saw a young lady staring at him with empty eyes; she had a pistol in her hand. It contained a silencer. His eyes went wild, but he had no place to escape. He stood as if cemented to the floor and stared.

"Please, Dumas, I have another plan, a worthy one... hear me out!"

* * *

Ten minutes earlier, Claude and his group had landed at ORLY. They found out where Dumas was located. They had located the same rental agent who leased the car to Rene Dumas that the tall man from JASON, William J. Harper, had found. They were picked up by a black sedan and sped toward *Le Meridien Montparnasse*. They knew the countdown had begun and hoped they would get there in time this time. Teddy called Lieutenant Dubois on his new pre-paid cell phone.

"Nosey, it's one of the Old Duffers. Yes, I have information. Rene Dumas is at *Le Meridien Montparnasse* and William J. Harper of JASON is probably there by now as well.... What? ... It's a long story, Nosey, I'll tell you all about it if we live through this.... Thanks, bye."

Lieutenant Dubois collected six of his most skilled officers and sped toward the hotel. He was only about a half hour away from the time the tall man had entered Dumas' family room.

* * *

"Dumas, does she have to point that pistol at me?"

"Sorry, William, she must have thought you were someone else. Please sit down, I will listen to your new proposition."

The young lady stared vacantly at William but slowly put the gun down and held it in her lap, awaiting a verbal response from Dumas that corresponded to a message that had previously been sent to her brain.

The tall man sat down and told Dumas the reality of the situation and of his new plan.

"Will you consider my offer?"

"Yes, I had decided initially just to take the money, then I thought seriously about destroying the program along with the computer and all of the devices. However, I figure you are probably right. The powers within your group and the Pentagon would simply fund another project. Since some of the companies who helped with the original computer design probably still have the information on what they did initially for the program, it would not be too difficult to reproduce. All that would be needed would be to design the embedding device and the micro-miniature receiving devices, which I created. Even though they do not have my schematics, I do not think it would be difficult to obtain much of the needed information from the scientists and technicians who worked at my factory. I could never assassinate them to stop the process. Even I, as horribly evil as I have become, could never undertake that task. Ergo, your new proposal appears to be my only option."

"I am glad to hear that, Dumas. I believe as you do that it would take at most only a year or so to duplicate what has been done with the human-computer interface system, but it could be done. I am glad that you have taken up my offer of another two million Euros and we don't have to start over. I am quite disturbed with the direction of some within the JASON group, however. We have too many foreign members now that want many of the original goals of the group replaced with some of their ideological goals. Fortunately, the new goals are unacceptable to the majority of our members. They felt the Arab's new goals would be a danger to too many non-Arab citizens all over the world, and especially the Jews."

"William, how many of the JASON group and the Pentagon know of the ultimate use of humans in the project?"

"My special group of four, but only one high-level officer in the Pentagon knows of the intended use of the project and approves. The new anticipated use of the project pushed by the minority JASON group, however, is known to only our group."

"I see, and you are sure that their proposed use is as you have stated?"

"Yes, I firmly believe that the use of the GITMO prisoners for our original reasons has been superseded by this group. They have another more clandestine use that would be devastating to the United States and her allies, but mostly to Israel," William stated. "The prisoners from Israeli jails and citizens in the Israeli cities would probably be the first of their project humans. Other Jews, even innocents in the United States and Europe, probably in the thousands, could be injected for use in the future."

The two continued discussing the problem and the new direction of the project with the lady staring vacantly when a knock was heard at the door.

"It must be Henry," William stated.

As he said this, Dumas ran into the other room and typed new instructions into the computer. The lady became alert.

William let Henry Hammer into the room. Henry noticed the lady staring into empty space immediately and shuddered. The door to another bedroom opened and Dumas stepped into the room.

"Well, I suppose you are the other man from JASON. Where are the other members of your sick group?"

"They are not sick, Dumas, William and the other JASON members are," he stated as he looked over at William. "It is the Jews who are responsible for the chaos in the Middle East, not the Arabs. Until we overcome the leaders in Israel, we will never have peace in the area, or in the world."

William sighed and looked at Dumas. "We at JASON have been the patriots of the world, we have always kept it in order. We created the means for all of humanity to live in prosperity. We only created wars to rid the earth of evil vermin, the despots and tyrants of the world. We are the reason the world is still in one piece. If not for our devices, like gunpowder, bullets, missiles, even the atomic bomb, the world would have ended eons ago." He turned to Henry. "To blame the Jews for the Mideast problem is ludicrous, Henry, it is the Islamic terrorists who are the problem."

Henry smiled, then frowned. "I agree that man was not programmed for peace, William, just look at the behavior of the human species, always fighting, always killing each other. I also agree that only by continually destroying the evil ones can the world continue to exist, and we all know that the true evil ones are the Jews. Judaism is the scourge of the world, Islam is the savior of it."

William flinched, then looked at Dumas who stared at the man. Then he spoke in a low, gravelly French-accented voice. "Some men are evil, that is true, and because of that, they perhaps deserve to die. However, only a handful of pure evil souls are responsible for the majority of the chaos and horror in our world. They do not protect it; they destroy it. Their sick minds create illusions of logic and sanity, but in fact, they are illogical and insane. The Germans were some of those of whom I speak. The Islamic terrorists are the other insane ones in this world. Your plan to do what you want to do to Israel is insane as well."

"You who have murdered in cold blood, and would even consider murdering me in cold blood, makes you the sane one?" Henry screamed. He grabbed a gun from behind his back and, before the lady or Dumas could react, he shot Dumas and then the lady, right in the heart. She winced and fired a shot at Henry, hitting him in the shoulder. She tried to shoot again, but fell heavy upon the carpet.

While the gunfight was going on, William had grabbed the computer and started to run out of the room. Henry ran to the door and shot him twice in the back. He then took the computer and the other devices and left. The eyes of the female were vacant, but William was still alive. He moaned, got on his cell phone, and made a phone call, dying halfway through the conversation. After a few moments, Dumas awoke and felt a searing pain and burning in his lower right leg. The bullet had gone through his left knee and blown out part of his patella. He was bleeding profusely.

He painfully got up and went to the bathroom, tore a towel in strips, and put a tourniquet around his leg. He looked at the woman and William, picked up the suitcase, took out the money, and stuffed it in a bag. He then hobbled out of the hotel through the back fire escape.

After slowly making it down three stories, he came back into a hallway and saw a lady with a large pushcart filled with piles of clean towels coming out of a freight elevator. After she turned the corner, Dumas hobbled to the elevator and went down to the basement. The pain in his leg was horrible and he was soaking wet with perspiration. The towel was soaked through with blood. He knew that once he lost over 30% of his blood he would die.

About 15 minutes after Henry had gone down the back fire escape stairwell and five minutes after Dumas had taken the freight elevator to the basement, Lieutenant Dubois and his group entered room 918. The Lieutenant looked at the two dead bodies and shook his head as the policemen went to the other rooms to see if there were any more bodies.

Claude and his group arrived about five minutes later and went up to the room.

Claude nodded his head. "Well, Lieutenant Dubois, it appears the man from JASON and the assassin are dead. Dumas is gone, too; perhaps he was shot. I see a lot of blood near the doorway. I don't see the computer, but there is a metal case sitting there." He opened it and found it empty.

"Lieutenant, I see a trail of blood going out to the back fire escape and one going down the hallway. It seems that another person was here besides Dumas. It appears they were both hurt since there are two different trails of blood."

About a half hour later when they went back down to the lobby, the desk clerk told them that when William Harper went up to his room, a short dark-complected man followed.

"I wonder if he or Dumas has the computer," Ephraim said.

"The pertinent questions now are who is the person who killed William and the lady, what happened to Dumas, and where are they going," the Lieutenant stated.

"Also, with whom is the other man affiliated?" Teddy asked.

"Since he knew either Dumas, William, or both were here, my guess would be that he is also part of the JASON group," Edward stated. "It is my guess that William probably was in communication with his group and then for some reason changed his mind about the project and contacted Dumas with another proposition. Perhaps someone in their group had other goals in mind."

"But why would a member of the JASON group murder one of their own?" Teddy asked.

"Now that is the billion dollar question," stated David. "I believe that may be the key to what happens from here on out."

Lieutenant Dubois and Claude's group continued to discuss the matter when a policeman came running into the room. "Sir, a woman was knocked down by a short Arabian-looking man with a bloody shoulder. That was according to a witness, an old bag lady. She helped the woman up. The bag lady said the woman fell and was stunned, but looked up and saw the man run into a building across the street."

"At least now we may know who to follow and possibly where!" Claude replied as he shook his head and looked at the Lieutenant. "At least as soon as we can decide which of the many buildings she saw him going into."

* * *

A private jet with three men and a woman were heading into ORLY immediately after the incident at the hotel occurred. The woman answered a cell phone. She listened intently for a short time before an expression of fear crossed her face.

"What is it, Sarah?"

The woman looked nervous as she glanced at the others. "The phone call was from William," she said softly. "He said he had been shot in the back. He said a female assassin and Dumas were also shot. He stopped talking mid-sentence... I think he is dead!"

"My God, what about Henry? Did he say where he went? Did that turncoat monk Dumas or the assassin kill William?"

"William said it was Henry who shot him!"

"What, William said that? My God, what is happening? What about the computer and the devices...?"

"William said they were taken... by Henry."

"I see. That means the foreign members in our midst have decided to obtain their goals even though we voted them down. This is horrible. As much as I hate to do this, I need to inform the NSA and Metsada."

* * *

The heated discussion was still going on in the lobby at *Le Meridien Montparnasse* when the ambulance arrived and Lieutenant Dubois and one of his officers got in their police car and drove off. Claude and his group stood on the sidewalk. Claude sighed and started to say something when a homeless woman pushing a grocery cart came up to him.

She bent over and whispered, "Claude, I am Claire Morel of the *Renseignements Généraux*. I have been working undercover in this area for two weeks now. I was near the woman who was knocked down by a short dark man. She told me he went into that building across the street." She pointed to a building across the street as she continued whispering to Claude. She then cackled and left, pushing the cart slowly.

Claude looked at the others. "I have the location of the building where the man went, gentlemen, let's get going."

David looked at him shook his head. "Was that a snitch or one of your girlfriends?"

"Neither, she is an RG undercover spy. Apparently the man went into the building across the street and he was bleeding profusely from his shoulder. She also said he was followed by a short, stocky man with bushy brown hair, dark glasses, and a limp. He was dressed in a dark green herringbone suit and wore an olive-colored Borsalino Rex Wool cap."

"What the hell is a Borsalino Rex cap?" Ephraim asked as the group started running across the street.

David smiled and said between breaths, "I happen to own two of them, one olive and one gray. They have two-inch snap-brims and are very durable because of the finely woven tweed. It is a driver-style hat and has warm quilted lining. It is great for the fall or early spring. It has a fabric sweatband and a partial leather inset for the forehead."

Ephraim stopped and stared at David with his mouth agape.

Edward laughed. "Aren't you sorry you asked?"

"How do you know about caps, David?"

"I own about ten Scottish wool hats and caps, they are my fetish. I happen to have a Men's Borsalino Calabria wool hat in my suitcase," he said with a smile.

"Davie also has about four of the same type of knobby tweed jackets that he is wearing now, along with some other things that he orders from Scotland. Am I correct, Davie?"

"That you are," he said, looking somewhat put out.

"Gentlemen, I think we need to continue to the building across the street, we need to search for these men!" Teddy stated as he pulled up his trousers and continued to run.

Ephraim approached the lady at the reception desk of the building and asked her about a dark man with a bloody shoulder and a short man following him. She said a man who was holding his shoulder went into the restaurant, but she didn't see the other man. They searched the restaurant and found he was not there. They did find another entrance from the restaurant into another street and saw some blood blotches on the cement. The man had disappeared. While searching the alley, David heard a cell phone ring and found it. It had been thrown away in a dumpster. When he retrieved it, he gave it to Claude who pushed a button to answer the call, but the call had already been terminated. He pushed a button and called the last number back.

"Hello?"

"Yes, who is this?" Claude asked.

The person on the other end hung up immediately.

"Who was it, Claude?" Edward asked, trying to catch his breath.

"They hung up as soon as I spoke. I need to get this cell to the agency immediately," Claude said as he looked around. The rag lady was standing nearby talking to some men and appeared to be selling something. He walked over to her, handed her a twenty-dollar bill, and surreptitiously dropped the phone in her bag. He whispered in her ear so the men couldn't hear him.

"Get the cell I put in your bag to Markham as soon as you can." The rag lady cackled, gave him a tiny bag of marijuana, and went back to her dealings with the other two men.

* * *

The three men and a woman from JASON arrived at ORLY. They got off the plane and went to the lounge where they sat down and ordered drinks.

"I have no idea what to do now," one of the men said. He was the older man in the group, thin and with years of experience "It appears that Henry has the computer and the devices and has disappeared. In my opinion the foreign goals are now going to be put into operation. I don't like what is happening. William talked to me about the foreign members in our organization about eight months ago and expressed some dismay about how angry they were about their inability to change our goals. I should have listened to him!"

"Do you think he was right?" one of the other men asked.

"It appears so, which means something has to be done. We are going to have to tell someone, unofficially and anonymously, about the situation, especially the Metsada."

"That means our plan involving the project will go down the drain," a robust man dressed in a light brown cashmere and silk suit exclaimed angrily.

"Yes, the project is probably now in the hands of a new enemy," the woman stated.

"Good God, we have to call someone immediately!" the thin man stated nervously.

"Yes, I am afraid so. I'll call Markham Tessier, the director of the RG, he is closest and is in Paris." With that, she picked up her phone and dialed.

"*Bonjour, peux je vous aide?*" A secretary asked.

"Yes, I need to talk to the director, Markham Tessier."

"Whom may I say is calling?" she asked in perfect English.

"Tell him that a person who knows all about the Pentagon Project and the assassinations is calling."

"Right away."

"Yes, who is this?" the director asked warily.

"That is of no importance, but what I have to tell you is."

The conversation went on for about three minutes and the woman hung up, leaving the director pounding his fist on his desk and shaking his head. He immediately called the directors of MI6, the CIA, and Metsada, and explained what he had just heard. He also called Claude Lambert.

"Yes, this is Lambert.... Yes, I see... yes, sir, that confirms our assumptions doesn't it! Uh... well, yes sir, I am still working with my group of ex-intelligence agents, a Lieutenant Dubois from the Paris Police, and an American on the assassinations you originally assigned me to.... Yes sir, I know you told me to drop it.... Yes sir! Oh good, I'm glad I will still have my job! ... Yes sir, we determined that it was Bourne and the other intelligence agents... yes, and the monk from the *Abbaye de Solesmes* as well. He is the one who we think assassinated around 12 people.... Yes sir, the group is responsible for all the data I gave you!"

"I can't believe that, why couldn't our intelligence agents have found out all of that? Well, no matter. Anyway Claude, the person who called me stated that a Henry Hammer, former name Hani Hamid, could have been the one who shot William Harper, the woman, and possibly the monk if he was there."

"Henry must be the man we have been searching for throughout the past hour."

"I take it you haven't found him or Dumas yet?"

"No sir, do you think this Hani Hamid is also a member of the JASON group?"

"Yes, and that causes me to believe that the person who called me was also someone from the JASON group."

"That could very well be true, how else could he have known that much about the project?" Claude commented. "But then why would he call?"

"That is what I can't figure out. It was a woman caller. My guess would be that this Hani Hamid or Henry Hammer is one of their foreign members, and from what I heard he is part of a radical group within JASON. Jeez, the JASON group, in my opinion, is as radical a group as you can get. I can't imagine it getting any more radical. I have a feeling that Israel and the world is in deep trouble. The JASON group has always been a friend of Israel in the past. It appears that may be changing now. I will get an APB out from here on Henry Hammer, or Hani Hamid, after we get on the computer and find his full description as well as his picture. You and your group keep looking for him. I will also set up some officers and agents at the train stations and airports. I should be able to send each group the full description of Hamid in a very short time. You should have it well before you reach your destination." He explained a little more about the new use for the computer-humans before he hung up, and reminded them to keep looking for Dumas.

"Anything else, sir?" Claude asked as he nodded his head in disbelief.

"Yes, you and your group might want to pray if any of this does take place! It could lead to the third world war."

"Ah, yes sir. All we need now is to have some foreign power to have the human-computer system in their hands to destroy Israel's leaders through assassinations. I wonder if they are in affiliation with the Islamic terrorists?"

"Hard to say, but that's what I am afraid of." The Director said his goodbyes in a tired voice and hung up his phone. Moments later, he answered an incoming call from the Director of the CIA.

"Yes George," stated Markham Tessier in a very quiet voice. "It appears to be true."

"Have you called Dan at the Mossad?" The CIA Director asked in a frustrated voice.

"Yes I have George, we also need to notify the other allied intelligence agencies immediately," Markham stated in a weary voice. "I can Contact Fritz from Bundesnachrichtendienst, Marcel at SV/SE, and Sam at the CSIS."

"Okay, I'll contact Adamo at the *Agenzia Informazioni e Sicurezza Esterna*, Ichiro at the Cabinet Intelligence and Research Office, and Alyona at the FSB," George stated.

"What about the Arabian General Intelligence Directorate?" Markham asked.

George smiled slightly. He knew Markham did not particularly like the Arabian sheik, and did not trust him, either. "Yes, I guess I can call him!" George obliged. "I'll contact Sam first, though. After Bourne being part of the Pentagon NSA plot, then his arrest, escape, and assassination, this is all he needs to totally destroy his year."

"Yes, I think it is all any of us need right now, George. Especially Dan, of the *ha-Mossad le-Modiin ule-Tafkidim Meyuhadim,* he has too much on his plate now with the latest conflict with Hamas. I swear I don't know how much more that country can take and still function. Do you think that is where it will all start?"

"That would be my guess, if the leaders in the Arab countries, even those who are moderates towards Israel, can gain an upper hand there it would be a terrible blow to the little country. It would be a victory for Hamas and all of the terrorists in the world."

"Do you think it will spark a third world war?"

"My guess would be yes, and possibly even an atomic one. Israel will never give up this time. They will go down fighting even if it means the death of Israel along with the Arab nations and some of the rest of the world. They will use their atomic bombs!"

"*Condmanez-le tout a l'enfer!*" Markham exclaimed in frustration.

"Yeah, you got that right. We have to find that damn computer and the embedding devices or the whole world is in for one great big trip to hell!"

"I have to call Claude and see what he has to say about Henry Hammer, or as we now know, Hani Hamid. I just hope that little group of his can find him."

"Who is in this group he is working with?"

"Claude said he is working with a police Lieutenant from Paris, three retired intelligence agents, and a professor."

"My God Markham, a bunch of has-beens, a policeman, and a citizen professor? What were you thinking?"

"Well actually George, they are the ones who have put the whole damn thing together... by themselves. It is quite a group. Anyway, that all may all be moot now, we no longer have the JASON group, the unholy assassins, NSA, or the Pentagon involved. At this point, all we have is a man named Hani Hamid and his JASON splinter group, and the Monk Dumas who is also missing."

"Markham, we are all in a leaking boat and about ready to float over a waterfall of crap now, that's for sure. Do you want me to contact some of my agents in Paris to help you?

"No, hold off on that for now."

"Alright, I will hold off for now, but keep in touch when you get something."

"I will George, I just hope I get something good to tell you about."

"Yes, I know. Goodbye for now, Markham. I'll get on the phone and contact the agencies. Uh, I will not mention the group that is working on it for now if that is okay with you."

"Yes, George, I understand. But Claude is one of my best agents and if he is comfortable with them, I am too. Goodbye for now."

Chapter Eighteen
The Computer Disappears

Hani stumbled as he ran around the corner of the building. The bullet in his shoulder was starting to hurt terribly and he was weak from a massive loss of blood. He stopped for a short time and saw a small man with bushy brown hair, dark glasses, and a limp coming around the corner. Hani pulled back so he was in the shadows and couldn't be seen. He watched the man, who looked up and down the street and then tapped his mahogany cane with a gold handle on the pavement. Two men came out of the shadows. He whispered something to them and they took off in different directions. Hani wiped his brow with a handkerchief and leaned against the cold wall. His shoulder was hurting so much he almost fainted. He pulled out his cell phone and made a call.

"It is Hani, I have the computer and the devices, but I have been shot and I have lost a lot of blood."

"Hani, will you be able to get to the flower market at *Place de la Madeleine* at the end of the Rue Royale?" the man asked in Arabic.

"I will try. I will try to catch a cab."

Just as Hani got into a cab, the man with the limp saw him. He hailed one as well and followed behind him. He got on the phone and made a call. He spoke in French.

"This is Andre Billen of the SGRS Belgium. I have found Hani Hamid and am following him in a cab as we speak. He is heading toward the Eiffel Tower area. Send some men to the general area and I will inform you with a more precise location when I arrive there."

"Monsieur Billen, how is that you know of Hani Hamid and what are you doing in Paris?" Markham asked from the other end of the line.

"We have been tracking him for two years now. We believe he was the financial backer of terrorist cells in Antwerp, Bruges, Brussels, Leuven, and Sint-Niklaas. We raided the cell in Bruges, killed the terrorists, and found data that confirmed our suspicions and gave us information of some others in a group called the JASON group. We found Hani Hamid's name in some files associated with the terrorist cell. We also found a recently signed and un-cashed check from him for ten million dollars to another terrorist organization in the area. Unfortunately, the ten members of the cell decided to fight instead of surrendering and they are all dead now, so we could not get any more information from them. However, we found data that led me to Paris, and *Le Meridien Montparnasse*. We will be raiding all of the other cells in a short time. Anyway, I arrived at the hotel and found the room a person named Dumas had scheduled. When I went to the room, I was too late and I saw only bodies and Hani escaping down the back route. I thought all the others were dead, so I did not check to make sure. Anyway, Hani was ahead of me and got away. Regrettably, I am somewhat slow with my cane not aiding my leg in a running mode. I eventually saw him getting in a cab and am following him in another cab."

"Okay, Monsieur Billen. I will send some men to the area of the Eiffel Tower and will await your instructions. I appreciate your call and your help."

"You are welcome, Monsieur Director, it is my pleasure."

"Please, call me Markham. I am at your service."

Markham called Claude immediately after Andre hung up his phone. "Claude, Markham here. I have good news for you. Hani was the one who was shot and is heading toward the Eiffel Tower area. I should have better data on the location in a short time. I was given the information by a Rene Billen, an agent with the Service Général du Renseignement et de la Sécurité, also known as SGRS."

"My God, how did Belgium intelligence get involved in this mess?" Claude asked.

"It's a long story, but get your group heading toward the Eiffel Tower immediately! I will send some other agents to the area."

Rene Billen got out of the cab just as Hani disappeared abound a corner. He tossed twenty Euro into the front seat of the cab and walked as fast as he could after Hani but lost sight of him.

Hani eventually stumbled into another alley and fell behind a large trash bin. The blood that he had lost was finally taking its toll. His shoulder was still bleeding profusely but the pain had gone. He looked up to the sky, then his hand let loose of its grip on the suitcase containing the computer and devices and it slipped to his side. In a few more moments, his eyes looked vacantly at the cloudy sky, no longer seeing anything. Minutes passed by and an unknown homeless woman searching the dumpsters in the alley walked up to Hani. She stared at him for a short time, looked suspiciously around the alley, then gave his body a gentle kick. Getting no response, she kneeled down next to him.

"Well, you got yourself into some pickle of trouble, didn't you monsieur?" she stated to the body in French.

She felt in his pockets and found his wallet, which contained about five thousand Euros. She whistled and looked around as she removed the large bills and quickly stuffed them into a bag in her cart. She glanced at the man again and slipped the Rolex from his wrist and put it on her own. She then took a ring with a yellow pyramid-shaped diamond with emeralds all around it and put it on her thumb. She smiled as she looked at the ring.

She started to leave when she noticed the suitcase on the other side of the body. She lifted it up and opened it. She recognized the laptop computer but not the other devices. She closed the case up and put it in her cart as well. She started running and pushing her cart out the other side of the alley as fast as she could go after hearing a noise.

"Well, Mary," she said to herself, out of breath and wheezing from running. "This is the best day you have ever had. That old crystal gazer was right saying I would be having good luck this month." With a huge smile on her wrinkled face, she started whistling as she walked quickly, pushing her cart toward the street.

* * *

A few moments later, Rene Billen walked into the alley and saw a man lying next to the garbage bin. He walked over to the body, looked down at Hani, and shook his head. He called the director and told him he had found Hani.

"Yes, he is dead. He lost a tremendous amount of blood. I am in the alley next to the Rue Royale restaurant just a hundred meters from the *Place de la Madelene*. The cross street is *Rue de*

St-Honore. Uh, we do have a problem here though... there is no computer!"

"What? How could it be that there is no case?" Markham asked.

"It is a puzzle, but all indicators say that someone found him and he was robbed."

Markham had put the conversation on all of the agents' cell phones and Claude was listening in. He looked at his group. "The alley where Hani is located is right around the corner."

When the group got there along with several other agents, Rene Billen was leaning next to the wall smoking a long, thin cigar. He looked up, shook his shoulders with his palms up, and pointed to Hani. "He has only been dead for a very short time, three to five minutes at most, so whoever took the case containing the computer should still be somewhere in the area. My leg has given up on me, so I will have to rely on you to catch him."

The RG agents left immediately to search the general area. David looked at the body, then looked around the ground. "Someone with a cart has been here very recently, look at the wheel tracks that have gone across the blood. They left us a trail."

"Very good, Davie!" Teddy exclaimed. "That probably means it was a garbage dipper."

"A garbage dipper, what is that?" Rene asked, looking puzzled.

"It's an American term meaning someone who searches in the garbage for food or other things, quite often aluminum cans or glass bottles they can turn in for money. A garbage dipper is usually a bag lady, although some homeless men indulge in the questionable career, too."

"*Un qui recherché dans les ordures?*" Rene asked.

"Yes, in America bag ladies are always searching in garbage bins and trash cans," Teddy answered.

Rene shook his head. "If it is a bag lady, that means she must be around the area someplace."

"Unless she obtained a lot of money from the wallet and took a cab!" David commented.

Claude got on the phone and asked for an ambulance and more men to search the area for a bag lady.

Up the street, a group of grim-looking protestors were marching solemnly down the Rue de Rivoli. The bag lady was running as fast as she could, pushing her cart toward the same street. Just as she approached the intersection, her cart went out of control and swung right into the group of protestors. She looked up and saw the group wearing black hooded robes and white facemasks with painted blood running down their cheeks. Around their necks were white cardboard placards with names of dead children, Tibetans, Iraqis, and children from African nations.

One of the protestors grabbed the cart and the lady so she wouldn't fall. She then handed the cart back to the bag lady. The bag lady smiled, thanked the protestor, and handed her the suitcase. She said in French, "You are so kind, I wish to give you something for your cause. Please take this."

She grabbed her cart and continued running down the Rue de Rivoli into another alley between some old apartment buildings. She took off the ring and watch and put them in her pocket. She then went from the alley to the Park, *Jardin des Tuileries*, where about 15 homeless were sitting around a fire in a garbage can.

"Mary did you have a good day today?" one of the men asked.

"Fair, Marcel, fair. Tomorrow will be even better." She smiled a toothless smile.

She mused to herself that she would hock the ring and Rolex tomorrow, which indeed would make it an even better day. She knew the girl in the small café near the park that would do it for her for a small price. She knew that if she did it herself, the thief of a tradesman at the *boutique de preteur sur gages* would cheat her.

* * *

Claude's group and the RG agents searched high and low for a bag lady, but didn't find her. The bag lady and the computer had disappeared.

"Well, there is possibly one good thing Claude, none of the bad guys have it, and no one else knows how to use it, so we are probably safe!" David stated.

"That may be true, but then maybe a computer-type will eventually end up with it and perhaps there were notes in the case, with the devices, with instructions. Then of course, Dumas is still out there someplace, too."

"Lord, Claude, you know how to make a somewhat happy moment petty damn gloomy." Edward shook his head.

A group of protestors continued marching solemnly down the side of the street with their sad white masks covering their faces. They wore black hooded robes covering their bodies and had placards around their necks. They were marching to the heartbreaking beat of a single drum. It was a silent march except for the drum, which sounded like a funeral cadence. One of the females in the group was carrying a metal suitcase, which was quite incongruous to the somber demonstration. The agents failed to notice it.

Chapter Nineteen
The Computer Emerges

When will the dismal madness disappear? When
Will gentler times prevail, when will man cease
To murder his fellow man and when will the
Earth no longer be lost to fear?

It was only about 15 minutes after the death of Hani Hamid when the computer ended up in the hands of the protestor. The protest group eventually scattered in different directions, some back to school, some to their home countries, and many to other areas for more protest marches. One person in particular, Cathleen Fitzpatrick, after protest marches in France, Germany, and Italy, decided to look for a job and a new, more conventional life. She was the one who had been given the computer by the old bag lady.

Cathleen Fitzpatrick was given the name of a person who worked in the Pentagon by one of the protestors she met in London. He told her how well they paid and that she might be able to get some inside data for them if she could get hired as a translator. A short time after that, she left London for the United States to start her new life. She had had enough of the protest life for now, and didn't make any promises.

*   *   *

A short time after Cathleen arrived in Washington DC, she was hired as the senior translator for the CIA at the Pentagon. Cathleen could speak, read, and write in English, French, German, Greek, Italian, Russian, Arabic, and Spanish. She was a graduate of Alpha Beta Piccadilly in Merano and Bolzano, Italy, and studied Arabic at the London Arabic School. She also had a doctorate in linguistics from the Sorbonne at the University of Paris.

She had only become involved in the protest marches against killing after her brother was killed in the Iraq War, and a suicide bomb in Afghanistan killed one of her younger sisters who was a clerk in the Army. She now had a loathing for war and what it brought upon mankind, and an acrid distaste for those who engaged in promoting wars, especially those who promoted war for monetary gains and the amassing of power. She was hesitant, for that reason, to work for the CIA. However, an American she met during her interviews told her that most people in America were against wars, even though the history of America was dotted with the dark scarlet specks of war, and President Bush and his administration had started two of them. She told Cathleen that

President Bush did so because of 9/11 and the threat of terrorism. After the talk, she decided to give the agency the benefit of the doubt for now. Besides, the money was very good and the new incoming president said he was against war.

*   *   *

About two weeks later, when she finally found her new apartment in DC, she unpacked her things. For the first time in many months, she looked inside the metal suitcase that the French bag lady had handed her when she was in Paris. She took out the laptop computer. She knew her old laptop had seen its last days and a new one would be nice.

She was an ace on computers but had never seen one quite like the strange one she was staring at. She also looked at the devices in the case. She didn't understand the use of the tiny metal syringe-looking devices and put them back inside the case as she took out the computer. She turned the machine on and started to type. The words came out a garbled mess of what looked like symbols, unintelligible words, and odd sentences. They made no sense and seemed not to be in any language that she knew... and she knew a lot. It looked like it was an encryption of many languages. She tried several things with the laptop but all she got were the same weird figures and hieroglyph-looking letters. She finally gave up and put the computer back in the case and stored it in a closet. She decided she would buy the skinny new Macbook Pro as soon as she got a paycheck.

*   *   *

It was now summertime and there were no new leads of any kind in regards to the missing computer, the mysterious Monk Rene Dumas, or the Pentagon Project itself. The good news was there were no more assassinations, either. In the absence of any action on the Pentagon case, Claude Lambert was assigned to a new terrorist case and Lieutenant Dubois was deeply immersed in another murder case. It was not as interesting or weird as the assassination cases, which were still hanging up in the air, and he longed to get back on those.

David was back in DC finishing up his work on Kafka and starting his new novel about assassinations, the Pentagon, NSA, the CIA, MI6, Mossada, and a computer which interfaced with human brains. He had a big bite from his agent who thought perhaps it was a little far-fetched, but would pitch it when he finished it if the final product wasn't too far out and weird as it sounded.

The CIA, MI6, and Mossada were busy trying to find out how and why some of their assistant directors and agents got involved in such a nefarious project, and especially with a citizen group, without anyone knowing about it. NSA and the Pentagon were totally embarrassed when confronted with the fact that a top-secret black funded project at the Pentagon was being carried out without any of the big brass having a hint that it even existed. Heads were rolling or were on top of shaking bodies in heated meetings with Congressional oversight committees.

The three ex-spies were the only ones still interested in the case since they really didn't have much of anything else to do, except drinking wine and talking about the case. Unfortunately for them, chasing women was still not an option, much to their chagrin.

*   *   *

It was a hot, muggy, gray summer afternoon in London, typical of the city, when it happened. Teddy was drinking a pint of dark ale at his favorite pub when he looked across the table and saw a young man sitting at the table to his right. The lad was dressed in a black robe with a hood. He had an expressionless white mask pushed up on top of his head, and a white placard around his neck. He was taking a break from a sit-in protest across the street at a bank. They started talking after Teddy bought the man a beer.

"You didn't happen to be involved in a protest in France last spring, did you?"

216

The hippy-looking American, with dark stubble, a stringy goatee, and light blue eyes, smiled. "Yeah, man, I was in that group many months ago, man it was real ratty, you know, very cool. That guy on the drum made it all happen, man. You would really think we were at a funeral. Of course, that was the whole idea, wasn't it?" He laughed. "I mean, with all the dead bodies of those poor little kids turning up in Iraq, the Gaza Strip, and other places, man what a bummer, it just made me sick all over. But, you know what was a really strange and somewhat funny was what happened to Cathleen Fitzpatrick."

"What was that?" Teddy asked.

"Well this old bag lady came running like a bat out of hell out of an alley. She was running as fast as she could run, pushing an old rusty grocery cart. She was running out of control, you know, legs all going in different directions, right into our midst with the old cart about to topple. Anyways man, this cute protestor chick named Cathleen grabbed the poor old coot and her cart before she toppled over and made a mess of herself. The lady thanked her, shook her hand up and down a dozen times, and then handed her a metal suitcase. Then she tore off down the street into an alley, like some crazed banshee was after her. Cathleen didn't know what to do so she just kept marching along carrying the stupid suitcase. It was one funny situation, man."

Teddy's mouth went wide open and he asked if the event with the old bag lady and suitcase happened on a certain date. The date was the same date that Hani had died in the alley, and the suitcase with the Pentagon computer had disappeared. The youth said that was definitely the correct date, they always knew because they had a strict schedule for their protest events.

"Do you know where this Cathleen is now, is she still involved in protests?"

"Nah, she left right after that gig. She had been involved in about five events and decided she wanted to do something else with her life. She said she wanted to get a job and settle down with a conventional lifestyle. I don't know where she went. She was one bright and fantastic-looking broad, I can tell you that! You know, long auburn hair, beautiful brown eyes, gorgeous legs, full lips, and big boobs! Man I had one gigantic crush on her."

"You said she was bright, why?"

"Man she had a fancy doctorate from the University of Paris, spoke a bazillion languages, you know Arabic, German, Russian, you name it, and she spoke it, and read it, and wrote it. When we were in different countries, she always translated our messages into the language of the country we were in."

"Do you know anyone that might know where she is now?" Teddy asked excitedly.

The young man scratched his scraggy goatee and then nodded his shaggy head. "Yeah man, maybe, she used to bunk with a Russian girl named Irina, she might know where she is now."

"Do you know the Russian girl's last name?" Teddy asked, trying to contain his excitement.

"Let's see, yeah, Vodka... no that's not it. Maybe it was Voronkova. Yeah, that was her name, Irena Voronkova."

"Do you know where she is and what happened to her?"

"Yeah, she married another guy in the protest group, a real nice Russian guy named Boris Babanov, he was really into the anti-war, anti-killing thing. He was smart too, had a science degree."

"And where is he now?"

"Back in the good old USA, he was an environmental engineer and went to work for some green firm in Falls Church, Virginia. I don't know what the name of the firm is. Oh, oh, hey I gotta get going back to work, the boss is back. We are ready to march now. We always march after doing a sit in!"

When the man got up, Teddy found out his name was Danny Hale. Teddy gave him 50 Euros, thanked him and shook his hand, then walked back to the bus area. The young man stood there with his mouth open as he looked at the bill in his hand. He smiled a big smile, put the bill into his pocket, and waved. Teddy waved back, then got on a double-decker bus, and phoned Edward from the top area.

"Edward, you won't believe what happened at the pub today."

"You found yet another ale you like?"

"No... well yes, I did that too, but I found out that one of the protestors along the Rue Royale in Paris was given a metal suitcase by a bag lady this past spring."

"What? On the correct date?" Edward asked excitedly.

"Yep, it has to be the suitcase with the computer inside."

"Who was the person and where is he?"

"It's a she, her name is Cathleen Fitzpatrick."

"Where is she now?"

"No idea, but the guy I met at the pub said her friend Irina Voronkova married a guy named Boris Babanov and they live somewhere in Virginia now. Boris is an environmental engineer and got a job with some green firm in Falls Church, Virginia."

"Holy cow Teddy, that is fantastic. Davie lives pretty close to Falls Church. I'll call him right away! Are you on your way back to my place for dinner tonight?"

"Yes, I'm on a bus heading that way right now. Won't Ephraim be excited to be back in the saddle again?"

"Yeah Teddy, we all will be, it was getting boring around here, ole chap." Edward laughed. He got back on the phone and called his nephew.

"Hello, David Heywood."

"Davie, how would you like to get back on the Pentagon Project case again?" Edward asked.

"You mean you guys have a new lead after all of these months?"

"You got it, Davie, we have the name of a girl that the bag lady gave the computer to."

"How in God's name did you ever do that?" David asked incredulously.

Edward explained the whole story to him, embellishing things here and there for impact.

"Wow, Uncle, that is great! I should be able to narrow the firm Boris works for in a short time. I'll call you back if I talk to the girl named Irina."

"Okay Davie, be good and I'll talk to you soon. By the

way, how is Kafka going?"

"Well, I have him burrowed out of the isolation of his irreligious cage in less than 40 days, he hasn't turned into a dung beetle yet, and the trial isn't over so I guess things are going well!" He laughed.

"Davie, you are a kick. By the way, wasn't he a Czech?"

"Yes he was, but he published in German which is why I had to learn how to read German as well as French when I studied existentialism for my doctorate. It seems most of the existentialists were French, German, or European. I guess they are a dark lot! I didn't know you knew about him."

"Well only from my high school days where I was forced to read Metamorphosis. I never did get why that guy turned into an ugly beetle." Edward laughed.

"On one level it had to do with his abiding belief that the father is the authority and if you conform you are safe, and if not... you might turn into an ugly, meaningless insect. It actually had to do with Gregor Samsa, his character in Metamorphosis, and Kafka's inability to be a significant part of his family as a child. His stories often dwelt on the conflict between spirit and matter and the comparison of man to the universe, but usually dwelt upon the family from which he was unusually estranged."

"Well, I am now very sorry I asked. Anyway, it is all a bit over my head old chap, so I will say adieu to you."

"Yes, Uncle, goodbye," he stated as he shuffled a pile of papers on his desk, trying to ferret out his copy of *The Giant Mole* hiding under the pile.

*   *   *

Cathleen Fitzpatrick was sitting at her desk at work translating a memo discovered in one of the destroyed houses in Iraq when Ed Smythe leaned on the door.

"Are you busy?" he asked.

"Ed, I am always busy, but what do you have for me?"

He gave her a suggestive little smile, which she dismissed with a little frown and a nod of her head, which was covered with beautiful auburn curls that bounced when she moved. He cleared his throat and came into her office looking serious this time.

"I have a translated memo from German to Arabic to French or something, which appears to be quite odd in the final translation."

"Odd, how so?"

"It reads: the purple dog has left the alley." He laughed.

Cathleen looked at him and laughed too. "You are kidding me, right?"

"No, look at the memo." He handed her the translated memo along with the original, making sure he touched her soft, velvety skin. Touching her always gave him an electric spark and a pink face.

She took the memo and read it. "Hm, in French that is the message. Let's see what happens when I translate the French back into Arabic." She studied the memo for short time. "That's odd, it could translate now into 'the imperial robe worn by the traitor has left.' " She frowned and then translated the Arabic into German.

"That's even stranger... it now could be translated to read 'the leader who has gone is the traitor."

Ed looked at her and smiled. "That's it, Cathleen, that's it! A German spy, Fritz Fruehauf of the German Federal Intelligence Service, the BND, recently disappeared. They discovered after he disappeared that he was involved with a CIA agent, Gary Hart, and a Doctor Steven Bourne, the Technical Manager of NSA in a secret project here in the Pentagon. Gary Hart and Bourne were assassinated in France last spring. It is believed that it all had to do with humans who had been programmed by means of a computer with a message to assassinate people, or something like that. How is that for the beginnings of some conspiracy novel by a nutty author! Anyway, it was believed by some in the CIA that the assassins were actually innocent civilians who had micro-miniature receiving modules embedded in their brains without their knowledge. It was these modules that received messages from a transmitter in a computer and caused them to behave as directed. Altogether there were more than a dozen people actually killed by assassins with modules in their brains. The word is that the secret project started in NSA with Bourne, but many in the CIA figured he was not the true head of the plot. It was believed that the head of the plot was a civilian in a secret group called the JASON group. My former boss, many years ago in the Renseignements Généraux, was one of those who helped track the renegade agents and the others involved in the scheme. It all ended close to five months ago when a top member of the JASON group was killed and a sophisticated Pentagon computer, as well as a monk who was involved in the project, disappeared."

"Ed, that all sounds like some futuristic alien plot! What was the actual impending use of the system?"

"Only those involved knew what the aim was, and they are all supposedly dead."

"I had heard there had been a lot of probing at the Pentagon as to how a secret project could have been initiated and funded there without any of the top brass knowing. I had no idea the project was such a weird one. I translated some memos in regard to the project when I first got here. They were coded but once I translated them I found they were also initially written in both French and Arabic," Cathleen said. "It reminded me of the way Nostradamus wrote. He always wrote in about three different languages and placed them in odd ways for secrecy."

"Why would he do that?"

"So he wouldn't be tried as a heretic by the Catholic Church."

"Yes, that makes sense. Anyway, it seems that a civilian named Henry Hammer, an Arab, was the last one who had the computer." He went on to tell Cathleen when the man was killed and an odd-looking metal suitcase with the computer had disappeared.

* * *

The specific date and odd-looking metal case that Ed described to her didn't register until she got through with her hot bubble bath at home early that same evening. When it did occur to her, she quickly dried off and went to the closet to pull out the metal case.

She placed the suitcase on a table and took out the computer again. She turned it on and typed something into it. She got the same odd cryptic code as she did months ago. She then realized nothing that she had typed was being placed into the computer. She determined that there was already another message in the computer, and that was what kept coming up on the screen. This time, she used her decoding and language skills to translate what was written. She found that the message was a combination of French, Arabic, and German placed into a symbolic code.

After about three hours, she had the code translated. It read: "When a dark-complected man named Henry Hammer appears in the room, wait for a nod from me then shoot him and the tall man."

She turned ashen as she realized that this was the computer used to program the assassins; this was the Pentagon Project computer. The so-called conspiracy farce was a real project. She then looked at the metal syringes filled with tiny microscopic particles. She shuddered and put the computer and other devices back in the closet. She went to the living room, fixed herself a stiff drink, and sat down on the sofa to think about what to do next.

* * *

"Yes, this is David Heywood, I am looking for a Boris Babanov. He is an environmental engineer." This was the eighth firm he had called with no luck. He was tired and it was getting late.

"Yes, Boris works for us. I believe he is on his evening break right now. He is the manager of the second shift. I'll see if he is available."

David smiled and sighed with relief. "Thank you," he said and waited patiently.

"Yes, this is Boris Babanov. I don't recognize your name, do I know you?"

"I was given your name by Danny Hale."

"Oh my gosh, are you involved in the anti-war protests?"

"Not actually. I am looking for a Cathleen Fitzpatrick, Danny Hale said she and your wife, Irina Voronkova, were friends during the protest marches."

"That is true, what can I do for you, Mr. Heywood?"

"I would like to talk to your wife to see if she knows where Cathleen is now. Can you give me her phone number?"

There was a hesitation and then Boris said, "Give me your number and I will have Irina call you back, is that okay?" He sounded somewhat suspicious.

"Sure, that would be fine." He rattled off his number to the Russian.

"Good, I'll have her get hold of you as soon as she can."

"Yes, that would be great. Thank you."

Within 20 minutes, David's cell phone rang – well, actually, it barked. David loved dogs and programmed his phone to bark. Now you know just how silly philosophy professors are! "Yes, this is David Heywood."

"Mr. Heywood, this is Irina Babanov, Boris said you were trying to contact Cathleen Fitzpatrick."

"Yes, thank you for calling back. Do you know her whereabouts?"

"Yes, in fact I just got a letter from her last week. She just moved to an apartment near the Pentagon, she works in the CIA as a translator. Are you a friend?"

"Actually I am not. I am trying to see if she was the protestor in France who was given a case by a French bag lady."

"Oh my gosh, is that a problem?" she asked suspiciously.

"I have been looking for the case for some time now, uh, it has my special laptop computer in it. It was stolen the day of the protest march."

"Yes, I saw it the night after she opened the metal case. I was right behind her when the funny-looking old bag lady gave it to her. Is the computer important?"

"Yes, it is very important. I need to find it right away. It was lost during an altercation I had in an alley. Do you have her address?"

"Yes, let me get it."

After David got the address, he thanked Irina and said he would tell Cathleen that she said hello. He clicked the phone off, shook his head, and made a call to Edward.

"Uncle Edward, I talked to Irina. I have located Cathleen Fitzpatrick; she works at the Pentagon now and lives in the Casey Apartments nearby. It is probably too late now to go visiting, but I'll go there first thing in the morning."

"Fantastic, David. I will be waiting for your answer."

After Edward hung up his phone, a surveillance device in London clicked off.

A dark-complected man smiled at another man sitting opposite him. He spoke in Arabic. "The lost Pentagon computer has emerged! We have an address of where the computer is located as well. It was very fortunate that you decided to bug Edward Jones' manor house or we would never have known. He just received a call from his nephew in Washington DC, David Heywood."

"Very good, call Fritz in DC and give him the address, it shouldn't be too far from his safe house. I want that computer!" The man picked up his phone, made a call to America, and smiled.

After David had hung up his phone, he glanced at his watch and decided to go see Cathleen right then. He decided that tomorrow would be too late to satisfy his heated up curiosity. He looked at a map, wrote the address down, and went out to get in his car.

There was a dull illumination of the whole area by a full moon peeking through filmy clouds. The atmosphere was still warm and quite humid, which was usual for this time of year. Bright stars sparkled as they illuminated the sky. He loved the nightly scenes of the heavens in Washington DC. However, there were things in DC that he really hated. The horrible, damp, mushy humidity during the summer was one thing, and the icy, cold, bone-rattling, freezing rain during the winter was another. He could never get cool enough in the summer because of the hot temperatures and high humidity. It was like living in a sauna all day long. In addition, in the winter getting warm was impossible because of the freezing rain and intense winds that blew the icy cold right through your clothes and into your bones.

He thought about a recent offer to teach philosophy at a small private University in Santa Barbara, California and figured he might just take a trip to look at the campus. He had heard that Santa Barbara had a Mediterranean climate, with nice warm summers. It was also said that the area had nice mild days all year long, and very rarely any freezing days in the winter. The salary was not that good, but since he had made a ton of money on his conspiracy novels, he had no worry about money. He would probably make another pile of green if his new novel concerning the Pentagon and human-computer systems sold like the rest.

After talking to David Heywood, Irina decided to call Cathleen and tell her about the conversation.

"Irina, what did this David Heywood say?" Cathleen asked nervously.

"He just asked about the computer he had stolen from him, and if you were the one who got it from a bag lady in a protest march in Paris. He gave me the same date of our anti-killing protest march. He sounded so nice and sincere that I gave him your address then I thought about it and decided I had better give you a call. He said it was urgent, and that he really needed the computer."

"Thanks, Irina, I'll take some precautions just to be sure. Thank you, bye."

Cathleen went to the closet, took out the computer and the other devices, and put them in one of her personal luggage bags in another closet. She took some heavy things and wrapped them in old socks, then placed them in the metal suitcase. She closed it and placed it on the floor in the living room.

Fritz pulled into the parking lot at the Casey Apartments, took his Heckler & Koch .45 out of his glove compartment, put it in his belt, and buttoned his suit jacket. He went into the office and talked to the apartment manager. He said he was Cathleen's brother from Ireland and came to surprise her. He was told that she lived in apartment 377. He thanked the woman and started up the stairs to the third floor. When he approached the apartment, he heard a woman talking. The voice was muffled and he couldn't make out the words.

He waited for a few minutes, then knocked on the door.

"Yes, who is it?"

"It is David Heywood, Miss Fitzpatrick. I talked to your friend Irina Babanov about a computer that a bag lady gave to you during a protest march in Paris." Fritz waited calmly.

"Oh yes, one moment please."

Cathleen got back on the phone with her friend and coworker, Ed Smythe, who lived on the fourth floor in apartment 477.

"Hello, are you still on the line?" Ed's voice came through the receiver.

"Ed, I think I have a problem... someone is at my door, he said his name is David Heywood, and he knows I have the computer!" she whispered.

"What computer, Cathleen?"

"The one we talked about... it's a long story Ed, can you come down to my apartment immediately? Bring your gun."

"Yeah, I'm on my way."

He hung up his phone, grabbed his Glock, and put it in his shoulder holster. He then ran down the stairs.

"Miss Fitzpatrick are you there?" Fritz asked, getting somewhat angry.

"Yes, I am sorry, just a minute please," she called out from the living room.

She then went to the front door and looked through the peephole... she couldn't see anyone. She opened the door and peeked out. Fritz had moved away so she couldn't see him. When she opened the door, he immediately pushed her aside and walked into the apartment.

He looked at her and said, "Miss Fitzpatrick, I believe you have something my Intelligence Agency has lost." When he said that, he flashed his office ID.

Being in the CIA, Cathleen recognized immediately the ID of another Intelligence Service. "That is the ID of the BND, Germany's Intelligence Service! What are you doing here in

America?"

The man blinked but recovered instantly. "We are working with the NSA and the CIA on a case which has to do with the National Security of both nations." Fritz moved closer to her. "I need that computer now, Miss Fitzpatrick, where is it?"

Cathleen moved back and pointed to the metal suitcase sitting beside the couch. The man smiled, quickly went over to it, and picked it up. At that moment, Ed came through the front door and saw the man with the suitcase. He started to take his gun out of his holster, but Fritz drew his pistol and fired. The bullet hit Ed in the chest, knocking him flat. Cathleen screamed and Fritz fired at her but his gun jammed. He cursed, then ran out of the room with the suitcase in his hand. Cathleen called 911 and then went over to Ed who was lying on the floor.

"Ed, oh God Ed, can you hear me?"

"Yeah what the hell did that guy shoot me with, a cannon? I thought my new flak vest would take any hit, but man, that bullet knocked me flat. I think I am going to have some cracked ribs. Who was that guy?"

"He said his name was David Heywood."

Just at that moment, David looked into the room.

"Hello, I'm David Heywood... Irina said you lived here, what is going on?" He saw the man on the floor and furrowed his brow.

Ed looked up and started to grab for his gun, but David kicked it aside. "Hey, don't shoot me, I am not the enemy."

Cathleen looked at David. "The man who shot Ed said he was David Heywood, he showed me his ID."

"What? He said he was Heywood, did you look at the name on his ID?"

"Yes! No... I don't know, it was an ID from the BND, Germany's Intelligence Service. I am afraid I didn't really look at the name on it."

David took out his car license and showed it to her. Realization struck and he said, "Oh my God, that man was the one that was running down the stairs as I got out of the elevator. He was carrying a suitcase, please tell me that the computer was not in that suitcase!"

Ed moved to a chair. "Who are you and what is this all about? I am Ed Symthe and I am with the CIA at the Pentagon, and so is Cathleen. What is this computer thing of which you spoke?"

"It's a very long story, Mr. Symthe, but needless to say it has to do with a secret Pentagon Project gone awry."

Cathleen looked at David. "Does all of this have to do with Bourne of NSA and some intelligence agents who worked with a computer-human interfacing system?"

"Yep, you got it. I have been working with Claude Lambert of the French Central Direction of General Intelligence along with my uncle, an ex-MI6 agent, Ephraim Yatom, a retired agent with Metsada, and Teddy Dell, a retired CIA agent. We were tracking the computer and the people who used it to assassinate about a dozen people. We were investigating weird happenings involving the computer. Then it disappeared in Paris during a protest march against global killing. That is when you, Cathleen, were handed a case with a laptop computer inside. We had no idea who had the computer at that time until Teddy accidentally met a fellow named Danny Hale at a pub in London."

"Danny? He met Danny Hale? Oh my gosh, we were in the protest march together with Irina and about a dozen others."

"Yes I know, Danny is the one who told Teddy that it was you who was given a metal suitcase by a bag lady. That was the start of our new quest to locate the computer, and you."

Cathleen shook her head just as two EMT's ran into the room. They took off Ed's flak vest and looked at his chest. They decided he needed to get to the hospital. It appeared he had a broken rib, which could puncture a lung.

"Will you be okay, Cathleen?" Ed asked nervously as he was carried away.

"Yes, I will Ed, don't worry, and I'll get over to see you in a short time. Thank you for being so brave and wonderful!" She squeezed his hand and kissed him on the cheek. Ed turned red and smiled.

Cathleen turned back to David and smiled. "Don't worry

about the computer, David. I switched it, along with some weird-looking devices, to one of my luggage bags. It is in another closet." She got up, went to the closet, and brought out the bag.

David opened it and pulled the computer out. "It is a laptop, but it doesn't look like any other laptop computer I have seen."

"Well, in a way it is similar, but in most ways it isn't. Watch what happens when I turn it on and type something on it."

David's mouth went open when he saw the weird-looking letters and hieroglyphic symbols appear when she typed. "What the devil is all of that?"

Cathleen laughed and said, "It is a combination of French, Arabic, and German in code. I didn't type in anything, it just repeated what had been written in it some time ago. One probably needs to push some key or something on it to actually begin to enter a new message. The inability to type directly into the computer is probably to make sure that anyone using it wouldn't be able to do any damage accidentally. No one accidentally seeing what was being typed into the computer could understand what was written, either. It would preclude anyone without knowledge of the system and the code from ever using the computer. I happen to be a translator of languages and cryptology and even considering that I just kind of fell into translating the code, the fourth time around. The first time I saw it I couldn't make heads or tails of it. Does this computer really send messages to a person's brain causing them to follow what is typed?"

"I am afraid so, Cathleen, and so far about a dozen people have died because of it."

"Oh my God, David what was the Pentagon going to do with it?"

"Well, first, most in the Pentagon had no idea it even existed, and those who planned the project are all dead, at least we thought so. That is a question now, since your visit by an agent from Germany. We surmise, though, that some people in the Pentagon, NSA, the CIA, MI6, and Metsada were involved in a plot involving assassinations. One unproven theory is that they were going to embed the receiving devices, that's what is inside the metal syringes there," he said pointing to the syringes, "into the brains of some terrorists and then send them back to other nations, or perhaps even terrorist cells or camps. Once there, they could be instructed by the computer to assassinate people, probably their leaders. It could be even more far reaching of course, but that is our preliminary assumption. Then a monk named Rene Dumas took the computer and used it to program assassins to kill some pedophile priests who molested his nephews. The nephews had committed suicide over their sins, as eventually did their mother. It is a very long and somewhat complicated story. Then Henri Hammer, who it is believed was a member of the JASON group, possibly wanted it to program some other people, probably Israelis imprisoned in Gaza someplace. One theory, since he was affiliated with Islamic terrorists, is that he wanted to free Israeli prisoners in Arab states, embed them with the brain modules, and send them back to Israel and have them assassinate the leaders there. Man it is all so complicated it is hard to explain."

"And just think, I had the stupid thing all this time," Cathleen stated as she stared at the computer and shook her head. "Yes, but I wonder with whom that German agent is affiliated, and I wonder how he found out about it. How would he even know that it was here? I will have to call my uncle and have him check his house for bugs, and I don't mean the insect variety. With your permission, I would like to take the computer and devices now."

"Yes, of course. Which agency are you going to give it to now?"

"That is a very good question. We still do not trust any intelligence agencies here yet. We probably need to vet all of the new directors a little more. No evidence has been uncovered that any of them are part of the original plat, but we can't take the chance just yet. At this point, we don't really know who to give it to. We may just decide to destroy the computer and devices. Claude Lambert of the RG and his director are the only ones we trust so far. Oh yes, and a Paris police lieutenant named Dubois."

Cathleen shook her head, sat down, and asked David if he would like a drink. He declined and said he needed to get back to

London immediately with the computer. He told her to call the CIA and explain what happened in regards to the German Federal Intelligence Service agent and the shooting. He said she should ask for some protection for a while since the agent might come back when he finds the computer missing.

She called a number and told David that two agents would be sent over in about 20 minutes. David thanked her for her help and asked her to keep the information he had given her secret. She promised. He took the laptop, put the computer and devices in a bag, shook Cathleen's hand, and headed happily out to his car.

He couldn't believe that the long trail had finally ended and the good guys had won. When the CIA agents pulled into the parking lot, David was already near his car prepared to leave. He put the sack with the computer and devices on the ground next to his car and placed his key in the lock to open the door.

Unfortunately for him, he failed to see a moonlit shadow near a dented white van two cars down from his, as well as the person right behind his car. When he opened the door to get in, he felt a tap on the nape of his neck. A dark shroud covered his consciousness. When he awoke, the computer and brain modules were gone. Someone had the deadly brain control system once again and he had no idea who.

Chapter Twenty
Strange Occurrences

The spring storm rages again, as darkness
Remains indoors contemplating the
Inadequacies of life, perhaps even death.
Where are the greedless and those who
Are unselfish? Where are the men of peace?
Where can we find compassionate people, in a
World so fractured by war and chaos?

It had been almost four months since David Heywood had the computer and devices stolen from him in the parking lot near the Casey Apartments. Boris and Irina Babanov, originally of the anti-war protest movement and recently of Green Environments, Inc., disappeared from Falls Church, Virginia that same night. Boris never returned to work, nor did he and Irena return to their apartment. They left in a white van to places unknown.

*   *   *

The three old retired spies had settled down to look at new things in which to meddle, but couldn't find anything as intriguing as their case involving the Pentagon Project. They settled with talking about the case in the past tense and formulated all sorts of weird outcomes. They couldn't understand why there had been no evidence of any questionable activities going on indicating that the Pentagon computer was in use again. They kept checking to see if any suspicious assassinations had taken place, but none had. They mainly did a lot of toasting and tasting of exotic wines. They still didn't have the energy to chase beautiful women.

*   *   *

Later on that year, the media started reporting about odd and unique sets of events taking place in various parts of the world. The events baffled even the most erudite intelligence personnel as well as the leaders of the world. The major question they all asked was why a plethora of past bloodthirsty terrorist ideologists and cruel despots started promoting peace and nonviolence in their areas.

Past dictators of small, poor nations now worked hard to help the destitute people in their countries. Known terrorists now pleaded with groups fighting each other to seek peace among their people and stop the killing. Terrorist leaders in Africa, Afghanistan, Pakistan, Burma, and many other nations that had been under siege walked with olive branches among feuding chiefs and promoted peace and the end to the killing of their brothers. The Taliban had thrown down their arms and had rejoined the Afghanistan government. Iran allowed inspectors and engineers to come into their atomic facilities to dismantle their bomb-making systems. The Chinese leaders gave the Tibetans their freedom and talked openly of allowing free elections in China in the following year. North Korea signed a peace treaty with South Korea and started to resume peaceful relations with America and her allies.

An especially odd occurrence was a peace treaty between Israel and Palestinians.

It was during the new Israeli-Hamas hostilities in the Gaza Strip that Mahmoud Bayt Dajan from Hamas and Nadav Ben-Aharon from Israel were sent to a secret neutral site in Egypt for a meeting. They were supposedly sent to initiate and write up a new truce and peace treaty, and were given total freedom to negotiate such a treaty between Palestine and Israel. However, the leaders of Hamas and Israel knew full well that the two they sent would never agree on anything because of their mutual hatred for each other and the nations they were to negotiate with.

It was well-known in high-level Palestinian circles that Mahmoud, a renowned and fanatic Hamas terrorist, abhorred the Jews and would never sign a peace settlement that would not totally benefit Hamas and aid in the total destruction of Israel. It was also well-known among the Israeli secret services that Nadav, an anti-Palestinian Israeli Army General, could not abide Hamas and had been a top level voice against any peace settlement with Hamas for years. He had even advocated that the Israelis take back the whole Gaza strip and oust all Palestinians from the land forever. The military powers in Israel knew that he would never sign a peace treaty that would not totally benefit the Israelis to the detriment of the Palestinians.

During the first week, extremely heated, contentious, and acrimonious negotiations almost caused the sides to come to physical blows many times. After a non-military plane landed in the darkness of the night, with no one aware of its arrival, Mahmoud and Nadav suddenly disappeared from the two delegations. Each nation blamed the other for the abductions and both brought the remainder of their delegations back to their respective nations. They declined to send other negotiators to Egypt in an attempt to secure a peace agreement. They also hardened their stance toward any peace agreement. This was after the United States, the United Nations, and Britain, as well as other Arabian nations, pleaded for them to sign a truce.

The two negotiators suddenly appeared later in the week as mysteriously as they had disappeared. Both men stated that a truce and peace settlement had been accepted and signed by both negotiators. The world was told of the treaty through various news agencies.

The two antagonistic nations were in shock as they brought their negotiators back to their own countries to interrogate them. They had their top attorneys read the peace settlement to determine the ramifications of the agreement, and determine if they could void the treaty. If they could not find a legal way out of the peace agreement, they knew they would have to abide by it since the world knew of the treaty and there was an international promise by the two nations when they went into negotiations to abide by the issues outlined in any treaty.

Both nations had agreed in writing, unconditionally, to accept a truce and peace treaty prior to sending the two deadly antagonists to negotiate. They, of course, had firmly believed that no pact would ever be signed, and the promise was a ruse. However, since a treaty had been signed and it was determined for both factions that there was no legal way to invalidate the agreement, they had no choice but to accept the conditions of the peace agreement and stop killing each other. Neither side was happy!

After the treaty had been signed, twelve people dressed in white, featureless masks and black-hooded robes stood quietly by a small plane. One was a short, stout, pious Frenchman. He had a cane, a considerable limp, and a gravelly French-accented, melodic voice. He had come a long way from the darkness in his mind to what he was now doing. The younger men and women smiled and gave each other high fives as they got on the plane during the darkness of the night. The somber Frenchman nodded to the others, took his seat in the rear, and started softly chanting prayers. It was so soft that the others could not hear his pleas.

"Dear God, forgive me of my sins for I have sinned against you and against man, I am not worthy to live... please accept my new actions as an atonement for my sins."

The monk's agonizing prayers went on for hours as they others slept peacefully.

*   *   *

In an ornate office in an Israeli government building, a day after the Palestinian-Israeli treaty had been signed, one man with a red face was berating another vociferously in Hebrew. "My God Nadav, what have you done, you damn fool? How could you have done this to us? You are a traitor, you have ruined Israel!" The Israeli Prime Minister screamed at the top of his voice. "You have tied our hands behind our backs and placed a blindfold over our eyes! We can no longer protect ourselves from the Islamic terrorist monsters. We will all be destroyed because of what you have done. You are an anathema to Israel!"

Nadav, looking at the Prime minister in an extremely calm manner, simply shook his head. "War is never an end to any nation's process of becoming. It is the thousand-year lie of those who have never had the ability or intelligence to see the world as a place for all people to live in peace and prosperity. It is the lie of those who live in anger, hatred, greed, and arrogance. War is not an answer to any problems, and especially not ours!"

The Prime minister became even redder in the face and slammed his fist on his desk, but he had no immediate rejoinder to Nadav's comments. He eventually calmed down, looked up at Nadav's serene face, shook his head angrily, and ordered him out of his office.

At the same time, a heated conversation in Arabic between Mahmoud and the Prime Minister of Hamas was also taking place. The Prime Minister, his face crimson with anger, glared at Mahmoud after the peace treaty had been explained to him. He then screamed at the top of his voice.

"You have ruined us, you stupid, ignorant fool! You have destroyed our holy Jihad. How could you do this to us, Mahmoud? We trusted you to do your job, which was to stop any truce, any peace treaty! We can no longer attack the infidels with our rockets or any other means now. We can no longer kill our deadly enemies. You have put a curse on us to live in peace with the Jews who will invade our land with their apartments and foul breaths until we have no land left! How could you have done this to us? You are a traitor to Palestine, to Islam, the Koran, and our sacred Jihad!"

Mahmoud gazed at the Prime minister and simply smiled. "As Kahlil once said: Deliver me from him who does not tell the truth unless he stings; and from the man of good conduct and bad intentions; and from him who acquires self-esteem by finding fault in others."

The Prime minister turned beet red and sputtered, but could not say a thing to rebuff the famous and revered poet's words. He finally rose and ordered Mahmoud out his office.

The following day, the war was over, the Israelis started withdrawing their tanks, destroyed the remnants of their half-built settlements, and ceased all bombings. Hamas immediately stopped firing rockets from Gaza into Israel and started destroying all of their rockets and rocket launchers, as well as their explosives used for suicide bombings. The Israelis opened up all of the borders between Palestine and all of the other surrounding nations, and humanitarian supplies started flowing into the Gaza strip to aid the Palestinians. When some Iran militants attempted to smuggle in more rockets, Hamas agents stopped them and destroyed the rockets that were brought in. They also arrested all of those in Hamas who remained militant and who planned to fire rockets into the Israelis. The Iranians were astounded.

The Israelis sent tens of millions of dollars into Gaza to rebuild what they had destroyed, and sent millions of dollars of humanitarian aid to the Palestinians. They also tore down the walls separating Israel from what was once the enemy area. They opened up their cities to hire Palestinians to allow them to live among the Israelis. The world was in shock.

Nadav and Mahmoud met regularly, mostly alone but sometimes with their superiors and representatives of the free world. This was to assure that the peace accord between the two nations was firmly maintained, the conditions of the agreement were carried out, and a peaceful coexistence was strictly preserved. Nadav and Mahmoud told their countries that they would ensure that the peace would be never-ending, and that the world would know the truth if any obstruction to the peace process occurred by either country. The world of nations stood by in amazement, not understanding how such a miracle had occurred.

The whole area was now at peace and a mutually accepted and negotiated peace treaty tightly bound the Palestinians, Hamas, and the Israelis together for the first time in thousands of years. The treaty was becoming a new bargaining system for many countries at loggerheads in their relationships. Many of the leaders were influenced by a group of protestors who flew into their nations in the dark of the night. The leaders' eyes were cloudy and their actions were saintly. It was a new world that was taking place, and no one knew why.

Chapter Twenty One
A Turn of Events

Although the rhetoric of change continues
The reality of change is always fleeting,
Always somewhere in the distance in the
Minds of those who create chaos.

Edward Jones was the one who first noticed the odd demeanor of several of the leaders who were now promoting peace on one of their TV appearances. They appeared to be in a deep meditation-like trance. The people of the world simply saw the appearances as godly, serene manifestations, like that observed in Gandhi, or the Dalai Lama, and left it at that.

It was at their bimonthly dinner during the summer that Edward mentioned the anomaly.

"Take a look at these still pictures that I got from the TV station." He looked at Teddy and Ephraim. "What do you see in them that appears odd?"

Ephraim and Teddy looked closely at the blown up photos Edward had placed in front of them. The pictures were of Mahmoud Bayt Dajan from Hamas and Nadav Ben-Aharon from Israel. They were the two negotiators that had surprised their nations and the world by signing a binding peace accord. Ephraim and Teddy nodded their heads and shrugged their shoulders until Edward took out a magnifying glass and pointed to the eyes.

"Oh my God, it can't be, can it?" Ephraim stated wide-eyed as he bent over to look closer.

Teddy then looked at the photos with the magnifying glass. "My God, Edward you are right; there is something definitely odd. They all look like they are in some type of trance, they have a vague, vacant look in their eyes."

"Yes... just like the assassins!" Edward commented.

"You are right, *exactly* like the assassins. Do you think the anti-war group were the ones who stole the computer from Davie? I wonder how they learned to use it to promote peace? I thought it was determined that only Dumas knew how to use the computer?" Ephraim asked.

"To answer your first question, yes, I believe someone in an anti-war group probably stole the computer from Davie. Didn't Irina and Boris Babanov disappear the same night that David was put to sleep and the computer was taken?" Edward stated.

"Yes, and they were once a big part of the anti-war movement marches. Do you think they are the ones involved?" Teddy replied.

"They sure could be. What do you think we ought to do now?" Teddy asked.

"Absolutely nothing," Edward answered. "I can't think of a better use for the secret Pentagon Project, can you? To get back to the second question, how did they learn how to use the devices? I believe in their midst is probably a short, stout Frenchman who used to be a monk. He taught them how to use the computer or uses it himself."

The other two old spies nodded their heads back and forth then lifted their glasses of wine for a toast to peace. It was the fifth toast of the night and they were feeling very good; in fact, they were all quite tipsy.

"Here's to the dark monk, may he be able to achieve atonement for his sins!" Edward stated, weaving a bit.

The others raised their glasses. "Here, here!" they shouted and drank the glasses dry.

"And let's hope he doesn't go mad again and decide to use it for nefarious purposes in the future!" Ephraim stated as he nodded to the others.

They looked at each other and shook their heads solemnly.

* * *

In Darfur, six people in black, hooded robes and expressionless white masks stood in the shadows and waited for the leader of a sect of Islamic terrorists who had been raiding camps, killing the men and raping the women. When the terrorists appeared, they were put to sleep with a strong mist of an ether derivative. In a few minutes, microscopic modules had been embedded into the brains of the leader and two of the next in charge.

Six people waited in the shadows as the group awakened. Boris typed in three different messages at specific frequencies. The leader looked at his men and said in Arabic, "My loyal followers, I have had a vision from the great Mohamed. He told me that what we have been doing is evil, and is a mortal sin against the Koran. We must stop killing and help the dark people of Darfur."

Two others of the group got up, broke their rifles against the side of the jeep, and cheered their leader. Other terrorists who just arrived gathered around the three men, gazed in disbelief, but then joined the three and destroyed their weapons as well. The leader looked at his followers, and in a trance-like state, faced the east and began to pray for peace. All of the terrorists kneeled and followed his chanting.

The same thing would soon occur in countries from Algeria to the Congo, from India to the Ivory Coast, from Nepal to Somalia, in all nations in war or chaos. The self-assigned task of a gentle and trusting group with a lack of worldly sophistication was to control those involved in evil by a using a computer that was once planned for assassinations and war. The age of computer generated peace was now in the hands of those who protested against killing and war.

They were always dressed in silly, sad white masks and black hooded robes, and wandered to and fro from one country to another to engage in peace marches, and with their computer send initiated subliminal messages of love and peace. A short Frenchman paid for the cost of their voyages and provided the plane to fly them all over the world. He used a cane and had a noticeable limp, and watched as the others participated in the marches. He spent his time, when he was not working with the computer, chanting prayers. He had a deep, soothing French voice. He kept telling his fellow protestors that the world would never be the same!

*   *   *

David Heywood completed his book on Kafka and accepted a full professor's job at a private college in Santa Barbara. He convinced Beverly to come with him and take a job at the CIA office there. A very large diamond ring went with the proposition.

Claude Lambert was appointed the Head of the *Renseignements Généraux* (RG) when Markham retired. Lieutenant Dubois was selected as the new Paris police commissioner and the three old duffers were wondering what else they could get themselves involved in that would make their golden years a little more exciting. They were too old to chase women, even though occasionally they gave it a heroic shot.

The JASON group went underground even deeper than before. The Pentagon started taking more measures to assure that the Secretary of Defense knew what projects were going on in his realm of responsibility.

Sister Murray still prayed and attended lectures and conferences on the combining of science and religion and had no recollection of her past activities as an assassin. The monastic life at the *Abbaye de Solesmes* went on as it had since 1010 and Gregorian chants still softly perfumed the nave and sculptured halls as in the past. If one looked very closely at the marble face of Mary, they would notice that she was smiling.

The CIA, DIS, Mossad & Metsada, BND, MI5 & 6, NSA, and other intelligence agencies continued probing every nook and cranny in their agencies to make sure no one was involved in any clandestine activities, at least those they had not initiated.

Epilogue

A private plane carrying a group with sad white masks and black hooded robes was heading toward another nation in turmoil. Huge, dark clouds covered the plane like a black pall. It was spring again and it was raining, the thunder of falling lightning could be heard in the far reaches of the mountains. In some areas of the world, dark nefarious entities of war and chaos had retreated into the bowels of the earth, at least for now. The mystery of life and death remained an enigmatic riddle.

Somewhere, some people were also conspiring to do evil. Unfortunately, it has always been this way since the beginning of time.

Father Dumas' cheeks were covered with tears. They ran down his craggy chin and dripped to the floor. He was on his knees again, praying for forgiveness. His knee ached unmercifully, but he accepted it, even welcomed it, as part of his atonement. His mind was never at peace. However, as he continued to purge his dark actions from his mind, he was usually successful. One could only hope that it stayed that way... the alternative would not be pretty.

A world that contains an inexplicable mystery
Is much more desirable than one where each
Day is so small in scope that we can continually
Understand the nuances of each hour.

About the Author

Dr. Piatt earned his B.S. and M.A. from California State Polytechnic University and his doctorate from BYU. Prior to his retirement, he was a missile engineer and launch-conductor, a science teacher and alternative high school principal, a Junior College professor of psychology, engineering, and philosophy, as well as Dean. He was also a College Professor of Education and an administrator of Master of Education programs. He has published over 350 poems, 31 short stories, and seven essays in over 60 magazines and anthologies.

Broken Publications published his debut book of poetry *The Silent Pond* in 2012. Write Words Inc. published his debut science fiction novel *The Ideal Society* in 2012. His poetry book *Ancient Rhythms* is scheduled for release by Broken Publications in 2013. All are or will be available on Amazon.

www.ingramcontent.com/pod-product-compliance
Lightning Source LLC
Chambersburg PA
CBHW071302250626
47159CB00004B/1282